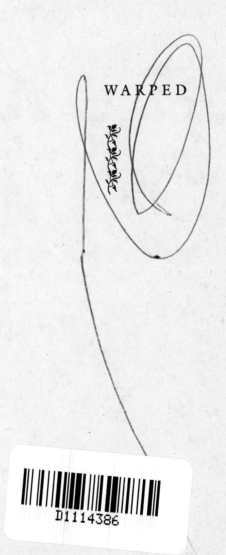

WARPED

WARPED

MAURISSA
GUIBORD

EMBER

Text copyright © 2011 by Maurissa Guibord
Cover art copyright © 2011 by Monica Alina (girl);
V & A Images/Victoria and Albert Museum (tapestry)

All rights reserved. Published in the United States by Ember, an imprint of Random House Children's Books, a division of Random House, Inc., New York. Originally published in hardcover in the United States by Delacorte Press, an imprint of Random House Children's Books, New York, in 2011.

Ember and the colophon are trademarks of Random House, Inc.

Visit us on the Web! www.randomhouse.com/teens

Educators and librarians, for a variety of teaching tools, visit us at www.randomhouse.com/teachers

The Library of Congress has cataloged the hardcover edition of this work as follows:
Guibord, Maurissa.
Warped / Maurissa Guibord. — 1st ed.
p. cm.
Summary: When seventeen-year-old Tessa Brody comes into possession of an ancient unicorn tapestry, she is plummeted into sixteenth-century England, where her life is intertwined with that of a handsome nobleman who is desperately trying to escape a terrible fate.
ISBN 978-0-385-73891-0 (hc : alk. paper)
ISBN 978-0-385-90758-3 (glb : alk. paper)
ISBN 978-0-375-89646-0 (ebook)
[1. Time travel—Fiction. 2. Tapestry—Fiction. 3. Magic—Fiction.
4. Great Britain—History—Henry VIII, 1509–1547—Fiction.] I. Title.
PZ7.G938334 War 2011
[Fic]—dc22
2009053654

ISBN 978-0-385-73892-7 (tr. pbk.)

RL: 6.0

Printed in the United States of America

10 9 8 7 6 5 4 3 2 1

First Ember Edition 2012

Random House Children's Books supports
the First Amendment and celebrates the right to read.

For Ron,
Luke, Genny
and Danielle,
with all my love

warp (wôrp), n. 1. the set of yarns placed in a loom that forms the lengthwise threads of a woven fabric. 2. a hypothetical eccentricity or discontinuity in the space-time continuum.

—from Webster's dictionary

PROLOGUE

On a hillside stood three figures. Black cloaks billowed over them from head to toe, while hoods cast a pall of darkness over their faces. These walking shadows were the Norn. Some called them by another name: the Fates, the three sisters who eternally spin and weave and cut the threads of human life. They had lived and worked here forever, beneath the huge ash tree named Yggdrasil, whose branches reached up so far they seemed like roots embedded in the sky.

The one called Spyn knelt beneath the twisted tree. She scooped her hands together and gathered a mist that drifted down from its branches. The mist was the color of snow, holding prisms of winter sun trapped within. Her spindly fingers jabbed and twiddled and pulled at the translucent material until it became a gauzy mass. From this, Spyn drew one long, shimmering thread. She passed it to Weavyr. Weavyr took it, and her dark fingers flew as she wove the thread into a fabric that lay upon the ground. This fabric flowed out in all directions from the hill, turning and folding, coiling into whorls here and twisting spirals there. This was the Wyrd. The threads of human life were here, endlessly woven and tended by the Norn. Each thread was a mortal soul whose destiny was made by their thread's winding path in the Wyrd.

"Something is not right," Weavyr announced. She crouched lower over one spot in the Wyrd and tugged, redirecting the threads. In the moments that followed, throughout the world hearts were broken, brilliant careers were launched and dreams were dashed. A volleyball serve also went awry.

"No," Weavyr muttered from beneath the folds of her hood. "Still wrong."

Spyn drifted closer to examine her sister's work. Beneath the cloak her bony shoulders shrugged. "Life is often messy."

"You sound like one of them," Weavyr observed.

"Human, you mean? Don't be vulgar," Spyn retorted.

"What is it?" A deep voice, like an echo from an empty crypt, interrupted the discussion. The third sister was called Scytha, and her tall form loomed over the other two, eclipsing them in her shadow. From the sleeves of her own cloak Scytha's hands hung down: large, thick-fingered and pale. Scytha held a pair of heavy shears whose razor edges glinted so brightly that it stung to look upon them. "Why do you stop your work?" Scytha demanded.

The calloused pads of Weavyr's fingers tapped together in irritation. "It's all wrong," she said, pointing to the troublesome spot in the vast fabric. "But it's not my fault. It's the missing threads."

"The missing threads," Spyn repeated in her thin, wavery voice. "Five hundred human years have passed and still they plague us. Out of the billions, the myriad, to think that seven threads could matter so."

"They do," Weavyr replied. "You know they do. The loss of those threads created rifts, knots and tangles in the Wyrd. Things that were not meant to be have come to pass. Proper destinies have not been fulfilled. I've had all I can do to maintain order."

Spyn's answer came on a whispery sigh. "Yes. You're right, of course." Her long fingers knit the air. "But what can we do?"

"Nothing," said Scytha. "The threads are lost. They are gone from the Wyrd and therefore beyond our control." She dragged one pallid finger across the fabric, and in the human world, a hundred souls shivered, as if each had felt the tread of footsteps over his grave.

"Not lost. Stolen," Weavyr said, with a bitter snap.

"Yes. The threads were stolen." Scytha pronounced this slowly. She did all things slowly, except for one. "Let us hope that someday they will be found."

"And whoever stole them . . . ," Weavyr began.

"Will be punished." Scytha's fingers inched over the shimmering threads and then stopped. She plucked up one of the threads and pulled it taut. "But for now, Sisters, we have work to do." As if to demonstrate, Scytha's fingers moved with a quick and dreadful economy. The flashing blades gaped. *Hssst*. The thread was cut. A human life was ended.

The other two Norn nodded and returned to their duties as Scytha had bidden them. Spyn's nature was energetic, and full of drama. Weavyr was careful and workmanlike, just like her fingers. Scytha was final.

"Still," said Weavyr. The dissatisfaction rang clear in her tone, even as her dark fingers worked, weaving the paths of human lives. "The stolen threads. I do wonder what has become of them."

Chapter 1

Cheever's Fine Auction House was packed on a stormy spring afternoon. The auctioneer's voice carried over the patter of rain drumming on the high, dark-beamed roof of the former dairy barn. "Number ninety-four. Last lot," he announced to the crowd.

"Thank God," said Tessa Brody under her breath. She'd been sitting there so long, she'd probably have an impression of the chair slats engraved on her rear end. Auction butt. Not good.

"Nice collection of books from an estate sale," the auctioneer boomed. "Some old leather-bound editions of the classics, and some more unusual stuff too." Beside Tessa, her father leaned forward in his seat, making the flimsy wood creak. "Four boxes," said the auctioneer. "Nope, make that five," he added as his assistant lugged out one more. This was a wooden crate instead of cardboard like the others. The assistant set it on top.

"These are the ones I want," Tessa's father whispered.

"Really?" Tessa eyed her dad. Jackson Brody twirled his bidding placard, which looked like a Ping-Pong paddle, between his fingers while his knees jiggled and his heels tapped the concrete floor.

Tessa smiled at him. "Way to be nonchalant, Dad."

She shifted to give the elderly man on her other side a little more elbow room, and rattled the last of her ice in a sweaty paper cup. If she'd had any patience, which she didn't, it would have been gone about three diet colas ago. She and her father had been there for hours, since the preview, and had watched the bidding on what seemed like every Kewpie doll, vintage bedpan and tarnished tea service in greater New England, waiting for the collection of books her father was interested in. Naturally, it *would* be the last lot.

The auctioneer's assistant took the top off the wooden crate and pulled something out. It looked like a faded, rolled-up rug.

"Look at that," said the auctioneer. "You get a bonus with this lot. Open it up, Charlie. Looks like an old piece of tapestry was tucked in with this last crate of books."

Tessa narrowed her eyes and shifted to see as the assistant lifted the piece up. It unfurled with a faint puff of dust to reveal a woven fabric about three feet square. A brilliant white unicorn was poised against a darker background. Across the length of the auction hall the unicorn seemed to glare at Tessa from the tapestry. Its eyes were a blazing golden brown.

A feeling of dizziness swept over Tessa. Her eyes fluttered closed and the cup of ice slipped from her hand.

Hoofbeats.

Tessa heard them. The distant but clear sound of hoofbeats rose above the murmured noise around her. Louder. The air shuddered with the sound of hooves pounding against the earth. They were coming closer, faster.

Hoofbeats. Savage. Frantic. Closer.

"Tessa."

Tessa gasped. Her eyes flew open.

"You okay?" Her father was concerned, the fine lines at the corners of his eyes crinkling as he peered at her.

Tessa didn't answer for a moment. She listened. The sound of hoofbeats was gone, but her breathing was ragged and her heart pounded beneath the thin fabric of her T-shirt.

"I—I'm okay," she stammered finally. "I thought I heard something. Did you hear something?"

Her father bent to retrieve her fallen cup. "Like what?"

Good question. Tessa brushed her hair back from her face, tucking it behind one ear. "Nothing." She straightened up. "I guess I zoned out for a minute. It must have been the rain on the roof. I'm fine."

"Do I have a bid of seventy-five dollars?" the auctioneer said. He nodded at a number of raised placards. "Seventy-five. Do I have one hundred? One hundred. Do I have one twenty-five?" In the front row a woman with a black beret perched on her gray curls shot an arm up. Tessa's father lifted his placard to raise the bid. This process went on briskly for a few moments, but gradually the hands became more hesitant and their number dwindled. Tessa's father settled back in his seat. He gave Tessa a half smile and shrugged.

He was giving up.

"Going once," said the auctioneer.

Tessa nudged her father. She wasn't sure why, but suddenly she wanted him to get this. It was important.

"Going twice. Two seventy-five." Tessa nudged harder. Her father winced. But he shook his head no. Without thinking, Tessa grabbed her father's hand and hoisted it up, still holding the paddle.

"Tessa!"

The auctioneer acknowledged the bid. "Three hundred dollars. Thank you in the back." The bidding went on.

Later, the rain had diminished to a fine, cold mist as Tessa helped load the boxes into the back of the Subaru. The last one, the wooden crate, was the heaviest. She hefted it onto her hip and tried to wedge it in with the others. "Why," she said, giving it a few forceful shoves, "does the last one never, *ever* fit?" She gave up and rested the crate on the bumper.

"Easy there," her father said. He took the crate from her and set it down with a grunt. His face was red from exertion, and he wiped his forehead with his flannel shirtsleeve.

Jackson Brody had a square, solid face that, over the last few years, had drifted toward pudgy.

"My wallet and I talked it over," he said, eyeing her. "You're never allowed near an auction again. You're a menace." He shook his head. "Must be all those teenage hormones."

Tessa glanced out at the parking lot, where people were loading stuff into their cars. She swiveled back and gave her father a level look. "Okay. Dad? Remember that list of things you're not allowed to talk about? Add Tessa's hormones."

"Right," her father sighed. "But the point is you can't act on every impulse you have, Tessa. It'll get you into trouble."

"Yeah, I'm a real wild one, all right." Tessa put her hands on her hips. "Imagine," she said, making her expression stern. "I spent my Saturday going to an auction with my father and buying a bunch of old books. The president should work on a special task force for that one."

Her father shook his head and smiled, as if despite himself. "You look just like your mother when you argue."

Tessa smiled too, and dropped the pose. Sometimes she wondered if her father knew she liked hearing that, and said it just to please her. But she *did* have her mother's features: pale skin with mahogany dark hair and wide blue eyes that were slightly heavy-lidded, giving her otherwise ordinary looks an exotic touch.

"Anyway," she said. "It was *your* impulse, not mine. You said you wanted them."

"Not four hundred dollars' worth," her father said dryly. "I thought you and the old lady in front were going to duke it out there for a minute."

"She looked pretty tough," Tessa said with a nod. "But I could have taken her."

She climbed into the back and tugged one of the cardboard boxes in farther. "Besides," she called out. "It wasn't four hundred. It was three sixty-eight, including tax. Dealer's discount, remember? And I'm sure there's stuff in here we can make a profit on."

"*I* can make a profit on, you mean," her father corrected. "The guy with the bookstore, remember?"

"Uh-huh," Tessa answered absently. She tucked a loose tendril of hair, curling now from the damp, behind her ear and fingered through the books before selecting one. *Plant Lore of the Middle Ages.* The tooled-leather spine wobbled as she flipped the book open. She wiggled a slim finger into the spot where the endpapers gaped and prodded gently. "I can fix that," she said. She liked to fix things; she was good at it too. But she frowned when she saw that one of the illustrated pages had been marred with someone's notes and cross-outs. "Great," she muttered, replacing the book with the others. "Looks like we had a scribbler. In pen, no less."

"No, I checked them over at the preview," her father said. "For the most part they're in good condition." He was staring at the wooden crate at his feet as he ran his fingers through his hair, sending the brown and gray mix into disheveled tufts. "You know, I really don't remember seeing this one then."

Tessa glanced at it. "Me neither." She pointed to the mark on the crate's side in heavy blue wax. "But it's part of the lot. Number ninety-four. See? It's the one with that old tapestry thing inside."

Her father nodded. "Yeah, well, it's not going to fit in the car. Let me go find some smaller boxes. We'll rearrange."

He disappeared back into Cheever's. Meanwhile, Tessa went to the glove compartment and found a screwdriver so she could pry the cover off the crate. They'd nailed it back on inside. She wanted to get a closer look at the tapestry. It might look cool hanging in the back of the store.

Tessa lifted off the plywood cover and wrinkled her nose as a dry, musty smell wafted up. Like crumbled dried flowers, or herbs. The tapestry was folded up and wedged in on one side, next to a stack of books. On top lay an old book. And not old as in used, Tessa saw immediately; old as in *ancient*.

The cover of the thick black volume had some red rot, the flaking decay that could make old leather crumble to dust. It would have to be handled with care. And certainly not taken out here, in the damp. She looked at the clouds overhead, which were threatening more rain.

Gently, Tessa pushed the book to one side and pulled the thick fabric of the tapestry from the crate. She shook it open with a snap; a small cloud of dust flew up, tickling her nose and scenting the air even more strongly with that sweet herbal smell as she spread the cloth over the open crate. She caught her breath.

Up close, the tapestry's deep, jeweled colors made kaleidoscope whorls of crimson and gold and emerald green, while in the center, the unicorn, woven in milky white, blazed like a pool of moonlight against the dark.

"Gorgeous," Tessa whispered.

It looked so real. The unicorn, with a long spiraled horn jutting from its tangled mane, was depicted rearing up on its hind legs as its front hooves raked the air. A violent, yet majestic strength was captured in the arched lines of its neck and the muscular shadows of its shoulders.

The unicorn was in a grassy clearing, hemmed in by denser forest. In the background a castle sat atop a distant hill, with turrets outlined against a brilliant blue sky. The scene, Tessa thought, was like something from a fairy tale. But definitely one of the darker ones. And probably not one with a happy ending. For she noticed that a dark cut was stitched on the unicorn's cheek, and from it flowed two crimson drops of blood. The unicorn's large golden brown eyes seemed to glitter. Tessa squinted. She felt strange, breathless.

She reached out and brushed her fingers over the tapestry. The threads were warm and soft, almost velvety beneath her touch. Then it happened.

A tingling sensation ran up her arm, quick and warm and so lightning fast Tessa didn't have time to snatch her hand back. Suddenly everything was gone. The tapestry, the car, even the *ground* was gone. It was as if a black fog had swept her up and was carrying her far away. She was drenched in darkness, blinded. But she could *hear* something. In the black fog, a voice spoke. Words swirled around her.

"Through warp and weft, I bind thee."

A shudder went through Tessa's body and she let out a low, trembling cry.

"What was that?" Her father's voice broke through the dark. Tessa's head jerked up. She felt herself fall with the sickening lurch of an elevator drop. Solid earth materialized beneath her feet as the darkness cleared. She blinked. She hadn't fallen, she realized. She was standing right where she had been a moment before.

"What?" Tessa breathed. She swallowed with difficulty against her dry throat and looked around, dazed. Besides their car, the parking lot was now empty. Evening was coming; it was getting cold. And dark. Beyond the edge of the building came the familiar sound of peeper frogs out in the woods. They sounded unnaturally loud. But even louder was the drumming of her heart. She glanced down, almost expecting to see its outline pushing from her chest, like in an animated cartoon.

Her father came up behind her. His shoes crunched in the gravel. "Did you say something?"

"Did I?" She hadn't spoken aloud, had she? She'd only *heard* something. That weird voice. Those words. "Something just came to me," Tessa answered slowly. "Part of a poem, maybe."

She raised a hand to swipe the corner of her eye. It was moist. She was crying? She turned to her father, tucking herself under his shoulder and hugging him tight. His stocky bulk felt warm and comforting.

He didn't let go but drew back a bit to regard her. Her father had gray eyes that might have been icy in color but were too bright and wondering to be anything but warm. "What's the matter, honey? Are you okay? You look kind of pale."

Tessa nodded. "I'm fine. I just got dizzy for a second." She felt silly now and loosened her hold on her father's waist to straighten up. What had just happened, anyway?

"You're probably hungry," her father said with a confident nod. He believed in feeding a cold, a fever and pretty much anything else. He ruffled her hair. "Let's get you home."

"Yeah, I guess so," Tessa replied uncertainly.

She stayed quiet during the ride, her forehead pressed to the cool glass of the window, her eyes unfocused on the blur of trees and road passing by.

Through warp and weft, I bind thee.

Tessa remembered the words she'd heard in the blackness. She hadn't been exactly truthful with her father. For one thing, she couldn't remember ever reading a poem like that in her whole life. And for another, she *wasn't* fine. She couldn't understand why those words should terrify her.

But they did.

Chapter 2

By the time they got back home, Tessa felt better. Her father told her not to worry about the boxes, he'd bring them in later, and Tessa didn't argue. From the push to get the front door open (it always stuck when it rained) to the jingle of the brass bell and the comfortable squish of her favorite armchair in the corner, everything felt normal again. Brody's Bookstore was home. Tessa closed her eyes and breathed deeply.

The scent of the little balsam-stuffed pillow stitched with the words "Don't Make Me Shush You" mingled with the fresh coffee Mrs. Petoskey, the part-time cashier, had brewing behind the register. Tessa sprawled back into the lumpy seat cushions and tried to forget about the weirdness at the auction house. Too much caffeine, she thought, or maybe the dust from all those old books, had caused some kind of short circuit in her brain. An allergic reaction, she decided. With special effects.

It was almost closing time, but there were still a few customers browsing in the store. Tessa noticed a little blond girl wearing a denim jumper walking slowly down the middle aisle. Heel-toe-heel-toe. Heel— The girl looked up and caught Tessa watching her.

"I like the creaky sound," she said, rocking back and forth on the dark, gleaming floorboards.

Tessa smiled. "Me too." She pointed out a worn spot in front of Mystery and Suspense. "There's a good one over there," she said.

The girl nodded, tugged on her ponytail and went to investigate. A tall woman carrying an armful of books peered out from the children's nook. She had blond hair too. "Sloane?" she called. Catching sight of the little girl, she hurried over. "Look what I found! About a mouse and a motorcycle. Should we read this one tonight?" She bent down close to the little girl and showed her the pictures. The two of them laughed.

Watching them, Tessa felt a familiar ache in her chest. Like a punch, only from the inside. She stood. "Dad," she called. "I'm going upstairs." Her father looked up and nodded from the front counter, where he was checking the day's receipts.

Tessa climbed the stairs to the second floor, went through the door to their apartment and closed it. It was kind of nice living right over the store, though sometimes Tessa wished they lived in a normal house. It seemed there was always something that needed doing in the store. She must have put a thousand miles on those stair treads by now.

In the kitchen she flicked on the lights and took a portion of lasagna out of the freezer for her dad's dinner. She wasn't hungry, and Hunter would be coming to pick her up at seven. Maybe she shouldn't go out tonight, Tessa thought, pushing the microwave buttons. She wasn't up for it, what with all the smiling and talking. Both would be expected on a first date. Her face hurt just thinking about it.

She grabbed a bowl of salad from the fridge and nibbled on a slice of carrot. Then again, she'd already told her father about going out. Now if she didn't go, he'd want to know why. *Here's the thing, Dad. I'm feeling a little weird and moody, and earlier, I hallucinated a teensy bit.* It could very well lead to a discussion about her menstrual cycle. God.

Tessa put a single placemat at the head of the table and arranged the plate and silverware. Ever since her mother had died four years ago, her father had done his best. She knew that. She frowned and adjusted the knife and fork to equal distances from the table's edge. But she was seventeen now. She could take care of herself. Besides, her father had something else on his mind lately. Or rather, some*one* else.

The timer dinged. She was fine, Tessa decided. She would go out. *Smiley talk, here I come.*

Her father came into the kitchen, carrying the wooden crate from the auction. "The store's all closed up," he said. "I left the other boxes downstairs. We can go through them tomorrow. But I thought you might want this up here." He set the crate on the table.

Tessa didn't answer. She stared at the crate. There was absolutely nothing scary about it. So why did her legs feel wobbly all of a sudden? She glanced down and loosened the white-knuckle grip she had taken on the kitchen chair.

Her father lifted the lid. He peered inside. "Tessa," he said in a low, excited voice. "Get me those cotton gloves in the junk drawer, would you?"

She got the gloves and handed them to her father, who put them on and reached in to lift out the large book. "Holy smokes," he murmured, turning the weighty volume in his hands. The book had thick, yellowed pages with the unevenly stacked edges of old-fashioned hand-binding. On the cover, in swirling, embossed letters, Tessa could make out the title:

TEXO VITA

"*Texo Vita*. What does that mean?" she asked.

"I have no idea," her father admitted. "It's Latin, I suppose. Hmm. *Vita* means 'life,' doesn't it?" He opened the book, then, nestling it in the crook of his arm, gently turned a few of the pages. Tessa stepped closer. The pages were covered with a thin, scrawled handwriting, but she couldn't make out any of the words. They were normal letters but all jumbled up and crowded, with way too many consonants and squiggles.

"I've never seen parchment like this," said her father, "except in a museum. I believe it's vellum. From sheepskin."

She nodded. "The cover has a little bit of red rot. How old do you think it is?"

Her father frowned. "I'm not really sure," he said, continuing to scan the text with a look of absorbed fascination.

His expression was priceless, Tessa thought. As if he'd just won the book lover's lottery or something. Her father closed the book and set it down gently on the table. His hands hovered over it for a moment, as if he were afraid it would fly away.

"You think it's worth a lot?" Tessa asked.

"Could be. But something like this is beyond my expertise. I know an antiquarian book specialist in Portsmouth. I could take it for an appraisal." He turned back to the crate and reached in again. "Let's see what else we've got here."

"Wait a minute. Don't—" Tessa broke off as her father lifted the tapestry out.

Her father peered at it. "Huh. Not in terribly good shape, I'm afraid."

"Really?" Tessa said, staring at the unicorn. She couldn't tear her gaze away from it. "I think it's amazing."

Her father glanced up. "You like it?"

Tessa wasn't sure if *like* was the word to use. "I've never seen anything like it," she said. "It's beautiful." She tilted her head, studying it. The scene was so lifelike; it almost seemed to be in 3-D. The detail was even a little unnerving.

"Here," her father said. "You take it." He held out the tapestry.

Tessa hesitated.

Her father chuckled. "You act like it's going to bite you. It's only a little dust."

She held her breath and reached toward the upper corner of the cloth. Her fingers touched the spot where a tiny bird was pictured, flitting against the distant sky. Nothing happened, of course. What was the matter with her? She took the tapestry from her father.

"Thank you," Tessa said. She held it in front of her, feeling the surprising weight of it. Again she had the sense of warmth and softness as she held the curled edge.

"We can go through the rest tomorrow," said her father.

Tessa nodded. "I've got to go get ready. I'm going out."

"That Hunter boy, right? I'll listen for him." Her father eyed the lasagna with suspicion. "That's not one of those diet dinners, is it?"

"Vegetarian. Enjoy," Tessa mumbled. She was already heading down the hall, still holding the tapestry at arm's length, considering it as she walked. She wondered if it could possibly be as old as the book. Despite what her father said, she thought it couldn't be. It looked too well preserved. The colors were so bright. She tried to imagine why anyone who owned it would have sold it.

Chapter 3

Lila Gerome leaned back in the leather seat of her private jet and tapped the rim of a cut-crystal flute in contemplation. She gazed out the window and took a sip of the chilled champagne. She enjoyed flying. She liked seeing the world down below her, as it should be seen. Far below were the tiny houses, bridges, cars and, even smaller still, people. Tiny, insignificant things, they were like so many pieces on a game board. She had been like that once. Not anymore.

She stretched out slim, silk-clad legs and let out a faint sigh. Had anyone been sitting nearby, they would have wondered that such an old, creaky sound could have come from such beautiful lips. Lila Gerome often made odd noises. On some occasions it had been amusing for her to let others hear them. For instance, she recalled a brief period of time—when was it? Oh yes, the 1970s. She had performed as the rock singer Belinda. She had rocketed to fame on her unique vocalizations and crooning ballads. And then, just as suddenly as her bright flame of stardom had flared, it was tragically snuffed out. Drug overdose. So sad.

To this day there were some fans who insisted on playing her vinyl records backward, listening for a prayer to Satan. Lila's laugh rattled deep in her throat.

She'd had many different lives, different names, over the years. Such was the burden and the delight of immortality.

Having to keep moving was a bitch, though. It was an inconvenience she suffered through every twenty-five years or so. Remain in one place too long and the neighbors would begin to wonder. Why does Lila Gerome never seem to age? For the years went by and still she kept the face and figure that would have been beyond the skills of Park Avenue's most adept plastic surgeons. So she had to move, disappear and reappear somewhere else. Always youthful, always beautiful.

She adjusted a heavy silver ring on one hand. It was a distinctive piece, with a lustrous yellow stone set in its center.

Across the narrow aisle she caught a glimpse of her countenance in the stainless steel galley. Silver-blond hair, perfectly sculpted features and luscious red lips. Her real self was perhaps revealed only in her eyes, which, though beautifully shaped, were somewhat small and strangely flat. Sometimes she wondered if anyone could glimpse her real self peeking out. Certainly no one would ever compare her to the shabby old weaver woman she had once been, so long ago. No, never.

It was truly delicious to be Lila Gerome. She could *be* whatever she wanted, *have* whatever she wanted. As long as she had the tapestry and the threads. And why not? She had worked hard enough, had paid enough. A long time ago she had paid the ultimate price.

The tapestry was snugly packed for shipping to her new home, wherever she decided that would be. She had seen to it herself before she had left the New York house. It was safe, along with the book. Lila smiled.

Her phone rang as they landed. She glanced at it and gave an irritated sigh as she flipped it open with a bloodred fingernail. "What is it, Moncrieff?"

"It's about the auction." Her assistant's voice was tense. "I—I think there may have been a mix-up. The chest in the master bedroom. It's gone, and I—"

"What!" Lila snapped. She lurched forward and champagne sloshed from her glass.

"I—I believe the auctioneer saw the book and thought it went with the others from the library. The book and the tapestry . . . are gone."

Her tapestry. Her unicorn. For a moment two feelings Lila had not felt in a very long time gripped her. One was fear. The other was helplessness, which was far worse.

With an effort, she quieted her mind. There was no need to panic. No one could do anything with the tapestry. *She* was the only one who could use it. Only she had the skill to control the threads. But to have it out of her reach was intolerable.

She spoke very quietly. "Moncrieff. Can you hear me? Get it back." She fumbled in the pocket of her linen jacket and her fingers found something there. A thread. Her fingers wound the thread, and pulled. "Get it back quickly, Moncrieff. Or else. Can you feel this?"

There was a choked gagging sound on the other end of the phone.

"If you don't find it," she said in a harsh rasp, "I'm afraid you're going to swallow your tongue."

Chapter 4

Tessa stood on a chair and held the unicorn tapestry up to her bedroom wall. It seemed like an outrageous splash of color against the plain, spare décor of her room. She frowned as she eyed the upper edge. She hated things to be uneven.

She turned to Pie, who sat on her bed. The cat watched Tessa with an expression of utter feline boredom. "Is this straight?" Tessa asked. Pie responded by flopping onto his side and swishing his tail back and forth. "You're never any help," Tessa remarked with a grin.

Turning to face the tapestry again, she saw the blurred mesh of the woven threads. There were lush greens and midnight blacks and, from the center, the glow of the unicorn in luminescent tones of milk and cream. She blinked.

It was odd; up close there seemed to be other layers, other colors, shimmering beneath the surface of the tapestry. And there were more details in the background too. A snake with yellow eyes lay coiled at the edge of the clearing, nearly hidden by a cluster of flowers and grass. Tessa narrowed her eyes, trying to focus on the threads, but they seemed to fade away. It must have been a trick of the dim lighting, but it almost seemed as if other creatures were moving, disappearing into the shadows of the forest. Strange.

She tacked up the corners and stepped down.

There was a hiss behind her. Tessa whirled to see Pie's bared teeth. His eyes were dilated black moons and his orange tabby fur stood up like it was electrified. He yowled at her, spat another hiss and sprang off the bed.

"O-kaaay," Tessa remarked. The sound of Pie's claws as he skittered down the hall trailed away.

Her cat was so weird.

Tessa glanced at the time. She had about fifteen minutes before Hunter would be there. But instead of getting ready, she turned back to the tapestry. Something about it mesmerized her. It was the unicorn. Once more she noticed the droplets of blood stitched along its cheek. It was bleeding, poor thing. She reached out and ran her fingers over the smooth, white surface of its neck.

This time when the rushing blackness took her, Tessa couldn't even cry out. In an instant she was flung through the dark. When the fog cleared, she was surrounded by brightness and the smell of fresh grass.

She was running.

There was a pebble in her shoe. The girl ignored it and kept running across the meadow's wet timothy grass, kicking out her skirts with each stride of her long legs. She dared to glance behind her. No sign of them yet. Still, she wouldn't stop for such a trifle. In fact, the little stone chafing her foot, the itch of the wool from damp, muddy stockings, even the bite of a mayfly in her ear, all these were nothing compared to the irritation this day had caused her.

A husband!

She was but ten and seven years of age, but to hear her aunt's chatter you would have thought she was a warty old crone.

"It's time you chose a husband. Or are you too good for anyone in the village?" Her aunt had sniffed. "Lam Doddle, for instance. He's a fine lad."

The girl vaulted over a clump of bracken and picked up her pace as if the hounds of Hell were behind her.

Lam Doddle. A beefy ox of a boy with wet, droopy lips and a lazy eye. Her aunt thought him a catch. His father was the village cooper, a respected tradesman. Lam had all the makings of a dependable barrel-maker too, she thought. He already resembled one.

She lengthened her stride and raced down the hill, ignoring the hampering weight of her skirts. Her aunt seemed suddenly determined to marry her off, and today's planting festival in the village had apparently fit in with her scheme. Even the games had conspired against her.

"Who's for Hare and Hounds?" The shouted question had been followed by a resounding cheer. Numerous mugs of small beer had already been quaffed and a mound of quince tarts devoured. Everyone was ready for sport.

"You'll be the hare," Lam announced, leering at her. At least, she thought he was leering. One never knew for sure. One of his blue eyes always seemed to be looking somewhere else altogether.

But she agreed to play. She loved to run; she was the fastest runner in the village. And she was quite sure she could outrun Lam Doddle with rabbit snares tied to her legs.

She was sometimes proud, as her aunt frequently observed. A feature that ill became a poor young maiden. Pride was sinful, and yet she felt sure she was meant for something better than warming a barrel-maker's bed. But what? What did she want? Whatever it was, somehow she didn't think she would find it in Hartescross.

Her breath puffed against the cool spring air. Her limbs felt warm and wonderfully loose. She could run forever. As the hare, she'd been given a one-hundred-count head start before the hounds gave chase. Lam wouldn't wait that long. Everyone knew that the only point of the stupid game was to get caught and be kissed. As if she wanted Lam Doddle to kiss her. Ugh!

She slowed her steps, catching a lock of her hair and twisting it around one finger. She was supposed to leave a trail for the others to follow. From the pocket of her apron she pulled a clump of knotty gray wool, cast off from this morning's spinning and too matted to be useful. She glanced around impatiently, and spotting a shrub of prickly pear, she pulled off a bit of wool and stuffed it underneath. There! Let the great oaf follow *that* for a trail.

Satisfied, she turned, only to find that her hair was caught on a thorny branch. It took but a moment for her to disentangle her long black locks, but she could scarcely afford the delay; she could hear shouts and laughter in the distance. Her passionate language as she freed herself was probably also ill suited to a fresh young maiden. It was a blessing no one was there to hear it.

Once she was free, her gaze traveled ahead of her to the deep green of the northern woods. She was surprised to see that she'd run this far. Her steps slowed and led her closer to the forest. The shelter and secrecy looked so tempting. But she shouldn't go in. Those woods belonged to the Earl of Umbric. They were to be used expressly for his pleasure in hunting. No one was to trespass.

Carelessly she dropped another bit of wool onto the grass. She was at the edge of the forest now, and could see the deep shadows beneath the oaks and chestnuts. A draft of cool, wood-scented air washed over her skin, reviving her like a tonic. Lam Doddle would never look for her in there, she thought. He wouldn't think her brave enough to dare it. Indeed, it would be completely imprudent. Unmaidenly, even. Ha! She picked up her skirts, imagining as she did the clucks of disapproval that the village women would make if they saw her. She ran between the trees and stopped, turning to peer out at the meadow. She froze.

A rider on horseback stood motionless on the rise of the hill. The girl narrowed her blue eyes, taking in the tall form that sat with an easy grace atop a huge black horse. William de Chaucy, the earl's youngest son.

The girl let loose a startled curse and stepped back, deeper into shadow.

What was he doing? Why wasn't he off studying, as usual? Everyone knew he fancied himself a scholar. The talk in the village was that William de Chaucy spent half of his time with his face buried in dusty books. Which was a pity, all agreed, because it was a handsome face. Clean-hewn, with a strong nose, and lips sculpted like a taut bow. And his eyes were a tawny golden brown, fringed with dark lashes. It was the sort of face, the girl thought, that made the village maidens stare.

But *she* didn't like to be made to do anything. So she didn't stare. In fact, the only looks she ever gave to Will de Chaucy were scowls. Not that he ever noticed.

For they were worlds apart.

Had he seen her? He would ruin everything. If she was caught in these woods, she could be punished as a poacher. A twist of nausea rose from her belly to her throat. Poachers had a thumb branded, or perhaps a hot nail pushed through their ear for their crime. Which would be worse? It hardly bore imagining. She peeked out again.

Another rider had joined William de Chaucy. By his short, square build he looked to be Hugh, the elder de Chaucy brother.

He *must* have seen her. Perhaps even now he was telling

his brother he'd spotted someone sneaking into the woods. What if they came after her?

She had no choice. She had to hide. Turning, she ran deeper into the darkness of the forest.

Tessa woke up. Well, not exactly *woke;* she was pretty sure she hadn't been sleeping. And not exactly *up;* she lay sprawled on the floor. She raised a hand to the back of her head. No lump. Nothing hurt. What had happened? She gazed around her room. The time glowed 6:46 p.m. on the clock radio. She hadn't been out for more than a few seconds. And she couldn't have fallen very hard or her father would have barreled in to see what was wrong.

She'd been dreaming. Images and sensations flooded back: of sunlight and shadows and the sweet smell of grass. Someone had been chasing her. Yes, a really vivid dream. A daydream. The details were disappearing. . . . She frowned, trying to remember. But it was like trying to grab a puff of smoke. The memories slipped through her fingers.

Weavyr let out a gasp. "Did you see that? Just now?"

"What?" replied Spyn, startled. She clutched a diaphanous golden cloud that was half spun and hurriedly twined it together with a brilliant black thread. Twins.

"There was a disturbance in the Wyrd. Here." Weavyr pointed to a fine blue filament. "This one. It folded back on itself. It's not supposed to do that." She smoothed the thread back into place.

"What does it mean?" asked Spyn.

"How should I know?" snapped Weavyr. "It's never happened before!"

Scytha floated up behind them like a draft of cold night air. "Show me," she intoned.

Weavyr traced the path the errant thread had taken.

"Back in time. Five hundred years," said Scytha. "To when the missing threads disappeared. Interesting."

"I'm glad you think so," muttered Weavyr.

"It is no coincidence," said Scytha. "There must be some connection to the stolen threads."

"That's what I've been trying to tell you," snarled Weavyr. "Nobody listens to me. And mark my words," she added with a grim sort of satisfaction, "this isn't the last of it. Something is very wrong."

Chapter 5

This is all wrong. Tessa felt the seat-belt buckle grind into her hip as Hunter Scoville leaned into the kiss, angling his head as if he meant to swallow her whole. He shifted one arm behind her while his free hand slid under the front of her sweater. The night air felt as cool as a splash of water on her skin, but his hands were hot, almost sticky. Hunter lurched forward again with hands and tongue. Tessa's head banged against the window.

Um. No.

"Stop." Tessa broke away with what she meant to be a gentle push, but it turned into a two-fisted shove. Without thinking, she brought one knee up.

Hunter drew back in surprise, then eased himself back in

the driver's seat. He ran a hand through his dark, cropped hair. "Sorry. Problem?"

"No problem." Tessa said. She winced as she unsnagged a strand of her hair from the door handle.

In the dim light she could see his flushed face, the sheen on his forehead as if he had been running. He'd gone from zero to sweaty in about ten seconds. *A sexual Porsche,* she thought. *Meanwhile, I'm . . . what? Pedaling along, waiting for . . .* What *was* she waiting for, anyway? She wasn't sure. But it definitely wasn't Hunter.

"What's wrong?" he asked.

"Huh?" Tessa stumbled toward an answer. "I'm not—" She broke off. *What? That kind of girl? Into you? Into having my tonsils excavated on our first kiss?* Anything she said at this point would sound lame. "Nothing," she said. She realized she was still balled up in a defensive position, like a nervous hedgehog. Awkward with self-consciousness, she straightened her legs and smoothed her rucked-up sweater.

Hunter leaned closer again. His breath was warm in her ear. "It's just, the way we met, right away I felt a connection. It was like fate brought us together or something. Do you believe in fate?" he asked softly.

Tessa frowned. "Fate? No, I don't think so."

They'd met when Tessa got hit in the face by one of Hunter's volleyball serves in gym. Not exactly the most romantic beginning. But Hunter had been very apologetic and really nice. And somewhere, she recalled, between getting an ice pack applied and having gauze stuffed up her bloody nose, he had asked her out. Of course she'd known who he was; he was one of the most popular guys in school. They even shared some classes. But Hunter had never seemed to notice her before.

"It was an accident," she said.

"A good accident," said Hunter. "Who knows, Tess?" he added. His smile was a gleam of white in the dark. "Maybe I really planned it all along."

Tessa frowned. She knew he was joking, but the idea of it bothered her. She hated being manipulated. Almost as much as she hated being called Tess.

When she didn't say anything, Hunter shrugged and leaned forward to change the radio station. Tessa cast a sideways look at him. He *was* cute. He had deep blue eyes and a slightly goofy lopsided grin that dimpled one cheek. And it was a beautiful night. Below them, the quiet waters of the cove were lit with color from Portland's city lights. The rich, salty smell of sea air drifted in from the shore. But she couldn't help feeling that something was just . . . wrong. She reached out and tapped the bobble-head baseball figure stuck to the dashboard of the SUV.

"Who's this?" she asked.

Hunter twisted to face her. "You're kidding right? That's David Ortiz. Red Sox? You're not a Yankees fan or something, are you?" he demanded.

Tessa smiled at the hint of actual outrage in Hunter's voice. "No. I didn't recognize him is all," she confessed. She glanced at Hunter with a half smile. "He's shorter than I expected."

Hunter frowned. "It's a collectible."

"Right. Sorry," Tessa murmured. "Guess I'm just not real

sporty." What was she doing here? *Note to self: never make social plans after blunt head trauma.*

A female singer's voice filled the silence of the car. The song was plaintive and moody. Something about losing her way in the dark. A path overgrown with broken hearts. Forever alone, forever apart. For some reason Tessa's thoughts returned to the strange tapestry. She just hadn't felt right since she'd first seen it. And the wild sensations and dreams, if that's what they were, were pretty strange.

Hunter drew her closer and Tessa tightened up. Her cheeks felt flaming hot and her lips felt raw, even though it had only been one kiss. "I'd better go home now," she said. "I haven't been feeling too well today." She grimaced and pointed vaguely to her stomach. "I'd hate to give you something. I've heard there's this bug going around school. Something gastrointestinal. Really bad."

Hunter shook his head as if in disbelief and leaned back. "Yeah. Okay," he replied. Tessa could practically hear the eye-roll. He started up the car and threw the shift into gear.

She couldn't think of anything to say to Hunter (and apparently it was mutual—wow, big surprise), so all the way home she concentrated on pretending she was alone. She was riding a city bus. She and the boy next to her were strangers.

It wasn't that hard.

At school the next day Tessa thought about all the words she would use to describe her social life: *Dismal. Awkward. Meager.* She was a walking thesaurus of pathetic.

Maybe she wasn't meant to date in high school. There were people like that, weren't there? Sure. They kept them in a glass case somewhere, right along with alien artifacts and mutant circus freaks. Hunter had treated her politely when he dropped her off at home, but he had definitely had that look . . . like he was visiting Area 51.

Tessa knew she wasn't the only virgin in the senior class of Prescott High School. But sometimes it sure felt that way. And now, after the weirdness over the weekend, she could add blackouts and hallucinations to her list of What Makes Me Special. Great.

Tessa shook her head and took a blank sheet of paper from her folder. She gazed out the window, chose a craggy-barked oak tree and began to draw. Usually the smooth scratch of pencil on paper could take her mind off anything. Not that she was talented. It was the sound she liked. It reminded her of her mother. At the breakfast table, on the beach, sitting cross-legged on the floor, her mom had always been sketching.

Opal slid into the seat in front of Tessa. It figured. The one day Opal wasn't running late and dashing in just as their English lit class started. *Look busy,* Tessa told herself. She hunched forward and kept her pencil moving diligently even as she stole a glance up at her friend. Opal wore a long, swirling paisley skirt and a lace-trimmed peasant blouse. A wide leather belt with a huge Harley-Davidson buckle cinched her tiny waist and complemented the black leather bolero. The combo wouldn't have worked on anyone in the world except Opal.

Along with being fashion fearless, Opal Kandinsky was

also Tessa's best friend, had been since second grade. Unfortunately she was also an information junkie of the worst kind, and she knew Tessa had been out with Hunter the night before. Tessa looked around, fuming. Where was Mr. Lawner? Whatever happened to teacher punctuality? Academic integrity? Early dismissal? Maybe if she was very quiet and really lucky, Opal wouldn't even—

"Well?" Opal was digging through the canvas messenger bag on her lap but shot the question over one shoulder. She stopped rummaging and cocked her head. Tessa could just picture the expression—one sharply curved eyebrow raised and a gleam of curiosity in her tilted green cat's eyes. Like a gossip-hungry pixie.

"Well what?" Tessa hissed. The pencil tip snapped under the pressure she was putting on it. She glanced down at the paper and frowned. She'd drawn only a series of wavy, crisscrossing lines. It wasn't even a decent doodle.

"Your *date*, dummy." Opal half turned and shot Tessa a questioning look. "How'd it go? I tried your cell last night but it was off."

"It went fine." Tessa folded the paper before her into a neat square, then got up to toss the scrap in the recycling bin.

"C'mon," Opal grumbled when Tessa got back. "You gotta give me something."

"Well, if you have to know . . ."

"And I do."

"It was a disaster."

At this Opal turned around fully. Concern clouded her

small, heart-shaped face, and she pushed back her pale blond bangs as she looked at Tessa. She seemed relieved by what she saw, because she relaxed and smiled crookedly. "Disaster, huh? How bad?"

Tessa let out a deep breath. "The truth? All I needed was CNN and the Red Cross. Maybe a helicopter with one of those grappling hook thingies."

Opal brought up a hand heavily beringed with silver and smothered a laugh.

"It couldn't have been *that* bad. I mean, Hunter Scoville?"

"He's nice," Tessa said. "But we have nothing in common. Nothing to talk about. Let's just leave it at that."

"Did you ever think," Opal said, her eyebrows tented together, "that the guy is nervous and not up to great conversation?" She looked away. "Maybe he's smitten."

"I don't think so." Tessa smiled to herself at the word. *Smitten.* So struck with love you couldn't function? She didn't think it applied to Hunter Scoville. Certainly not to his tongue. "That sounds so old-fashioned," she said softly. "I wonder if people even *get* smitten anymore."

"Fine. Tell me the rest later," Opal whispered as Mr. Lawner walked in the door.

"There *is* no rest," Tessa hissed back.

Opal gave a "yeah, sure" smirk and turned around but whipped back. "I just remembered," she said. "I've got a chemistry test next period."

"Right. Good luck," Tessa said.

Opal put out a hand. "Ahem?"

"Ahem?"

"The pig?" Opal gave an impatient huff.

Tessa's eyes widened. "Oh my gosh. Sorry." She slipped the pig off her wrist.

It was a bracelet of green jade beads knotted together on a black cord. The central, largest bead was carved into a fat, happy-looking pig. As a good-luck charm, the pig had been through math tests, piano recitals, even dentist appointments. When Tessa was wearing it, Opal kept her in her thoughts, and vice versa. Sometimes Tessa thought *that* was the real luck of the pig—having a friend who worried about you, who hoped you didn't screw up or get hurt.

"Here you go," said Tessa. "Though he wasn't much help last night."

Opal shrugged as she put it on. "Maybe the pig had an off night."

Tessa shook her head. "No. I think it's just me." She thought about the unicorn tapestry and the blackouts, or whatever those weird episodes had been. "Can you come over later?" Tessa asked. "There's something I want to show you."

"Sure."

Mr. Lawner gave the girls a stern glance as he finished removing some papers from his desk drawer. "Morning, people," he said. "Sorry I'm late. Now let's get started."

Chapter 6

William de Chaucy reined his horse to a halt but sat forward in the saddle, peering down the grassy slope. It was her. That girl from the village. He frowned, watching as she pulled at a bit of something in her hands and let it drop to the ground. What was she *doing*?

His eyebrows rose in surprise and then astonishment as she hoisted her skirts and went tearing across the edge of the meadow. Her hair was loose, and it swirled behind her like a dark, liquid banner. And then she disappeared into the northern woods. What was she *thinking*?

Will's horse, Hannibal, blew a gusty breath and stamped.

He was impatient with this interruption of their ride. But another rider was approaching, and Will held the horse in check. He turned in the saddle and let out a sigh. It was his older brother, pounding up on his charger.

"Where are you going?" Hugh de Chaucy demanded, panting as he reined in. Hugh always rode, Will had observed, as if *he* were doing the work, not the horse.

Will quickly surveyed the meadow. He relaxed slightly—there was no sign of her. Hugh hadn't noticed anything. "Going?" he repeated distractedly, "Oh. Right. Just going for a ride. No need to follow me."

"Alone? Why?" Hugh looked truly puzzled.

He never understood. Hugh liked to be surrounded by friends and noise and laughter. An hour's worth of quiet contemplation entailed two things he particularly despised: quiet and contemplation. But sometimes these things were all Will desired.

"I just wanted to ride," said Will, shrugging off his brother's watchful gaze and examining the distant line of trees. Yet he could feel the weight of Hugh's assessing look. Will wore a shirt of rough cambric, doeskin breeches and soft boots. A woolen cloak so old as to be of uncertain color was slung across his broad shoulders.

"You're not dressed to hunt," Hugh observed. His voice held a faint but unmistakable air of disappointment.

"No," Will said firmly. If Hugh thought there was the least chance of killing something, he would insist on coming along. "I just want to ride." He glanced to the meadow again, where jogging along awkwardly now was a portly youth who stopped and peered along the ground. He seemed to be searching for something. Will watched as the youth scratched his head and then his crotch.

"I just want to *think*," Will amended. Surely that would put Hugh off.

"Hmm. It must be a girl," said Hugh. When Will shot a frown at him, Hugh gave a triumphant grin that broadened his ruddy face and made his blue eyes nearly disappear in sparkling crescents above his cheeks. "It *is* a girl." He slapped his meaty thigh.

Will didn't reply but raked an impatient hand through his hair and silently cursed his brother. Would Hugh never leave? Will peered down the slope and frowned. Now the youth seemed to be entangled in a bush of some sort.

"Is it that short one from the village, the one with the hair in yellow ringlets?" Hugh sighed. "I love ringlets."

"Don't be an idiot," Will said, perhaps a little too quickly. He hoped his face didn't show anything. But he needn't have worried about revealing anything subtle to his brother. He had poked Hugh's temper, which was as quick as his smile.

Hugh reached out and cuffed him. Despite the glancing blow and the gloved fist, Will's head snapped as if it hung on strings, and his teeth rattled together.

"Watch your tongue, little brother," said Hugh pleasantly.

Indeed, Will checked his tongue, as well as his teeth. All there. His brother spoke with his fists. Fighting was a second language to Hugh, really, in which he was fluent. Foul-mouthed, but fluent.

"I forgot to say good morning," Hugh added, baring his teeth in a smile.

Will rubbed his throbbing ear, all thoughts of the girl in the wood, for the moment, driven from his head. "You do know," he said to Hugh, "you can't go around doing that once you're at court."

Hugh shrugged. "When we get to London, I'll let Father do the talking."

Right. Will frowned at the thought. That would not be a vast improvement. "Perhaps I should come along," he suggested, knowing even as he did that it was a wasted effort.

"Father's already told you no," said Hugh. He straightened in the saddle and announced, in a fair imitation of their father's deep, authoritarian boom: "'There must always be a de Chaucy at Hartescross.' Besides," he added, nodding toward the huddle of wattle-and-daub cottages in the distance, "what if one of the villagers has a complaint? Suppose there're weevils in the barley? Suppose somebody steals a chicken? Who better to deal with it than the earl's younger son? A young Solomon."

"You're very funny," Will told him. Then, more quietly, "You leave today, then?"

Hugh's face sobered and he looked out to the right, where the fields and the valley lay below. A shadow of worry crept over his features, and Will was shocked to see it. His brother was as stout-hearted as a lion.

"Aye," Hugh said, all trace of his usual bluster gone. "I just pray the king grants our petition."

"He must," said Will. "King Henry will listen to reason. He's an educated man."

Hugh brightened and grinned at him. "Well. We'll not hold that against him. Yet." He studied Will for a moment, then said with a nod, "We'll send news as soon as we have it. Now I'll leave you, little brother, to your *thinking* ride." He gave Will a swift punch in the arm for a farewell and wheeled his horse around. "And give the girl a kiss for me!" he called over his shoulder as he galloped away.

Will watched until Hugh became a distant figure. For once he didn't mind being left behind while his father and brother tended to the business of the estate. The land dispute would be settled soon anyway. Despite his rough ways, the Earl of Umbric was no fool. Neither was Hugh. They didn't need him.

Need him? Will's mouth curled into an ironic smile. They barely noticed him. As younger son, he wasn't master here at Hartescross (though everyone usually did as he bade them) and he wasn't servant (though he was told often enough what to do). Neither master nor servant. Neither idle nor employed. Just something in between. Would he ever find his place?

Will sighed. Somehow he didn't think it was at Hartescross.

He gave Hannibal free rein and trotted down the hill and into the meadow. The young man wandering there seemed put off at seeing the earl's son, for he gave a nervous tug on his cap and stumbled away.

After but a few steps, Will observed, the young man encountered a group of villagers, themselves running through the meadow with raucous shouts. Some exchange took place. It involved heated gestures toward Will and the woods beyond. And quite a bit more scratching. Finally the whole lot turned and walked with an air of glum resignation back toward the village.

Will shrugged and turned his horse toward the forest, where the girl had gone.

It was a foolhardy thing to do, he thought. Surely the chit knew it was forbidden. No one entered the wood without the permission of the earl. Not that his father would care if a young maid went wandering in the northern woods. But if the gamekeeper spotted her, she would likely have a thrashing. Miles was an ill-tempered sort. Foolish maiden or poacher, it made no difference, he would exact punishment first and ask questions later.

Will gave a puzzled look down at the grass to see what she had dropped so deliberately. A small tuft of gray wool. The girl was a mystery. A dark-haired enigma with huge blue eyes. He pretended not to notice her each time he rode through the village, something that he had found himself doing more and more of late. He didn't even know her name. But today, he decided, he would find out.

"Come out of there," Will shouted. More quietly, he added, "Hello?" He watched the wall of trees for a sign of her. When there was no response, he dismounted. He led Hannibal into the woods.

Chapter 7

After school Tessa walked home as usual. Meaning she ran. She barely looked up as she raced across Harbor Square; her feet had memorized every step long ago. Tessa's pace slowed as she approached the Artist's Shelf. Here she stopped and let her eyes linger for a minute on the display of starched white canvases, tubes of paint and sticks of rich oil pastels. She smiled at the tumbled array of colors, then sighed and kept moving. She was going to be late for work.

Their building sat in the middle of Portland's Old Port district. The handsome brick three-story had been built in the eighteen hundreds and stood on one of the "quaint winding lanes perched above a working waterfront." At least, that was how the summer guidebook described it. She glanced around the quiet street before going in. In the summer these streets were filled (or at least busy) with tourists. The bell over the front door rang constantly with the traffic. But this was spring, otherwise known as mud season, and it wasn't so busy. Dead calm, she thought, would be the nautical expression.

Tessa pulled the door, and the bell overhead gave a half-hearted jangle as if to say, "Okay. One customer. Big whoop."

"Dad," Tessa called. The wooden stool behind the front counter stood empty. He was nowhere to be seen. Typical. He was way too trusting. Anyone could have walked off with half the inventory. Tessa looked around with a despairing shake of her head.

"That you, Tessa?" Her father appeared above her, leaning over the railing from the loft section of the store, Maine History and Lore. He held a tattered, oversized volume in one hand and his glasses in the other. "How was school?"

"Fabulous," said Tessa, in automatic reply. She waited to see if details were needed. No. Her father's eyes were already back on his book.

How would he react, she wondered, if she broke away from their routine exchange and talked about something real? *Hey, Dad. Hunter wants to have sex with me and I'm not sure how I feel. About college—I don't want to major in business, or even go to the University of Southern Maine in the fall, for that matter. And oh yeah, I can feel a zit the size of a hamster coming out on my nose.*

"That's good, honey," her father mumbled. He was returning to the mesmerizing world of . . . Tessa craned her neck and peered to read the big letters on the spine . . .

Town Records—Livermore Falls. Really, was there anything her father didn't find fascinating?

Tessa sighed. She hung her backpack on a hook by the door, shrugged out of her denim jacket and rounded the corner of the counter, promptly slamming her leg into the large box tucked behind it.

"The last box from the auction is behind the counter," her father called down.

"Yeah. Got it," answered Tessa, rubbing her shin.

The bell chimed again as the door opened and Alicia Highsmith strode into the store.

Alicia Highsmith was a petite woman, but she carried herself like an army general. A very stylish, professional general, Tessa thought, wearing black woolen slacks, a pearl-gray sweater set and slingback pumps. Tessa became suddenly aware of her own appearance. Her hair was barely contained in a sloppy ponytail and she had on faded jeans, a Bowdoin College sweatshirt (the operative word being *sweat*) and worn-out Avias.

Alicia gave a smile and a brisk wave. "Hello, Tessa. Your father in?"

"Hi, Alicia." Self-conscious, Tessa felt herself straighten from her slouch as she returned a polite smile. "Dad!" she yelled to the loft.

Her father hustled down the creaky stairs, ignoring the fact that a heavy man should not hustle, anywhere. He looked practically giddy. "Alicia! I didn't expect you this early." He took Alicia by the shoulders and they exchanged a brief kiss as Tessa found something intriguing to stare at under the counter. Dust bunny to the rescue.

Girlfriend, thought Tessa, glancing up when their greeting smooch was done. It was not a word you thought of in the same sentence as *my father*. *My father's girlfriend*. No. It just didn't work.

It was little consolation, but Alicia Highsmith didn't seem the type of person who would appreciate the title either. For one thing, she was middle-aged, almost fifty, maybe. And the professional overachiever type, Tessa thought. She was CEO of a medical technology company in Portland that made prosthetics. She was attractive, with auburn hair cut into a sleek bob and big brown eyes that were currently fastened on her father's face. *Girlfriend*. Tessa sighed. It was too weird.

"Busy today?" Alicia asked.

"So far, you mean?" Tessa's father put his glasses back on and looked around. His chubby face looked hopeful, as if he expected a stampede of voracious book lovers to suddenly appear from behind the stacks. "Well. Not too," he admitted.

Alicia smiled. "You know, Jackson . . ."

"I know, I know." He raised a hand with a good-natured shake of his head. "We could turn a profit if we closed the store, kept the books in a warehouse and sold exclusively online. You're right." He beamed at her, his face animated and his eyes dancing. "My practical Alicia. But this is my dream job. Besides," he added, "we would lose the immense satisfaction of dealing face to face with the reading public. Not to mention all this charm. Right, Tessa?"

"Right." Tessa was still on autopilot. She looked around the store with a smile. Old books, check. Dust, drafty windows, creaky floors, all check. But charm? Maybe if it was dark, and you squinted, she mused. But the store was comfortable. And it was home.

Anyway, it didn't matter what "his" Alicia said, thought Tessa. Eww, by the way. The bookstore really *was* her father's dream. It would take a tsunami to move him out. He'd sat in a corporate cubicle for years but had always dreamed of having a bookstore. After her mother had died, he'd decided to pursue that dream. And he made no secret about the fact that he hoped Tessa would help run it, after getting her business degree.

Business. Such a weird-sounding major, when you thought about it. As in "I'm going to major in making money." Valuable, no doubt, but somehow it wasn't what Tessa thought her life would be about. Then again, she didn't have a clue what would be better.

Why was it so much easier to know what she *didn't* want than what she did?

"We're going to try that new Thai place down the street," said her father. "Would you like to come along?"

"No thanks. You guys have fun," Tessa said with a wave. "I want to hang out at home tonight anyway. Opal's coming over. We're doing our usual raid on the magazine rack."

Opal walked into Tessa's room and immediately sprawled across the bed. She kicked off her shoes and threw half of the carefully arranged pillows to the floor to make room for her usual supply of snacks.

Tessa surveyed the jumbled pile of cellophane-wrapped candy. "You are a nutritional disaster, Kandinsky."

"Not true," Opal mumbled around a licorice whip. She picked up a bag and shook it at Tessa. "I have raisins. Fruit."

"Those are chocolate-covered."

"Of course. For the antioxidants."

As they munched, Tessa looked through a glossy photography magazine while Opal flipped open a copy of *Guitar World*.

"Take a look at this Les Paul," Opal said. She pushed her wispy bangs out of her eyes and tapped the picture, as if she could make a riff come out of the glossy paper.

"Nice," said Tessa with a glance. She didn't know a thing about guitars, but Opal sure did. In fact, Opal could pretty much play any instrument she laid her hands on. She had a gift for music, and planned to go to the New England Conservatory after graduation.

Restless, Tessa dropped the magazine, got up and straightened the few items on her desk: a picture of her with her mom and dad, a calendar book and a small jar of multi-colored beach glass she'd collected over the years. Finally she walked over to where the tapestry hung on the wall.

Opal glanced up, and noticing the tapestry, she let the magazine drop from her hands. "Cool unicorn," she commented. Then she made a slight grimace. "Not exactly My Pretty Pony, is it?"

It was true, Tessa thought, considering it. The unicorn in the tapestry didn't look like the gentle creatures from fairy-tale illustrations. And definitely not like the chubby pastel versions that had decorated her pillowcases when she was a little girl.

It had a savage kind of beauty. Its eyes blazed like golden flames from behind the shaggy tangle of silver-gray mane. The black hooves on its raised forelegs looked long and sharp, more like talons. And she saw something she hadn't noticed before: in addition to the bloody cut on the creature's cheek, the tip of its long, spiral horn was dark, the color of dried blood.

As if it just gored the middle out of Bambi.

Tessa shivered.

"What's the matter?" asked Opal, looking at her.

"I—I don't know." Tessa blinked, breaking her gaze from the unicorn's eyes with an effort. "I feel kind of funny when I look at it."

"Probably the dust. Maybe you're allergic."

"Maybe," said Tessa. But she knew very well she'd shaken out and aired the tapestry. No. It wasn't any antique mold or mildew that was messing with her head. It was the unicorn itself. "What do you know about unicorns?" she asked Opal.

Opal tilted her head. "Let's see. Shy, imaginary creatures. Pointy headgear. Perennial favorite on the merry-go-round—"

"Ha-ha," Tessa replied. She hesitated, then asked, "Definitely not scary, right?"

Opal shook her head. "No scary unicorns." She pointed. "Except for that one."

Tessa looked again. It *did* look a little frightening, maybe because it seemed so real. As if the muscular forelegs could thrash through the air and the unicorn might leap forward at any moment. From the expression in its eyes to its defiant stance, the unicorn looked as if it was trying to tear itself free from some invisible restraint. "Does it look real to you?" Tessa asked.

"I guess," Opal replied.

"Do me a favor," said Tessa. She gave a nervous nod toward the tapestry. "Touch it."

"Touch it?"

"The tapestry. The unicorn. Just touch it," Tessa repeated. "Humor me, okay?"

Opal shrugged, walked up to the tapestry and put her hand on it.

"Feel it."

Opal gave Tessa a dubious look and then rubbed her hands all over the surface. "Ooh," she crooned. "Needlepoint."

Tessa watched her. "Do you feel anything?"

"Besides goofy? No."

Nothing had happened, Tessa realized. Opal hadn't felt anything when she touched the tapestry. Neither had her father. It was only her. Why was it only her?

"Can I stop with the touching already?" Opal asked.

"Yeah. Sorry," Tessa said. "I'm just— Never mind." She sat down and fiddled with the laces on her sneakers. "Opal, do you believe in reincarnation or past lives, that kind of stuff?"

Opal shrugged. "I dunno. I guess. Maybe."

"Do you ever have dreams about it?" Tessa asked.

"What, you mean where I'm Cleopatra or something? Nope. But I did have this dream last week that Bugs Bunny was chasing me through the school. Only he was a really mean Bugs. We had to have a lockdown and I hid under my desk." Opal frowned. "Sorry. Got sidetracked. Why do you ask? You think you're reincarnated?"

"No," Tessa said quickly. "Of course not. Just wondering."

Opal stepped back from the tapestry and frowned. "Are you really going to leave this up on your wall?"

Tessa shrugged. "Why not? You're always saying my room looks like an obsessive-compulsive nun lives here. That it needs redecorating."

"Uh, no, Miss Spartan-Pants. It needs decorating, not *re*-decorating. Like more of your own artwork," said Opal, giving her a pointed look. "Pictures of hotties. Democratic campaign buttons. Not gothic-looking fantasy creatures." She stared again at the unicorn. "That'll give you nightmares, Tessa."

Tessa let her eyes roam over the tapestry, past the unicorn into the deep shadows of the background and back again to the creature. She reached out to touch it, then stopped. She didn't know what was happening to her. But she was going to figure it out. "I'm going to keep it," she whispered. "It's so beautiful, and wild, and sad."

Opal bounced back down on Tessa's bed and opened the magazine. She glanced up once more and said with finality, "I think it looks rabid."

Chapter 8

Deep in the forest, William de Chaucy walked his horse along a rough path. Fallen branches and moss-choked rivulets crisscrossed the way and made it slow going. He had traversed these woods often enough, but it seemed different today. The darkness was surprising. Outside, it was a clear day, but here the trees made a green canopy, hung like a thick blanket overhead. All around him cool emerald shadows played upon black. It was a different world. A dark world.

He listened. Only the snap of twigs beneath his feet and

the moist snuffle of Hannibal's breath against his neck broke the heavy stillness.

Will shook his head. "What am I doing here?" he murmured.

As if in answer, the horse threw his great dark head, making his livery jingle.

"You're right, it's foolish," murmured Will with a smile, looking around. "I might as well hunt pixies." And he was talking to his *horse*. Hugh would be vastly entertained.

Then he saw her. Her face peeked out at him from behind a curtain of leaves. She didn't move, and for a moment he thought it was an animal, or some trick of the shadows. But no forest creature had eyes like that. They were deep blue, like faceted jewels. And they met his own and held his gaze for the length of a breath. Her skin was pale except for two spots of color on her cheeks where her exertions had made them rosy. Her dark hair was in a gleaming tumble upon her shoulders.

"Hello?" he said at last.

She bolted, tearing through the undergrowth with a faint cry.

"No. Don't—wait!" Without thinking, Will dropped Hannibal's reins and dashed after her. But he soon realized that he hadn't a prayer of catching her. He only glimpsed the flash of a pair of slim legs leaping over a bent sapling before she was gone, as quickly as a will-o'-the-wisp.

He'd frightened her. He hadn't meant to.

Will stopped running and listened. There was only silence, not even the chatter of birds. He took a deep breath, filling his chest with the liquid scent of the forest and letting it out again. His breath made faint plumes of vapor on the cool air. It was getting darker, and the girl couldn't know these woods. How the devil did she think she'd find her way back?

"Hello?" he called again. "Mistress?" Leaves brushed his shoulders, and small prickly vines tugged at his boots as if they were reaching out to embrace him, or to hold him back. "Are you there?" he shouted.

Then he came upon it.

Tucked among the trees there was a small—Will squinted at it—house? Little more than a hovel, really, and nearly invisible. It was hidden, not just by its location, which was some distance from the path and without any clearing of the surrounding trees, but by the curious way it was fashioned. The walls of the structure seem to be *woven*. Young living trees still rooted in the ground made up its framework, and between these were laced green leafy branches, to make solid walls. One rounded opening made a door, around which paler green vines twined, sprigged with small, bell-shaped yellow flowers.

Will went closer, examining the small cottage in amazement. He tore a leaf from one bough and fingered it. A living house.

"Welcome," said a voice from inside.

He went in, ducking his head.

In what might have been a trick of the darkness, an old woman seemed to appear before his eyes, taking form from the green shadows around her. Her frail, bent figure and her shabby clothes were unremarkable, resembling those of any grandmother from the village. Except for one thing. The old woman watched Will with the smallest, blackest eyes he had ever seen. They were flat and depthless eyes with no shine to them at all. The woman stood beside a huge loom. He glanced around the rest of the tiny room. It was empty.

"I have looked forward to this meeting, young *master*." The crone gave a curious emphasis to the last word and smiled, showing a dark, toothless mouth. "You are the earl's son."

"Yes," Will said, puzzled. "I am William de Chaucy. These are my father's lands." He straightened, and the top of his head nearly brushed the roof of the strange little house. He'd never noticed such a dwelling here before, nor this strange old woman. "You're not from the village," he remarked. "Who are you?"

"They call me"—she paused, with the air of trying to remember an unimportant fact—"Gray Lily. Just a simple weaver, milord." She beckoned to him with a withered hand. "Come closer. May I show you my work?"

Will stepped forward, wondering how many coins were in the pouch on his saddle. He would give the old woman something; it would ease the sting of having to tell her she must leave. But he pushed these thoughts aside as the object in the center of the room snared his attention. It was a loom, but unlike any he'd seen before.

The huge frame was made of a dark, oily wood. An unfinished piece of tapestry work was stretched upon it. The brilliantly colored yarns wove through thick, lengthwise threads of a white, glistening material strung through notches in the wood. The support threads reminded Will of something, but he couldn't say what.

Will drew closer, intrigued by the scene. A castle was on a distant hillside. The old woman must have used Hartescross as inspiration, Will thought, for it looked identical. In the foreground was an empty, sunlit clearing of grass, surrounded by dark trees and brilliant flowers. Small creatures were tucked here and there among the greenery. Will spotted a snake with yellow eyes that clung to one branch. It seemed to stare at him.

Will blinked. "'Tis fine work," he remarked. "But—"

The woman stepped forward. "You think it's missing something," she said. She pointed to the center, the clearing. "There."

"That was not what I—"

Will broke off, staring at the tapestry. He felt an odd dizziness. He took a step away from it. With the distance it seemed to him that his head became somewhat clearer. Curious.

"Have you seen a girl here?" he asked, turning to the woman. "I think she ran this way. She may be lost. She has blue eyes and long, dark hair."

The old woman's mouth closed, her lips flattened into a grim line. She threw a watchful glance to the opening of the hut. "Your sweetheart, is she?"

"No," Will replied. The remark annoyed him somehow. "She is a girl from the village. She may be lost."

The old woman smiled and raised a finger to her lips in a

playful, secretive gesture. "I've not seen her," she whispered. She shuffled closer. "Here, now." She reached out. In her hand she held a small lump. A waxy-looking yellow stone. She pressed the stone to his chest, over his heart.

Will looked at the old woman in surprise. The poor old thing was mad. She was staring fixedly at the spot where the stone touched him, whispering something.

With a short laugh Will reached up to push her hand away. But he found he couldn't move his hands. *He couldn't move at all.* The realization sent a deep bolt of fear through him. He tried to back away and run. He stayed. He was fixed to the ground as if nailed there.

"What—"

That was all he could say. His voice was silenced as if an invisible gag had been jammed down his throat.

"As I said, young lordling," the crone whispered while Will struggled silently, "I am a simple weaver. But the threads for my loom are priceless indeed. We are each given but one. One life. One thread."

Now the old woman's mouth opened wide. Her lips didn't move, but sounds came out. Not words, but foul grunts and guttural cries, like nothing a human voice should ever utter. The noises poured out of her gaping mouth, a language from Hell. Will's whole body shook with disgust as they washed over him.

Her touch was hurting him. Piercing him. Will stared down at her hand. The old woman still held the small, dull, yellowish rock to his chest. Through his shirt he could feel it, burning him with a searing pain. Not from hot or cold, but burning all the same.

Slowly, as Will stared, the old woman drew her hand away. Will staggered, his eyes wide. Something drifted out of his chest. A faint wisp of silvery thread.

Gray Lily let out a delighted cackle of laughter and spoke. "That's it. Come out." She took hold and pulled the silver thread, and as she did, Will felt himself being drained, being emptied. Of everything. Meanwhile, the woman's lightless eyes twitched back and forth and her tongue flicked out from her black mouth. The cold yet fiery pain seeped through Will's chest, and he could only stare as Gray Lily wound the thread over her hands, faster and faster.

The thread was his life, and as the thread left him, his body grew thinner. His flesh withered. His muscles shrank. The color left his cheeks, his hair, and finally even his eyes. For a moment he was a pale wraith. Then he was gone.

Only the old woman remained, clutching a skein of shimmering thread. "Strong young thing," she said, nearly cooing to it. She spoke as if the young nobleman still stood before her. "Your life is mine now." Her gaze drifted, became thoughtful. "I have been waiting for the proper thread to complete my work." Her gnarled fingers stroked the thread. "One such as you. Handsome, young and proud." Suddenly her black, lusterless eyes widened. She started to laugh. "You shall remain so. Forever."

The laughter changed and turned back into the dreadful sounds of her incantations. Her hands plucked and pulled at the strand of thread as she worked it. Faster. "This is the part I like best," she grunted. "*I* am creator now. Not *them*."

She worked the beautiful thread, using only her dirty,

crooked fingers and the power of the strange little lump of yellow stone. She remade the living thread into flesh. She crafted bone and blood. Wove hoof and horn and hair. And last, even breath.

Until finally the creature stood before her, its muscled haunches shivering like a newborn foal's. And so it was. So pure, so white. But the creature still had those large, lively brown eyes; those were the same, though they were now filled with pain and confusion.

"A unicorn," she whispered with satisfaction. "My unicorn. At last. The symbol of immortality made flesh. And when I weave you into my tapestry, I will have your youth, your strength."

The unicorn stamped and backed away from the old woman but couldn't go far in the confines of the small hut.

"Not so proud now, are you?" the old woman exulted. "But you should be. You're a creature of magic. And I am your master. When I pull your thread once more, it shall retain this form and all the power it possesses, and then you will live in my tapestry. A unicorn forevermore. Come here." She clapped her hands.

It might have been a cannon shot. At the noise Will let out a scream, but it emerged as a whinnying cry. He reared up on strongly muscled hind legs, and the sharp spiral horn that protruded from his forehead ripped through the roof, tearing boughs and leaves. He crashed down again on his front hooves. A torn, flowered vine fell and hung across his neck in a mockery of adornment.

Gray Lily reached out and grabbed for his thick, flowing

mane, but Will yanked his head back and hurtled past her. He crashed through the woven greenery, snapping boughs and tearing branches. The old woman let out a snarl as she watched him gallop away. The horse Hannibal laid back his ears and trotted nervously after the unicorn, his reins trailing on the ground.

"Run!" Gray Lily called after Will. "Run fast, young master!" Her voice dissolved into mad laughter. She drew in a deep breath and straightened. The boy's youth was delicious. She could only imagine how good it would feel to have all of it.

Her tongue darted from her mouth with a nervous energy. She glanced at the tapestry, at the empty space in the center. She had thought the unicorn would be more docile, easier to control.

"No matter. We shall have a hunt," she murmured. She would find a girl, a young maid from the village. Better yet, she would find the one with blue eyes and long, dark hair.

Chapter 9

"You look tired, honey." Tessa's father folded up the *Portland Herald* and laid it aside. Tessa sat next to him at the kitchen table, idly brushing the sesame seeds off her bagel.

She yawned. "I didn't sleep too well last night."

She would never in a million years admit it, but Opal might have been right about the unicorn tapestry. It had been almost a week since she'd hung it on her bedroom wall. Each morning since then she'd woken feeling groggy and disoriented, and almost surprised to find herself in her own room. Which was silly. Where else would she be?

Thank goodness today was the last day of school before spring break. She could sleep in for a whole week. Maybe that would take care of the strange dreams she'd been having.

Tessa broke away from her thoughts as she realized her father was still looking at her with concern.

"Tessa," he said, and stopped. He rubbed the edge of the table as if smoothing an invisible mar in the wood. "I know the fact that I'm *seeing* someone must be really difficult for you."

"What?" It took Tessa a moment to focus on his words. "Oh. Alicia. Right." She shrugged. "It's fine, Dad, really."

Her father shifted in his chair and looked at the ceiling, as if there might be a cue card up there for what to say next.

"I just wish you would give her more of a chance."

"What do you mean?" Tessa picked the last of the sesame seeds off one by one and took a bite of her bagel.

He sighed. "You know what I mean, Tessa. You've made no effort to get to know Alicia."

"*I'm* not dating her, Dad. It's not exactly a requirement."

"It might be," her father said.

Tessa shot him an inquiring glance. "As in?"

"As in Alicia and I enjoy each other's company," he replied. "And I plan to see a lot more of her."

"Yuck."

"You know what I mean," her father said wearily.

"Okay, cheap shot," admitted Tessa. "Sorry. But do we have to make a big deal out of this? I just don't see what the big attraction is. She's older than you, isn't she?" Tessa kept her other questions to herself. Like why he needed to be so demonstrative toward Alicia, so gaga all the time. It was embarrassing.

"Alicia is three years older than me," her father replied. "Not that it's a big deal."

Tessa blew on her tea and tapped her fingernails on the sides of the mug, making a ceramic clink that seemed loud in the quiet kitchen. She waited, staring at the amber-colored liquid. Then she said it:

"She's nothing like Mom."

It was a casual observation. That was all. And if she could have taken the words back . . . well, she wouldn't. But the cold silence that followed in the Brody kitchen could have halted global warming. Tessa didn't look up. She knew the hurt her remark had caused; she could feel it too.

"No. She's not like your mother," her father answered at last. "Nobody is." His voice sounded tired. As if he was saying something to humor her, something that was obvious and didn't need saying. And it made him sad.

"Dad," Tessa began. "I—"

Her father stood. "Hadn't you better get to school?" he said, putting his dishes in the sink. Tessa glanced up. His mouth was pressed into a tight, unforgiving line that said *I don't want to talk about this anymore.* The expression made Jackson Brody look older; it made him look like a tired, middle-aged man. And Tessa had to deal with the fact; she was the one who'd put it there. She got up and left.

After school the bookstore was busy. Tessa's father stayed at the front counter with customers while she threw herself into cleaning a small stack of used books in the back. She dipped a rag into the pot of cleaning paste and rubbed hard. Gradually the black grime lifted away and a clean, fresh-looking cover of *Wuthering Heights* emerged. But the work didn't give her the usual feeling of satisfaction. She laid that book aside and went on to the next. Why did she have to make that stupid comment that morning? *Way to be mature, Tessa.*

Getting up to stretch, she decided to forget about it. Later, she would apologize to her father. It would all be fixed.

In the meantime, she would do some research. Tessa pulled all the books she could find that included unicorn folklore from the shelves. Maybe reading about unicorns would put her weird dreams to rest. Or at least put a better spin on them.

By break time Tessa was settled in a back corner of the storeroom with her dinner, practically barricaded in by a stack of thick volumes that constantly threatened to topple over without an occasional steadying nudge from her sneaker. She selected one called the *The Legend of the Unicorn.*

She skipped the prologue, took a bite of veggie wrap and read from chapter one. The earliest description of a unicorn was recorded there, by a historian from 400 B.C.

> *The unicorn has only one horn in the middle of its forehead. It is the only animal that ventures to attack the elephant; and so sharp is the nail of its foot that with one blow it can rip the belly of the beast.*

"Okay," Tessa murmured. "Maybe that's not what I needed to know." She skimmed ahead a few centuries. She had never realized unicorn lore was so extensive. The book said that in the Old Testament there were references to a unicorn called *re'em* in Hebrew. And in Japan the word for unicorn was *kirin*. It had a lion's face and a body covered with scales. The Persians even had a unicorn, known as a *shadhahvar*. Apparently the shadhahvar looked cute and gentle; it lulled the unsuspecting with lovely music it created by channeling wind through its hollow horn. Then it cut them to shreds.

"How sweet," Tessa commented, closing the book. She picked up another that looked more promising: *The Compendium of Fantasy and Folklore.* At least this one had more pictures. An illustration on thick, glossy paper in the segment on unicorns looked more like what she'd always pictured them to be. A white horse, basically, with an elegant spiral horn. It was grazing in a moonlit meadow. It looked so peaceful, so pretty. "That's more like it," she murmured. But on the facing page another picture caught her eye. Interestingly, it was a picture of a tapestry entitled The *Unicorn Hunt.*

In this one a wavy-haired maiden with a pouty mouth and vacant eyes sat in a clearing in the middle of a forest. A silvery unicorn knelt by her side. And it was wounded; a long spear hung from a gash in its side. Its anemic-looking head was nestled in the girl's lap. One of the girl's tiny hands was resting on the unicorn's head, as if she was petting its mane. The caption underneath read: *Medieval legends tell of the unicorn being hunted for its horn or its blood. Both were said to cure disease and even bring immortality. Hunters could capture the unicorn only by placing a virgin in its haunts.*

A virgin in its haunts. Tessa frowned. She'd heard about that part of unicorn legend before. But now something really bothered her about the whole thing: the cruelty of it. And just how did the unicorn *know* the girl was a virgin, anyway? Tessa glanced again at the maiden in the picture. She looked kind of spacey—she was gazing off into the distance. She didn't seem to even notice that the poor unicorn was bleeding to death in her lap. What was her deal? Why would a girl do something so rotten as to trick a beautiful animal, to trap it?

Tessa closed the book.

A girl like that would have to be incredibly stupid, she decided. Or completely heartless.

Chapter 10

"Ms. Gerome?" Moncrieff's husky voice was deferential over the phone. A smile stretched Lila Gerome's crimson lips. Even after all the years he had worked for her, Moncrieff maintained this formality. She knew it was because he was afraid of her. She liked that about him. It was his most dependable characteristic.

"I've found your tapestry and the book," he said. "It took some time to track them down, but it seems a bookstore owner from Portland, Maine, bought them. As I said, it was an unfortunate accident. I'll contact him and get them back."

"Do it now," Lila ordered. "Get them. I'm flying back immediately."

"Yes," Moncrieff said. "We'll have to pay. Something considerable, perhaps."

"Pay it, then. Whatever it takes. Just do it quickly and quietly. I don't want to draw any attention to myself. You know that."

"Yes. I know."

Hartescross, 1511

The Earl of Umbric, Will de Chaucy's father, slammed a flagon of wine to the table. The echoing clang rang against the stone walls of the great hall of Hartescross Castle.

"Has the whole bloody world gone mad?" he bellowed. "What do you mean the boy's missing?" He righted a toppled goblet and said more quietly, obviously struggling to control his temper, "*How* could Will just disappear without word, without trace?" His glance shot to Hugh, demanding answers.

"No one has seen him since we left for London," said Hugh wearily. "Everyone at Hartescross assumed he accompanied us." He pressed his knuckles against his tired eyes. He had not slept since returning from court. He had questioned every inhabitant of the castle, from the char sweep to the falconer, as to the whereabouts of his younger brother. Will was gone. As completely as if he had been spirited away.

"What of his horse?"

Hugh shook his head. "Gone."

"A fortnight, then?" The earl's fists tightened. "My son

has been missing a fortnight while I have cooled my heels at court, waiting for King Henry to deign to see me?" He finished in a low mutter, "All to plead my case for my own bloody land."

"There is more," said Hugh.

The earl gave a curt nod for his elder son to go on.

"There's been talk in the village." Hugh's usually ruddy face was pale, and the circles beneath his eyes told of sleepless hours. "Talk of a beast. In the northern woods."

"What kind of beast?"

"A unicorn," answered Hugh softly.

The earl stared for a moment, then let out a dismissive cry. "Madness," he said. His expression registered something between disgust and despair.

Hugh hesitated. "Perhaps," he said. He paced before his father's massive oaken chair as if to wear a groove in the flagstones. Hugh's nature was one of action. He despised talk. He halted, and then, speaking in a curt monotone, said: "There's an old woman come to the village. A traveling weaver. She says she saw the unicorn at the edge of the northern wood. She followed it into the forest and saw it attack a young noble. The description she gave sounds like Will." He looked at his father with anguish. "I would say the old woman is raving, except that some of the villagers say they've seen it as well—a unicorn with a blood-tipped horn. And Will was . . ." Hugh broke off and cleared his throat noisily. "He was going into the northern woods on the day we left." He lowered his head. "I might have stopped him. Or gone with him."

The earl rubbed a heavy hand over his eyes. He was a

brusque man with a titan's temper. But his sons were as dear to him as his own breath. He looked at his elder son. "This is no fault of yours, Hugh. Gather a hunting party. Capture the beast. I will see it with my own eyes before I believe a word of this tale."

Hugh shook his head. "The crone says the unicorn cannot be captured by ordinary means. A trap must be set, and then the creature must be fettered with iron shackles."

"Trap? What kind of a trap?" the earl asked. His eyes brightened, seemingly despite himself, at the prospect of a challenging hunt.

"A virgin must be placed in its haunts," said Hugh.

"Then make it so," said the earl. "And if this is true, if there is such a beast," he went on in a commanding tone, "kill it, Hugh. With your own hands, kill it. It won't bring Will back to us, but such a thing must not be suffered to live. It's a danger to the village."

Hugh's breath was ragged with emotion, and wetness glittered in his eyes as he answered:

"I will destroy it."

Chapter 11

Tessa couldn't sleep.

No matter what shape she punched her pillow into, it wasn't comfortable, and every book she picked up she tossed aside. Her thoughts kept revolving around one idea: *something was wrong*.

Outside were the sounds of occasional cars passing, but the building was quiet. She was alone. Her father had called; he would be home a bit later. She'd heard music playing in the background as he spoke over the phone. "You're sure you're okay? I'm just around the corner, at Alicia's."

Tessa heard the carefulness in her father's voice, and the worry. "I'm fine, Dad," she'd said firmly. "And that thing I said this morning—I'm really sorry. It was stupid."

"The way you feel is never stupid, Tessa." He had paused as if to say something else but then seemed to change his mind. "I won't be too late."

Now Tessa heaved herself up from the bed and turned on the desk lamp. Her father was happy; it was a good thing. She should just focus on her own life. Or lack thereof.

She remembered what Hunter had said about the volleyball accident, about their having some kind of fate or destiny together. Tessa scowled. No. Hunter Scoville was *not* her destiny.

Anyway, she didn't believe in fate. If everything in this life were preordained, destined to be, well, that would mean that someone, somewhere, had decided that *Hey, on December 12, Wendy Brody will be in a head-on car collision on I-95 South. Make sure it's when she's coming back from a shopping trip. For Christmas.*

Tessa recognized the same painful twist of sadness she always felt when she thought of that day four years ago. She pushed it away.

As far as she was concerned, life was one big series of accidents. Some were good, like when you meet your best friend during your most embarrassing moment on the playground in second grade. Some were bad, like when you kill somebody's mom, somebody's wife, by falling asleep behind the wheel of a tractor trailer.

There was no such thing as fate, or destiny. Only what you could make happen. What you could swerve to avoid. What you could fix.

Tessa looked over at the tapestry. In the shadowy light

the fierce eyes of the unicorn stared at her. *What you can make happen.* Tessa stepped closer. She closed her eyes, reached out and touched it.

She was in a shady, wooded place. Here and there, spears of sunlight shot through the leaves to make pools of glowing, dappled color on the ground. She sat, resting on a swath of green moss. She let her eyes roam up over the latticework of branches high overhead. It was beautiful here. Peaceful.

Where was she? She couldn't remember. She knew only what she had been told: she must stay here and be very quiet, very still.

Her hands worked nervously, smoothing the thick folds of fabric in her lap. She looked down. The beautiful gown was not hers. The blue velvet felt heavy and constricting and the lacings of the bodice stole her breath. Or perhaps it was her uneasiness that made her chest so tight. Her breath sounded clamorous in the silence around her. *Be quiet,* she told herself. *Be still.*

There was a monster in the woods, a beast that must be caught.

They said it killed William de Chaucy. He had been killed on the very day he had followed her into these woods. Proud, handsome, bookish William de Chaucy was dead. She had hardly known him. They had never even spoken. And yet why, when she thought of him, did she grieve? Knowing he was gone from this world . . . it made something inside her feel empty and locked away. It was as if something had been stolen from her.

An old weaver woman had come to the village, telling everyone how she had seen the beast slaughter the young nobleman. Now the earl was set on hunting it, set on vengeance for his son. There had to be a young maid for the hunt, a virgin. She had been chosen for the honor. The village was small and the choices few, she thought wryly. And her aunt had not objected to accepting the heavy purse of coins the earl had thrust forward. It was a handsome payment.

So the girl had put on the fine gown she was given; it had belonged to the earl's wife, who had died. She unbraided her hair and brushed it till it shone in cascading ripples down her back. Dressed in finery as she was, and polished so, it was hard not to feel like bait. Or sacrifice.

You must wait here in the clearing. The unicorn will come to you.

The unicorn. That was the monster. A terrible beast with searing eyes and a single horn that could slash a man to ribbons.

But why should it come to her? Would it try to kill her too? No, they'd told her she was in no danger. She would be surrounded by armed men. They were hiding, even now, in the shadows.

The silence broke. She straightened, suddenly alert. There was a shout and a tangle of harsh voices nearby, then the blare of a hunter's horn. But it was the barking that made her jump. She stiffened, then leapt to her feet. The yelps and snarls came closer. She whirled toward the sound. Dogs. Of course there were dogs in the hunt. Her fingers curled into fists and her breath came faster.

She was afraid of dogs. She cried out and began to run. All the careful instructions she had been given were dashed away by fright. She ran from the clearing and into the denser forest, stumbling through brambles. Faster. She had to get away. She had to hide. She had no idea of her direction, nor where the hunters were hidden.

She plunged deeper into the woods, where black vines clutched at her ankles and the skeletal trees creaked and snapped overhead. She kept running.

Gradually the voices and barking grew more distant. But now there was another sound.

Hoofbeats.

There were hoofbeats behind her, along the path she'd just torn through. It was the unicorn, the monster. She'd been a fool to run from the safety of the clearing. Now it would surely kill her, just as it had the young master. She could feel the pounding of the monster's hooves on the earth as she ran. It drew closer. Closer, until she was sure she felt the creature's hot breath sluice down the back of her neck as she ran. She wouldn't turn to look at it.

But the gown! The mud-stained velvet twisted around her legs like ropes, slowing her progress. The tight laces of the bodice were iron bands, binding her breasts and making her breath come in short, exhausted bleats. She staggered at last, falling against a young sapling. She clutched the cold, yielding support of its trunk and pulled herself upright. She was about to die. She must see it. She twisted around, one arm raised to shield herself. The pale form exploded from the dark as the unicorn galloped from the dense cover of the woods, its head low, barreling toward her. She closed her eyes and waited for the pain.

But she felt only a rush of air and heat and the patter of a clod of dirt on her arm. She opened her eyes to see the unicorn land and shudder to a halt some yards away. She stared at it, dazed. She had never seen anything so beautiful. So terrible.

The unicorn looked like madness. Blood-flecked sputum frothed from its mouth, and its eyes rolled toward her, their whites showing all around. With a snort the unicorn reared and stamped down once more; the ground trembled. It stepped closer, tossing its head, and its long horn slashed the air like a sword. A step more and it would stab into her. But still she stood, frozen.

The unicorn stopped. It raised its head and its gaze locked on hers. She could not look away. There was something more than madness there. Something . . . familiar. The unicorn's eyes were a deep golden brown color. Strange. They weren't the eyes of an animal at all. They looked just like—

She screamed.

Tessa's eyes flew open. She was huddled on the floor of her room, her arms clutched closely around her knees, shivering.

The Norn stood together.

"Another disturbance in the Wyrd," said Weavyr. She sighed and bent over the fabric.

"There must be an explanation," said Spyn.

"This one." Weavyr spoke as she fingered a single strand in the Wyrd. "This girl. There is some connection between her and the missing threads."

Spyn bent closer to peer at the path the thread took. She nodded. "Yes. She was there when the threads were stolen. In another life, five hundred years ago. Now she travels back, in her mind."

"And makes another tangle in my work," grumbled Weavyr.

Scytha's hand hovered over the human girl's thread. "This can mean only one thing."

The other turned. "What?" they asked in unison.

"She was the one who stole the threads," Scytha replied.

Chapter 12

The next morning was Saturday. Tessa slept late. It was as if she'd been drugged. She could barely drag herself from bed. When she got downstairs, her father was sitting behind the store counter. He wore a puzzled expression as he hung up the phone.

"Tessa." He brightened and smiled at her. "It seems there's been some kind of a mix-up with the items from that auction." He nodded to the phone. "That was a lawyer who represents the estate. He says that old book and the tapestry were never supposed to be part of the lot I bought. The owner wants them back."

Tessa stared at him. "But they can't do that! Can they? You paid for them."

Her father ran a hand through his already-disheveled hair. "I know, I know, but just listen. . . . He seemed very upset about the whole thing. He began by offering to pay me the full amount of what I paid for the entire lot. But he only wants those two items back. Apparently the owner, a Ms. Lila Gerome, is moving to England. The book and the tapestry have been in her family for generations. I get the impression she's kind of a demanding woman, a bit eccentric, and loaded. So get this," he said, lowering his voice.

"What?"

"I told him I'd already taken the book to be appraised and you'd taken a liking to the unicorn tapestry. That's when he got really worked up. Guess how much he offered me?"

Tessa shook her head.

Her father grinned. "Ten thousand dollars." He stood up and did a little shuffling dance step.

Tessa's gaze traveled up as she thought of the tapestry hanging on the wall in her bedroom. "Wow," she said in a flat tone.

Her father's smile faded. "I thought you'd be thrilled, Tessa. Ten thousand dollars would cover a good chunk of your tuition for college this fall."

"Yeah," she answered slowly. It *was* a lot of money. But the thought of selling the unicorn tapestry left Tessa with a sudden feeling of . . . she wasn't sure exactly what.

"What did you tell him?" she asked.

Her father threw his hands up with a perplexed look. "I didn't really have a chance to tell him anything. He said he's on his way here. Driving from New York. He'll be here tomorrow morning. If it was an honest mistake, I think we should give them back. Don't you?"

"I—I guess so," Tessa answered. But she wasn't so sure.

"Well, it didn't sound like the fellow was taking no for an answer. I'm going drive down to Portsmouth and pick up the book from the appraiser.

"Polly should be able to handle the counter. Just give her a hand if things get busy. I'll bring home some supper."

After her father left, Tessa went up to her bedroom and closed the door. She walked over to the tapestry. She wondered how old it was. She hadn't given it a lot of thought before, but it must have been made hundreds of years ago. Weird to think that a real person, living so long ago, had made this. And now it was here, in her room.

Now someone was going to waltz in and take it away, Tessa thought angrily. She bet that lawyer had just realized how valuable the tapestry and the book were and wanted them back. Maybe he even wanted to sell them himself. It would probably end up in some locked display case in a mansion somewhere. Maybe even a museum. It wasn't fair.

Tessa felt a stab of sadness and knew: she wanted to keep the tapestry. *She was meant to have it.* The weight of the feeling brought sadness but also a fierce burst of pride; her gaze drifted over the tapestry. Then she noticed it.

A loose thread was dangling from the bottom. It was a single strand of silver, drifting in the air like a piece of a spider's web. Tessa caught it and twined it around her finger. She hesitated for a second. It was only a tiny thread; she wouldn't damage the tapestry. Besides, it was the kind of thing that would drive her crazy. She tugged. It didn't snap off. *Pretty strong for something so fragile-looking.*

She stepped back and pulled harder. The thread, rather than breaking, drew out of the tapestry in one long, glittering trail. As it came out, Tessa felt a blaze of heat run from her fingertips, race along her arm and rush through her, leaving a warm, tingling sensation in its wake.

Before Tessa could react, a deep rumbling noise began and the floor beneath her feet tilted with a sickening lurch. She staggered, fighting to keep her balance. The whole room began to shake. Tessa gave a strangled cry and reached for the wall to steady herself—but where her hand should have met the firm surface of the tapestry and the wall beneath, all she felt was a cool, moist . . . nothing.

Tessa, thrown backward by the push of some unseen force, crashed into her dresser and fell. Her whole room shook as though it were a dollhouse in the hands of a giant toddler. The floorboards rose and fell like piano keys as their nails shrieked. The room pitched to darkness as a violent, tearing noise shredded the air. Then, quiet.

She was on the floor. The lights flickered on. Tessa let out a groan and eased herself up to a sitting position. Her shoulder was sore where she'd jammed it against the dresser, and she'd fallen pretty hard on her rear end; otherwise, she was okay.

Tessa looked around. Everything was still, and except for

some books fallen from her bookcase and a spill of papers from her desk, her room looked pretty normal.

"What the—?" she whispered. "When was the last earthquake in Maine?"

Then she realized she wasn't alone.

A young man crouched on the floor beside her, gasping for breath and shaking. Tessa stared as he raised his head to look at her. Dark blond hair fell in coarse tangles across his forehead and reached to his shoulders. His eyes, an intense, startling golden brown, were ringed with dark lashes.

Tessa was so surprised, her scream came out only as a strangled gasp. She scuttled backward, away from him, and scrambled to her feet. Her heart was pounding. "Okay, wake up," Tessa told herself. "Wake up."

The guy stared at her. He was panting in deep, heaving breaths, as if he'd been running. He stood. He was tall, and dressed in a gray cloak and suede pants and boots; all were torn and muddy. His lean, tanned face was dirty too, and he had an ugly gash down one cheek.

"You," he said, in a choked voice. He took an unsteady step toward her, then stopped and looked down, staring at his feet. He stared up at her again. "Sweet Jesu," he breathed. With that, he toppled forward, collapsing to the floor.

"Hey!" Tessa took a step forward and stopped. The young man didn't move but lay with long arms and legs splayed out.

"Hello?" Tessa said nervously, then repeated it a little louder, took a step closer and gasped. "Oh my God." Her thoughts were spinning in frantic circles. "Okay," she said, looking around. "We had an earthquake. We had an earthquake and a strange guy in weird clothes collapsed in my bedroom." She closed her eyes tight and shook her head. What was happening? This was way too real to be a dream. Even for her. And too strange for reality. She opened her eyes. There was still a guy on the floor.

"Hey," she said again, in a voice that she hoped sounded tough, authoritative. But the young man didn't move. Tessa took another cautious step forward.

"You're hurt," she said, forgetting caution and kneeling over the young man's body. This was no dream. Being hurt was real. "Are you okay?" Tessa shook his arm. He still didn't move. With an effort, she tugged at the dirty clothes and rolled him onto his back. A sudden memory of the CPR training she'd had the summer before came to her. "ABCs," she whispered to herself. Right. "Airway." Tessa reached out and gently moved his jaw to open his mouth. She knelt closer, swept her own hair out of the way impatiently and brought her ear close to his lips. Warm breath tickled her skin, and she could see the faint rise and fall of his chest. "Breathing," she murmured. "Breathing is good." Circulation. She pressed two fingertips to the firm column of his neck, where a pulse beat in a fast but steady rhythm. "Okay, you're alive," breathed Tessa, with a sigh of relief. She sat back on her heels and looked at him. Really looked at him.

He had a face of strong lines—clean, angled jaw and arrogantly sculpted nose. A deep, ragged scratch tore across one cheekbone, and a streak of dried blood was crusted on the middle of his forehead. His skin was tanned, and his tousled hair and eyebrows were touched with a paler color than the dark lashes that shadowed deep-set eyes. He smelled, but not really unpleasantly, Tessa realized, of musky sweat and campfires and something else . . . horses?

Good-looking despite the dirt. So good-looking, in fact, that if he hadn't been filthy, he'd hardly look real. Especially dressed as he was, thought Tessa, in some kind of costume from a medieval fair. She reached out a tentative hand to touch his clothes.

He woke up fast. At her touch, his hand struck out like a whip and captured her wrist. Tessa gasped as he leapt up, hauling her up with him. He gripped her by the shoulders and nearly carried her as he propelled her forward to push her against the wall. Tessa swore, struggling to get her knee up and wrench herself away, but he only tightened his hold and pressed closer, pinning her to the wall.

"Where am I?" he demanded. "And what are *you* doing here?"

But Tessa ignored the questions and let out a high-pitched scream. He clamped a hand over her mouth. "Quiet!" he hissed. "I'm not going to hurt you." His face as he looked down at hers was pale, giving his tanned skin a waxy look. His eyes were furious.

His eyes. Tessa stared, blinked and slowed her struggling. She *was* dreaming. She had to be. That face, those eyes, definitely came from her dream. Didn't they? And it was impossible, but she could have sworn that she saw recognition in his expression as well. She nodded once. *Okay.* Slowly he took his hand from her mouth.

"Pray don't scream," he said, examining her closely. "It was you who released me?"

"Released you?" Tessa whispered, still staring into his eyes with confusion. She trembled as an eerie sort of understanding crept over her. "The tapestry." She turned her head.

The tapestry hung on the wall, smooth and intact. But in the center of the picture, the clearing was empty. The green grass had been replaced by a shadowy darkness of tangled threads.

The unicorn was gone.

Chapter 13

At the same moment that Tessa Brody pulled a loose thread from an old tapestry, something else happened. Over the ancient tree Yggdrasil a knife of green lightning split the sky. A tiny rift appeared in the Wyrd. The endless, flowing fabric was torn. Ripples cascaded from the spot, across centuries, across continents.

The shock of it struck Weavyr into stillness. Her dusky fingers seized up as she watched her precise patterns, the symmetrical forms, become hopelessly tangled.

"By the powers!" she shrieked. "Not again! Come. Help me, Sisters!"

The other two Norn came swiftly.

"What is happening?" Spyn cried.

"Look for yourself. The Wyrd is torn." Weavyr gasped. Her fingers began to fly, clutching at threads to straighten paths, to restore order.

"How?" Scytha demanded in a booming voice.

"The stolen threads," Weavyr replied. "Hold this. No, not that one. No, too late. Here."

"They've been returned?" asked Spyn.

"No," Weavyr answered, working frantically. "Not returned. But something has happened. A terrible disturbance. It must be because of the stolen threads, or one of them."

"Can you repair it?" Scytha asked.

"I'm trying," said Weavyr. Her cloaked hood shook as if she was shuddering beneath it.

Lila Gerome strode across the concourse of Logan Airport, her high Prada heels clicking on the tiles and her shiny hair swinging. Abruptly she stopped. Her face contorted into a shocked grimace. She let out a grunt. Clutching her stomach, she lurched forward. Surprised travelers swerved out of her way as she ran into a nearby washroom.

Lila hung over one of the stainless steel sinks as a fiery pain scorched through her chest. A pain like she'd never felt before. "Wh-what's happening?" she croaked. Her voice. It wasn't smooth. It was as coarse as tar paper. It sounded *ancient*.

She clutched her chest, her breath coming in wheezing

gasps. Her hands. She lifted them up and stared. The slim fingers thickened and twisted as the joints swelled. Blue, cordlike veins rose beneath the spotty skin. In a moment her hands had shriveled into clawlike fists.

"The tapestry," she said. The pain was subsiding now, and in its place was an overwhelming terror. Was she dying? No. Lila staggered forward to the full-length mirror on the wall. Slowly she raised her head. Staring back at her was a hunched old woman. Her fashionable suit hung on her rickety frame as if she were a misshapen hanger. Thin gray hair hung around her face, and her small black eyes were nearly buried in wrinkled folds.

"Shit," she said.

There was only one way for this to happen. It should have been impossible, but someone must have *taken* one of her threads from the tapestry. Taken her most precious thread, in fact, and released him. Her unicorn. He was her youth, her beauty, her strength. Stolen. Rage bubbled up, nearly choking her, and she let out a cry of frustration.

"Are you okay, ma'am?" A chubby woman in a floral caftan pulled her luggage on wheels up next to Lila, her face concerned.

Lila turned on her with a snarl. "Leave me alone!" she screeched.

The woman backed up, startled. "Well, fine," she huffed, and hurried away.

Lila straightened as much as she could. "Moncrieff," she said, nearly spewing the word. *He* had let this happen. Oh, he would pay for such incompetence. But first she must get the tapestry. And her unicorn must go back to its rightful place. And as for whoever had released him . . .

"I will find you," she promised. Yes. She would find the filthy thief and sing her black song and pull his life's thread. Not to weave it. No. She would destroy it. Tear it into tiny pieces. Send it into the Void.

Chapter 14

"You came from the tapestry," Tessa said softly, more to herself than to the stranger. He still stood close, his hands on her shoulders, his pale, tense face looking down at her. But whether he was trying to restrain her or steady himself, she couldn't tell.

"It's impossible," Tessa whispered. She closed her eyes tightly once again and shook her head. *Wake up, Tessa*. This *had* to be a dream.

"I thought so as well," said the young man. After a pause he added: "I had given up hope."

Tessa opened her eyes. He was still there.

"So you were the . . . ," she began. She couldn't even say it aloud.

The young man frowned. He took a hand from her shoulder to reach up and touch his forehead. He dropped his hand with a long exhalation and curled long fingers into a fist.

"The unicorn," he finished. "Yes. And no." He glanced around with a look of confusion and his gaze returned to her. "I thought I recognized you, but you are different. As is this place. It cannot be—" He broke off and shook his head. "Where am I? Where is the forest? Who are you?" he demanded.

"Who am *I*?" Tessa gasped. The question snapped her back, if not to reality, then at least to the recent highlights. "*You're* the one who just appeared out of nowhere!"

When he didn't make any move to release her, a headline flashed in Tessa's mind. *Local Teen Strangled by Escaped Lunatic Male Model.* She pressed both hands to the man's chest, which beneath the ragged clothing was firm and . . . not going anywhere. She tried shoving, but his hands only tightened their grip.

She went very still. "Let go of me," she said. It made her mad to hear how her voice warbled. She jutted her chin and stared up at him. "Right. Now."

He didn't budge, but something hot blazed in his eyes and Tessa saw them as she had before. It was impossible, but his *were* the golden brown eyes of the unicorn. They held a mixture of anguish and rage and fierce pride. She trembled, remembering a dream. Then it was gone. He dropped his hands and stepped back, his expression neutral.

"My name's Tessa," she said, rubbing her arms and sidestepping his tall form to sidle across the room.

"Tessa." He repeated it slowly, his gaze following her.

Tessa snatched up a small but heavy trophy from the bookcase. She held it by the gold-plated figure on the top and loved, *loved,* for the first time ever, that she'd won second place in the 2005 freestyle event at Crazy Wheels.

"That's right. Tessa Brody," she said, turning to face him. "And this is my room. My house." She brandished the marble base of the tacky Rollerblader at him. "So. Who are you? Forget it. Just get out. No." She hesitated, confused, torn between fear and curiosity. He just stood there, watching her. "Who are you?" she repeated finally.

The stranger glanced at her would-be weapon and raised his hands slightly. "I beg pardon, mistress," he said, although there was nothing remorseful in his cool tone. On the contrary, he lifted one brow, giving his lean, clever face a look of surprised amusement. "My name is William de Chaucy." With this, the young man in rags gave a short, formal bow.

Tessa stared at him. "William de Chaucy," she repeated as he straightened. The very polite escaped lunatic. She felt a little of her bravado melt and had the sudden and really urgent need to laugh. She sat down on the end of her bed. Or rather, she let her legs wobble out from under her. The bed happened to be there.

"What are you doing?" William de Chaucy said, his expression guarded.

"I think it's called going into shock," Tessa said. She looked up at the tapestry on the wall, then back at . . . Unicorn Guy, and choked back a giggle. "Cut it out," she told herself. She took in a deep, shaky breath and let it out.

He gave her a puzzled frown. "You speak most strangely, mistress."

"Really," she said, eyeing him. "So do you." He had spoken English. But not like Tessa had ever heard before. His voice was deep, with a strange accent. Not exactly British, not exactly French. Mostly Hugh Grant with a little Pepe Le Pew thrown in.

That did it. She was gone. Completely psycho.

"How did you bring me to . . ." He looked around her room once more and then shook his head. "How did you release me?" he demanded. Perhaps it was his accent or the way he held himself, but he seemed, thought Tessa, to act as though he owned the place. When she didn't answer, he raised his scratched, dirty hands, looking at them as if not sure of their substance. "How did you transform me thus?" he asked. His voice rose. "Cast a spell? An incantation? Where is Gray Lily?" He glared at her now, suspicious. "Are *you* a witch as well?"

Okay. That was really *it*. Time to muster up Tough Girl again. "Listen, *William*." Tessa stood up and jabbed her trophy at him, breathing hard. "I don't know what happened or where you came from. I didn't do anything. I mean, I—" She broke off. What *had* happened, anyway? Tessa frowned and went on. "I just pulled a thread hanging from the tapestry. One little thread." She stepped over to the tapestry and pointed to the lower edge. "From right there."

Instantly William leapt forward and pulled her back. "Don't touch it!" he hissed, gripping her elbow with a shaky hand. With a visible effort, he seemed to recover, and his hand steadied. He let go and stepped away, putting an extra couple of feet between himself and the tapestry. Though he looked like he would have preferred a couple of miles.

"I was trapped inside there for—" His eyes darkened and he swallowed. "I think a very long time."

Tessa stared at him. From his clothes to his odd, formal speech, nothing about him belonged here. "I think so too," she said slowly. Once again the sheer, ridiculous impossibility of the whole thing struck her. Maybe this was what happened when nice, practical girls lost their minds. But he was here. William de Chaucy was real. She could feel the warmth of him standing next to her, smell the green, smoky scent of him and see the quick flash of his eyes as they swept over her. She could reach out and touch him. Not that she wanted to.

"So. Where're you from?" Tessa asked brightly. Good old practical Tessa.

"From Hartescross," he replied. When this seemed to make no impression on her, Will stiffened slightly and added, "My father is the Earl of Umbric."

"Oh. *Right.* Okay." Tessa nodded, taking in the rough, grimy clothing the young man wore. It certainly wasn't very impressive. He looked as if he had just rolled out of a muddy stable.

"Hartescross. Is that in England?" she asked.

He gave her another sharp look. This one was wasn't so much suspicious, it was more like "Are you insane?"

"Of course," he snapped. "Cornwall."

"Just checking," Tessa said. It could just as easily have

been Tatooine. "What was the year," she asked slowly, "when you left?"

"It is the year of our Lord"—he frowned at her, then slid his eyes around the room and went on, his voice a little less sure—"fifteen hundred and eleven."

"Uh-huh." Tessa waited a beat, then nodded. "Okay. We need to talk. And then . . . I have to call somebody."

Scytha looked up from the Wyrd to her sisters. She traced the shining blue thread, her fingers crawling along its length like a monstrous spider. "We will contact this human. She will be made to return the threads."

Spyn's fingers trembled and twitched as she worked. "You do it," she said querulously. "I don't like talking to humans. They never understand anything. And they always have to ask the question. Always the *same* question. It makes a buzzing in my head."

Weavyr spoke. "We must find out how this happened. How did this mortal winnow the threads from living beings? Has she destroyed them? Is that what caused this mess?" She waved a frustrated hand at the Wyrd.

"No," answered Scytha. "The threads are not destroyed. We would have sensed the pain of the souls that were ended."

Weavyr and Spyn nodded.

"We will get the threads back." Scytha's voice seemed now, more than ever, to carry the gloom of a deep abyss. "Or there will be consequences."

Her shears flashed.

Chapter 15

"So you pulled a thread from the tapestry. Room starts shaking. Bing bang boom. Guy lands on the floor."

"Right," Tessa said into her cell, to Opal. "Stop repeating it, okay? He's from England in the fifteen hundreds, and practically royalty. According to *him*, anyway." Tessa added this in a low voice. She watched as William de Chaucy paced her room, examining her books, her photos, the computer, smelling a felt-tip marker with a look of distaste. "He's really from the past," she went on. "He doesn't know anything about our time. Cars, planes, phones, nothing. This Gray Lily person, who sounds like a real piece of work, put some kind of a spell on him and took a thread with his soul or his life or something, and used it to make him into a unicorn. The unicorn from the tapestry."

"Was he naked?" Opal asked.

"*What?*"

"Was he, like, all naked when he came out of the tapes-try?"

"No. He wasn't naked!" Tessa hissed in an undertone. "Opal, have you been listening to me?"

"I dunno. I just thought—"

"Look, I'm serious. I mean, I'm not crazy or anything. But maybe I am. And if I am, I need your help even more." Tessa stopped and took a deep breath. She tried to ignore William, who had turned and was now watching her, arms folded, leaning against the wall.

"And you really buy all this?" Opal asked. "You believe him?"

"Yes," Tessa said simply. She *did* believe him. She wished she had told Opal about the strange visions she'd had when she touched the tapestry. She didn't know how or why, but she had seen William de Chaucy's world. Some-how she'd *been* there. "I can explain more when you come and see for yourself."

"It just sounds weird," Opal said.

Tessa looked at the tall, muddy guy in her bedroom, who had just noticed the light switch. He flicked it off and on again. A look of shock came over his face, then a delighted smile.

"We passed weird a few stops back," Tessa answered. "This is real."

"Okay. I'll be right over."

❧

Tessa touched the wet facecloth to the dirty, torn flesh on William de Chaucy's cheek. He never moved, but she winced as the dried blood and grime came away, revealing a ragged cut that traveled from his cheekbone to his jaw.

"This is a mess," she said, staring at it. Winced again. *Not the best thing to say, Florence Nightingale.*

Opal hovered over Tessa's shoulder. "Did Gray Lily do that to you?" she asked.

"No," William de Chaucy answered, staring straight ahead. His voice was as expressionless as his face, but both still relayed a clear message: *It's none of your business.*

"You should probably have stitches," Tessa said. She waited to see if that broke his cool. A lot of tough-looking guys went surprisingly weak-kneed about stuff like that. But the comment didn't seem to faze de Chaucy.

"Here, put some of this on it." Opal handed Tessa a tube of antibiotic ointment. Tessa began to daub it along the wound, but William shied away from her hands. He stood up.

"Enough," he told her.

"But it could get infected," Tessa said indignantly.

"What is *infected*?" he asked, glaring down at her. His tone was suspicious.

"You know, germs," said Tessa. "Pus, gangrene, flesh-eating bacteria?" Now he was looking at her like that again. As if he didn't trust her. "I don't suppose my lord has ever heard of a *tetanus shot*," Tessa finished, sounding harder than she meant to.

She didn't feel afraid anymore. Mostly, Tessa realized, she felt kind of helpless and, for some reason, angry. And the angry had nowhere to go but toward *him*.

William stared at her. "Most of your words I cannot construe," he said. "But I take your meaning. The wound will heal. I don't require any further attentions. And I am not a lord," he added. The faint curl of his lip made Tessa wonder if he was making fun of her or himself. "Being the younger son of an earl, I am only an esquire."

"That's cool," said Opal. She'd been ogling him with transparent awe ever since she walked in. "William de Chaucy, Esquire." She grinned.

"Please. Call me Will," he said to her. He flashed an easy smile, grimacing slightly as it caught up to his cheek. He had a crooked front tooth, Tessa noticed.

But Opal was charmed. She grinned even wider, showing gums that had probably never seen daylight before. Tessa scowled and wiped her hands.

"I thank you for your help, Tessa, Opal," Will said, nodding to both of them. "But I must go now. Just get me some food and ale." He crossed to the chair where his cloak lay, covering the distance in two long strides. He grabbed the cloak and slung it over his broad shoulders. "I'll take one of your horses."

"Oh really?" snapped Tessa. "Well, we don't happen to have any horses in the old corral at the moment." She flung the bloody cloth to the floor. "Do you always order people around like this?"

"*Yes,*" he said, with stormy emphasis, as if pleased that she finally understood.

"Fine," Tessa shot back. "But it seems to me, having just been *rescued* or *released* or whatever"—she threw her hands up—"you could be a little nicer."

Opal stood by, looking at Tessa with wide eyes. Blinked. Looked at Will.

He never took his eyes from Tessa's face. "Perhaps I have my reasons," he said quietly, his expression unreadable. "But it is true. I do believe I owe you my life, mistress. Such as it is."

There was a bitter irony in his tone, in his words, that baffled Tessa.

Before she could react, his expression changed. He smiled again and laid his hand on his chest. "And so, if my manner has been surly, please accept these, my sincere apologies. I shall try to be, henceforth, *nice*." He bowed once more, but this time it was deep and, no mistake, mocking. His eyes were trained on hers, glinting a challenge from under tousled hair.

Tessa tried to ignore the strange little hiccup in her pulse. "Okay then," she managed. "But I still don't see how you can go off on your own. You've got no money, no food. And there's presumably somebody out there who could . . ." *Take your life and basically turn it into macramé.* "Hurt you," she finished.

Then she remembered something else. "The woman who owned the tapestry," she said. "She wants it back. Maybe she knows something about it, something that could help." She frowned, trying to recall the name.

Meanwhile, William de Chaucy's face was set in firm lines that seemed to express cool disdain for the idea. "Thank you, but I shall take my own counsel on the matter," he replied.

"We should find out, at least," Tessa argued. "Besides," she reasoned, "where would you go?"

"Home," Will said, as if it were just that simple.

Opal looked back and forth from Tessa to Will. "You know, the two of you are acting like this isn't totally whacked." She waggled a finger between them. "Do you think you could both be crazy together? I've heard of stuff like that happening—mass hypnosis or psychosis. Hysteria, that's it."

"Hello?" said Tessa, raising a hand. "Not hysterical here."

"I am standing before you, Mistress Opal," said Will dryly. "And that"—he pointed to the empty clearing in the tapestry—"is where I *was*."

Tessa allowed herself to gaze at the tapestry once more. She took a step toward it. "What is it like?" she asked. "Inside there?"

Will de Chaucy regarded her gravely. "As you see. A forest," he answered. "Exquisitely beautiful. And deadly. And endless."

She stared at the dark center of the tapestry, then said in a quiet voice, "I wonder if there might be a way for you to go back?"

He stiffened. "Is that what you wish?"

"No," said Tessa simply. "I didn't mean—"

"I will *never* go back into the tapestry," Will said. He glared at her. "I would die first."

Opal shook her head. "A unicorn," she said, eyeing Will. "People just don't get turned into unicorns. I mean, this is a mythical creature we're talking about."

Will picked up a snow globe from Tessa's desk and turned it in his hands, studying it. "I don't know how Gray Lily performed the witchery." He looked at Tessa closely, and again she saw distrust in his eyes. "Or how *you* managed to reverse it, mistress. But I am, as you can see, real. And as for the unicorn," he added to Opal, "it is not mythical. It's legendary."

"Okay. So what's the difference?" said Tessa.

Will shrugged and set down the globe. "Mythical creatures are imaginary. A fiction. Legends are based on something real."

"Right," said Opal, nodding agreement. "I get it. Kind of like Elvis."

Will turned to her. "Who?"

"The singer. Elvis." Opal held up an invisible microphone, slicked back an imaginary pompadour and swiveled her skinny hips.

Tessa smiled despite herself. This was getting crazier by the minute.

"Elvis is a legend, right?" said Opal. "But he was a real guy first. The King of Rock and Roll."

Will nodded thoughtfully. "Yes." He turned back to Tessa. "I am like Elvis."

Tessa gave in to a helpless laugh at his serious expression. William de Chaucy cocked his head, looked at her and raised one brow. Someone knocked on the door.

"Tessa?" her father called. "May I come in?"

"Oh. Just. Perfect," Tessa bit out under her breath. Then she yelled, "Uh. No. Wait a minute, Dad. I'll be right out!"

She grabbed Will by the arm and pushed him toward her closet. "Come on, *Elvis*. I don't want my father to find you. I am so not ready to have that conversation."

Will allowed himself to be pushed, but ambling backward, he shot a smile down at her. A real smile that went straight into her eyes. "That was *King* Elvis, I believe," he said in a low voice as she shut the door.

"Is Opal staying over tonight?" Tessa's father asked when she scrambled downstairs to the kitchen.

Staying over? Tessa thought, suddenly panicking. *Was* he? Where was she going to put him? What could she do with the sixteenth-century-tapestry-unicorn-turned-really-good-looking-though-very-disturbing-and-kind-of-snotty guy upstairs, hiding in her closet?

"Staying over? Yeah, I think so," she choked out. "Is that okay?"

"Of course. I wanted to tell you about what the appraiser said." Her father sat down at the kitchen table. He wore white cotton gloves, and he carefully picked up the old book that had accompanied the tapestry. Through the protective plastic sleeve Tessa saw the title once again: *Texo Vita*.

"Believe it or not," her father said, "this book seems to be from somewhere around the sixteenth century."

"Really," said Tessa. She turned away, opened the fridge and peered inside. She could have probably narrowed its age down a bit more than that. But she wasn't ready to tell her father what had happened.

Jackson Brody watched as his daughter took out cheese, milk, sliced ham, pickles, mustard, mayonnaise, two sodas. "I'm sorry, honey," he said. "I promised you some dinner, didn't I? You must be hungry."

"Starved." She pulled a loaf of whole-grain bread from the drawer and grabbed a thick handful of slices from the bag. "So's Opal." She began constructing sandwiches and piling them on a paper plate.

"I guess I haven't been paying too much attention to you lately, have I? I'm sorry about that, Tessa. You know, about Alicia and me—"

"Dad," Tessa interrupted. "You don't need to say anything. Please. I'm fine with you guys going out or whatever."

Her father gave her a perplexed look and shrugged. "Okay. But we're going to have to talk about the 'whatever' sometime."

Tessa's eyes dropped. "What were you going to tell me about the book?"

Her father tapped the spine of the thick tome. "Professor Waterhouse has never seen anything like this or even *heard* of anything like it. He also can't explain the level of preservation. The paper, the binding, even the vegetable inks are all consistent with this book being roughly five hundred years old." Her father shook his head. "The paper should be crumbling by now, but it's not. And the text is in Medieval English, interspersed with Latin. It seems to be a journal, detailing local tales around a particular region in Cornwall, especially about witchcraft but also, strangely enough"—her father frowned—"about weaving." He laid the book down and pulled off the gloves.

Tessa stopped. "Weaving?" A cold tingle of fear passed from her core along her arm to her fingertips, retracing the streak of warmth she'd felt when she pulled the silvery thread.

"Yeah." Her father came over, popped a gherkin into his mouth and munched. "Very intriguing. In fact, translated, *Texo Vita* means 'the weave of life.'" He frowned. "Waterhouse was really disappointed that I took it back. He'd already contacted someone at Yale to do further testing."

"Listen, Dad." Tessa worked nervously, slapping bread on the last sandwich and squishing the whole stack down. "We can't give the book back. Or the tapestry. At least, not yet."

"But Tessa, we've discussed this already." Her father's plump, easygoing face looked puzzled as he watched her. "I have to return it. The lawyer for the Gerome estate will be here first thing in the morning."

"I just—" Tessa hesitated. She looked away from her father, plucked up a dish towel to wipe her hands and smoothed it out on the countertop. "I just have the feeling something isn't right," she said. Now, that was completely true. Down to her Jell-O-y bones she knew something was not right. Like the whole world, maybe. She wasn't lying to her dad. She was just . . . not sharing. Yet.

Her father smiled. "Well, I certainly wouldn't want to mess with a woman's intuition. Why don't we see what this lawyer fellow says in the morning? Maybe we can work something out. But you know, we could really use that money."

Tessa put the food and drinks on a tray. "Okay," she said with a puff of relief.

Her father leaned over and gave her a peck on the cheek. "Night."

"Night, Dad," mumbled Tessa. She hardly heard him walk out. She was staring at the red and white checkered dishcloth spread out on the kitchen counter.

It was moving.

The small towel wriggled as if it were covering a bed of snakes. As Tessa watched, the red and white threads of the cloth began to writhe and separate. They crossed, twisted and rearranged themselves with furious speed. Then they suddenly stopped and the dish towel lay flat once more. Tessa backed away with a little cry, staring at the pattern that had emerged. Stark white letters on a red background said:

Give them back.

Chapter 16

Tessa clutched the tray of food in her trembling hands and walked upstairs. As she balanced the tray on her hip and levered the bedroom door open, she could hear Opal's voice:

"U.S.A. The United States of America. Actually, we were part of England and then broke away in 1776. We had a war and everything. But we're cool now. You kind of missed the whole thing."

Opal was sitting cross-legged on Tessa's bed while Will stood some feet away. They both looked up when she entered, and by their expressions, Tessa realized how she must look. Maybe as if she'd just seen the ghost of dish towels past.

"What is it?" said Will sharply.

Tessa only shook her head and put down the tray with a

clatter. Half of the sandwich pile flopped over and a pickle rolled onto the floor. She couldn't speak but held her icy hands together, blew on them and turned to look at the tapestry. With its center of tangled black it wasn't beautiful anymore. The background was the same, with the forest and the distant castle, but the spot where the unicorn had stood seemed dark and full of secret dangers. She was afraid to look too closely at the shadowy threads but afraid to turn her back on them as well.

"I just got a message," she said in a shaky voice. "In a dishcloth."

Opal gaped at her. "Huh?"

Will said nothing, but his face was watchful, wary.

"It flopped around and remade itself right in front of me," Tessa went on. "The threads made letters. It said, 'Give them back.' Dish towels are *not* supposed to do that," she said, turning to Will. "Just in case you're wondering if it's some twenty-first-century thing. This is insane." She slumped onto the chair and put her face in her hands. "I'm babbling."

"No," Opal said doubtfully. "Well, maybe a little. Babble-ish."

"Where is this cloth?" Will asked.

"In the kitchen. I didn't want to touch it," Tessa confessed. A shiver began low in her spine and she straightened, trying to make it stop. "I guess it's still down there."

"'Give them back'?" Will repeated. "What does it mean?" His glance swept to the tapestry and back to Tessa.

The shiver started again and Tessa hugged her arms tight

to her body. Why couldn't she warm up? "It means the tapestry, I guess," she answered. "And the book."

Opal frowned. "Freaky. So you think it's a message from the witch that did the unicorn thing to Will. Right?"

"*What* book?" demanded Will.

Tessa nodded to Opal. "I guess so."

"What *book*?" Will repeated, clipping off each word like an angry elocution teacher.

"I'll show you." Tessa stood. "But you have to stay here." She hesitated at the door. Suddenly she couldn't bear the thought of going down to the kitchen again. Especially alone. "Opal, would you come with?"

"Yeah. Right behind you," Opal said, grabbing a tennis racket that leaned against the wall.

Tessa padded downstairs and flicked on the kitchen light. The dishcloth lay exactly where she had left it on the countertop. Except now it was normal. It was just a plain old red and white checkered towel.

"The letters are gone," Tessa said slowly.

Opal lowered the racket from a batter's stance and they stared at the towel for a moment.

Opal shot Tessa a reassuring glance. "I believe you," she said.

"Thanks," said Tessa. "I'm not sure I do." She took a deep breath, snatched up the dish towel, stepped on the pedal of the trash can and with a quick toss, threw the towel inside and let the lid slam down. She looked at Opal and both of them broke out in nervous giggles.

"This isn't funny!" Tessa gasped.

"I know, I know. Why are you laughing?" said Opal, and bit her lip.

Tessa shook her head and sobered, tugging her fingers through her hair as she thought about what to do. She turned and looked at the book on the table. "C'mon," she said with a sigh. "Let's bring this upstairs. Maybe we'll find some answers."

The *Texo Vita* lay open on her desk, illuminated by a greenish pool of light from the adjustable lamp. Outside, the wind rattled against the dark pane of the window as Tessa turned the crisp yellowed pages with a gloved hand. The lines of black script were so small and ornate, they looked like spiders crawling off the page. She could make out some of the letters here and there, and some dates. That was about it.

Opal leaned over Tessa's shoulder. Will paced behind them, finishing the last of a ham sandwich.

"Do you recognize any of this writing?" Tessa asked him, turning and leaning back in the chair.

"No," said Will, giving the book a brief glance. "Should I?"

"I suppose not." Tessa closed the book with a sigh. "I don't know how this can tell us anything."

Will stopped pacing. He reached over her and plucked the book away. "I said I did not recognize it," he said quietly. "That does not mean I am incapable of *reading* it."

Tessa gave him an exasperated look. "You might have said so."

"You might have asked."

"Okay, kids," said Opal under her breath. "Let's all get along."

Will read the cover aloud. *"Texo Vita."*

Tessa recalled the conversation with her father. "That means 'the weave of life,' right?" she asked.

He ran a considering hand over the letters. "More precisely it means 'to weave life.'"

"Okay. That makes more sense," Tessa murmured. She looked at the tapestry. "Not in a good way, but more sense."

Will gripped the book by the spine and began to riffle through it.

"Hey!" Tessa cried. She peeled off the cotton gloves and shook them at Will, but he only turned away, completely absorbed in scanning the pages. She tossed the gloves down with a sigh. The book had survived for five hundred years. A little spicy brown mustard probably wouldn't hurt it now.

"It looks like a diary," he said after a moment. "Where shall I begin?"

"Anywhere," Tessa said.

Will put a finger on the page and read rapidly:

Thirteenth December, 1506

A baby born last night in village to whey-faced daughter of Winna Humphries. Girl child. Darkling. Well-formed and red-faced, took teat. I was paid four eggs and a plank of dried fish for delivering.

The weaving becomes harder. My joints ache so, and I am clumsy with the fine work. But I must keep working. I must find a way to obtain the threads.

Will turned a number of pages slowly, his eyes scanning the scrawled writing with apparent ease before reading again:

Dunnington. Nineteenth April, 1507
Guinea hens not laying for four days. Killed one for dinner and ate with mashed peas and soaked trencher of manchet. Teeth are hurting most painfully and bleeding some.
But it does not matter. I have discovered the key to obtaining my desire. It was sold to me by an Arabian trader.
The key was discovered on the shores of an eastern sea.
I now have the key. I have the craft. I shall soon have what I seek.

Seventh July
Have not yet mastered the way to bind them.
Harvested ten canes of young ash sapling. To be cured in sea brine and char wort, then thistle-smoked and dried on untouched stone. This shall be the frame. The path of the thread must pass through the center of the crossing weft.
Wove four cubits of linen broadcloth and sold at market cross for five shillings.

Will shifted his stance and his voice slowed:

Fourteenth June, 1510
Must find proper manner of warp fiber to contain the

thread. Saw a fine, long-legged calf in John Haysmith's pen. Sinew?

Will stopped abruptly and looked up. "There's no doubt of it. Gray Lily wrote this," he said. "This is the diary of the witch who trapped me." Will scanned quickly through several more entries. Then he stopped and read silently.

"What is it?" asked Tessa, going closer and peering over the edge of the page.

"This—this is some years later," he said in a low, hoarse voice.

Opal stood on his other side. "That's weird," she said. "The handwriting looks the same. But it's clearer. Less wobbly than the earlier pages."

"Read it," Tessa said. She glanced at Will's face and added, "Please."

In a slow voice Will began:

Hartescross. Twelfth September, 1511
The hunt is complete. I thought the older son, Hugh de Chaucy, would kill the unicorn. He is as brawny and stupid as a young bull. He thought of nothing but vengeance for his brother. I do believe he thought me mad with my laughing. 'Twas only that he did not know the jest. He cut a gash over the creature's face with his sword but was knocked aside, his shoulder split open to the bone by the unicorn's horn. The girl did not stay in the clearing as she was bid. She lost her wits from fear of the hounds and ran away. The unicorn followed her, stumbling and bloodied from

the lances. He laid his head on her lap. The girl did scream and cover her face....

Will's voice slowed and stopped. The muscles of his jaw were clenched, and his hands gripped the book so hard, Tessa could see the white of his knuckles straining through the skin.

"Stop reading," she said in a faint voice. The wound on his cheek had broken and two fresh drops of blood clung to it, bright and glittering as tiny rubies.

"No," said Will. He stared at her. "Listen." He looked down at the page and went on, sounding breathless now, almost as if he'd been running:

They put the iron shackles on the unicorn and it lay still. The villagers didn't want it killed. Some of them even marked how the creature did seem to have a keen look to its eye. Almost human. I laughed again at that.

Will stopped and let out a low breath, but his eyes stayed fixed on the words.

They stayed back—wisely enough, as they had seen how the thing had nearly flayed a man open with its horn. They cowered in fear as I took the thread from the creature.

I have my unicorn at last. He is woven into the tapestry and will remain imprisoned there forever. I am young again, beautiful and strong. I will travel far from this place, where no one will know me. My life is just begun.

Will let the book drop. The thud as it hit the floor made Tessa jump.

"She turned you into a unicorn," Opal breathed. "A real unicorn? And *then* she put you in the tapestry."

"Yes." Will wiped his hands on his tunic, as if trying to clean them. "She steals the thread of a life, and from it she creates what she desires. Then she pulls the thread once more to place that creature in the tapestry." He stared at the tapestry. "There may even be others trapped within her woven spell. As I was."

Tessa turned to Will as the realization of what had happened to him struck deep inside her. "They never knew the unicorn was you?" she said, looking up at his face. "The people of Hartescross, even your brother tried to—" She broke off.

He faced her and his eyes narrowed on hers with a golden stare, blazing and cold at the same time. He touched the wound on his cheek.

"Yes. They tried to kill me. My brother nearly succeeded."

Chapter 17

They read further, getting the rest of the story bit by bit. After capturing the unicorn and finishing her tapestry, Gray Lily had prospered. She'd moved from town to town, marrying and outliving (as she related in a gloating tone) a number of wealthy husbands. She became a lady of wealth and influence. And she never aged.

She kept the tapestry locked away from harm and prying eyes.

The last entry was dated October 12, 1842. Gray Lily was calling herself Madame Lillian Genoise and living in Paris.

"Gray Lily. Lillian Genoise," Tessa murmured, and yawned. It was two in the morning. She rubbed her eyes. They felt like they'd been rolled in kitty litter. Not even clean kitty litter. All at once she stopped and straightened up. "Lila Gerome," she said.

"Huh?" Opal's eyes were bleary too.

"Lila Gerome," Tessa repeated. "That's who my father said the lawyer was working for." She looked at Opal and Will. "Could it be her? Is Lila Gerome really Gray Lily?"

"Sounds like it," said Opal. She sat at Tessa's computer, tapping the keyboard, her eyes on the screen. "And she wants her stuff back."

Give them back. Tessa shivered as she remembered the message. She pulled her sweater tighter around her and faced Will. "So Gray Lily took your life from you, as a thread. How did she do that? What happened?"

Will gave her a strange, impassive look before casting his eyes down, remembering. "She spoke, making strange noises," he said, "like a demon from Hell. She held a small yellow stone. She touched it to my chest and a cold ache began. Here." He put a hand to his chest. "She pulled the thread from me, until there was nothing left." The memory of it seemed to bring back an echo of the pain. Will rubbed his chest absently, as if soothing a healed but still-tender wound.

"Then she used your thread to make the unicorn," Tessa said. "Why a unicorn?"

"I don't know," Will admitted with a weary shrug. "Perhaps as a creature of magic, I bestowed more strength to her."

"Immortality," Tessa murmured. In answer to Will's questioning glance, she went on, "I read about it. The unicorn symbolizes eternal life." She nodded. "Maybe that's how she's able to live so long. She used your life thread to make this magical creature, then she got the legendary power of the unicorn when she trapped you inside the tapestry."

"So what did it feel like?" Opal asked Will. "You know, when you were a unicorn?"

She sounded, thought Tessa, like a daytime talk-show host.

Will didn't answer right away. "I remember," he began slowly, "at first, the warmth of sun on my back. The hunger for sweetgrasses. The joy of galloping." He laughed, and for a second his lean face lost every trace of anger or fear. He looked like a little boy. "To be free was my happiness. But after I was trapped—" Here he stopped. The open, boyish expression vanished and his eyes met Tessa's with an impenetrable stare. "I was imprisoned in the tapestry. It was a living death."

Tessa said in a soft voice, "I'm sorry."

Will's eyes narrowed. "For what, mistress?"

The question took her by surprise. "That this happened to you," Tessa answered, with a bewildered expression. "That she *did* this to you." *What else would I be sorry for?*

"So what do we do now?" Opal asked.

Tessa shook her head. "I have absolutely no idea." She looked at Will, who had sat on the floor, back propped against the wall. One long leg was bent, and his elbow rested on his knee, forearm dangling. He leaned his head back. He looked lazy but elegant. There were shadows beneath his golden brown eyes, but he was watching her with a brooding intensity.

"I'll take the tapestry, as well as the book, and go," Will said suddenly. He spoke as if they had been having a silent argument about it and he had come up with the obvious and only solution.

Tessa reacted at once. "No. What do you think happens to *me*, and my father, if you take them?" she demanded. "The lawyer is coming tomorrow. He knows the tapestry and the book are here. He's offered my father ten thousand dollars for them. And if he doesn't get them—" She paused. "What will Gray Lily do?"

Will's eyes narrowed. "So. Ten thousand dollars." He turned to Opal. "It is a goodly sum in this realm?"

Opal nodded. "Pretty goodly. Not badly."

He turned back to Tessa, regarded her for a moment and then said, "Perhaps you think you could get more."

"What?" she sputtered.

"If it's money you desire"—Will de Chaucy spoke slowly, coldly—"I will pay you, once I return to my estate."

"I don't give a damn about the stupid money," Tessa said, angry that he could really think that about her. Why did he distrust her so much? Sometimes the way he looked at her, it almost seemed as if he felt nothing but coldness and contempt for her.

"I'm thinking about my father and me," she told him. "Gray Lily already proved what she's capable of doing, without even being present." As she spoke, Tessa remembered the eerie message woven before her eyes in the kitchen. "Who knows what she'll do if she gets really angry?"

"You could say I overpowered you and escaped. That I disappeared," he reasoned. "I shall take one of those flying machines you described. A 'plane,' was it not? I will go to Cornwall and find my home as well as my family. Or my descendants, as I suppose they would be now," he mused.

"I hate to tell you this, Will." Opal frowned, peering at the screen of the desktop computer. "I searched everywhere. I can't find a current Earl of Umbric or a Hartescross listed anywhere in the UK. And it looks like the last member of the de Chaucy family"—she paused, scrolling through one of the many genealogy sites they had checked—"was Gervais de Chaucy."

"That is my father," said Will.

Tessa peered over Opal's shoulder at the glowing screen. "He died in 1512," she said softly. "One year after the disappearance of his younger son. Who, according to local legend, was killed by a unicorn."

Will bent his head. He whispered something Tessa couldn't hear, but seeing the devastated look on his face was enough. She turned away.

"What about his brother, Hugh?" she prompted Opal.

Opal tapped the keys, then shook her head and sat back. "Sorry. There's nothing." She yawned. "I am so fried."

So was Tessa. She didn't want to think about witches or unicorns or anything else. And especially not about the boy sitting a few feet away from her, who was charming one minute and sneering the next. Totally cut off from his whole world and yet no part of hers. She was exhausted. The weirdness and danger hadn't gone away, but she had to sleep—she had to. Just a few hours of rest. Then, if he was still here when she woke up . . . well, she'd think of something.

Opal was already pulling a sleeping bag from the closet and unrolling it.

Both girls turned to look at Will. He was fast asleep.

Tessa dragged the puffy flowered comforter from her bed and tiptoed over to him. She covered him gently. She crawled into bed and reached over to adjust the alarm clock. Then Tessa burrowed her face and her fisted hands into her pillow and slept.

And dreamed.

She lay helpless where she had fallen, her ankle twisted and throbbing with pain.

The huge animal fell to its knees beside her and laid its head in her lap. Leaves and small twigs clung to the tangled mane, and blood seeped from a gash in the sleek jaw. Her velvet dress was stained with the dark, sticky fluid. She put out a tentative hand and touched the unicorn's side. She could feel the animal's shallow breaths. Her eyes widened as she saw her own hand stained with blood. The smell was thick, nauseating.

The weaver woman approached and bent over her. Her

wizened face was lit with eagerness as she looked over the unicorn. "You've done well, child. It will be over soon."

"No!" she cried. "Don't kill it! It's not a monster. It didn't kill Will de Chaucy. Its eyes—I think it's *him*."

"Clever girl," snarled Gray Lily. She glanced at her. "Don't worry, I'm not going to kill him."

Men came. They put a cuff of dull gray metal on each of the unicorn's forelegs and fastened them securely. "Iron will quell your spirit," Gray Lily said. "And hold you." She then took a small yellow stone from her pocket and pressed it to the unicorn's chest.

Awful sounds filled the air as Gray Lily chanted strange words. And then something impossible happened.

The girl watched as a curling, silvery thread drifted up from the unicorn's chest like a wisp of smoke. The unicorn shuddered and its eyes shot open, huge and dilated with fear. But it didn't move. The thread spun away, faster and faster. The unicorn's substance faded and finally disappeared. The silver thread drifted on the air.

Gray Lily held a tapestry. The unicorn's silver thread undulated through the air and traveled toward her as she spoke. As the old woman worked her magic, the thread wove itself into the tapestry. It looked like streaks of light rippling through dark water. Gray Lily closed her eyes and spoke again, and this time the words rang out clear in the stillness of the wood.

"Spirit transformed, I call thee.
Magic enclosed, I capture thee.

Through warp and weft, I bind thee.
Let your power be mine for eternity.
The tapestry is complete."

The unicorn was in the tapestry, frozen in a pose of wild torment. Its eyes stared out with a piercing sadness. *His* eyes.

The girl screamed. The men staggered back, muttering oaths. Several ran away in terror.

"You see? Isn't he fine?" said Gray Lily. She straightened, and she was no longer old but youthful, with thick fair hair and a lissome figure. "I told you I wouldn't kill him," she drawled. She ran her hands over her supple body with a smile of delight that was almost obscene. Then her small, dark eyes flickered up. "Now, *you*, on the other hand . . ."

She pulled a dagger from her cloak and advanced. . . .

Tessa moaned in her sleep. Her arms thrashed against the twisted covers. *Open your eyes.* It was dark. Strong hands gripped her arms. "Wake up." Will de Chaucy leaned over her, the darkness shadowing his features.

"I had another dream," Tessa rasped from her dry, constricted throat. "I saw Gray Lily. I saw what she did to you." *And what she was going to do to me.*

"*Another* dream?" he asked. His voice was so gentle. Just like the touch that brushed her tousled hair back.

"Yes," she whispered, suddenly very conscious of how close he was. "I've been having the strangest dreams ever since I first touched the tapestry. And now even if I'm not touching it. It was so real. It was like . . ."

"You were there," he finished. He straightened, drawing away.

Tessa sat up. "We have to do something. I can't go on this way."

"Agreed," said Will de Chaucy in a low tone.

Chapter 18

The next morning the bell on the door of Brody's Books jangled and a man entered. He was heavily built, with a thin salt-and-ginger-colored fringe of hair around a balding, freckled scalp. His dark gray suit looked rumpled, as if he'd slept in it, and he carried a worn leather attaché case. Tessa watched him from behind the counter, her fingers tapping a pencil on the morning newspaper.

The man's glance darted toward Tessa. "Is Mr. Brody in?" he said in a gruff voice.

Tessa nodded and pointed to where her father was occupied with a broom in the far corner of the store. "Dad," she called.

The man gave her a short nod of thanks and the corners

of his mouth pressed inward in a curt, professional smile. But his gaze lingered on Tessa's face. He had pale blue eyes, and there were bags of droopy flesh beneath them that gave him a gloomy expression. He strode past. Tessa wondered if the man could hear the knocking of her knees.

"Mr. Moncrieff?" said her father. "Hello." He set down a push broom and dustpan and nudged a large paper bag out of the way with one foot. He strode forward, hand extended. "Jackson Brody."

"Yes. I'm Moncrieff," the lawyer said tersely as they shook hands.

"I was going to call you this morning," her father began, his tone apologetic, "but I realized I didn't have your number. I'm afraid I've got some bad news."

"Of what kind, Mr. Brody?" Any trace of a smile, professional or otherwise, evaporated from the lawyer's face. A look of hard suspicion took its place.

"We had a break-in last night." Tessa's father pointed to a small side window, one that looked out onto the alley. A piece of cardboard was fastened on where the lower pane of glass used to be. "They stole quite a few valuable books," he said. "Including the one from the auction."

Moncrieff set his case down with a thump. "What?" he said, staring at her father. An angry flush rose in his neck and cheeks. He swiveled to look around the store, and his eyes, now sharp and accusing, raked over Tessa once more. "What the hell are you trying to pull?"

"Nothing," Jackson Brody replied. "We live upstairs but

unfortunately never heard a thing. Came down this morning to find . . . well, someone had broken a window, gotten in and robbed us."

"And you heard nothing?" the lawyer demanded.

"No," said Tessa's father with a shrug. "It's a large building, and the bedrooms are on the opposite end."

"But the tapestry," Moncrieff said, glaring. "Where is the tapestry?" His freckled lips worked silently as he waited for the answer. His hands tightened into fists.

Tessa's father looked taken aback but stayed calm as he replied, "The thieves got that too." He glanced at Tessa. "My daughter packed it up together with the book last night. It was all ready to go."

"That's right," Tessa said quickly. "I put them in the same packing crate they arrived in. It was sitting right here on the counter." She tried to sound matter-of-fact. Her pencil was still tapping the paper, though maybe a little faster than before. She set it down.

"You—you're lying!" The lawyer took a step and stopped. He raised a hand to his throat and swallowed.

"No, he's not!" said Tessa. She jumped up and whipped around the counter to stand next to her father. "It's true. They're gone. It's not my father's fault. It—it's mine. You can tell that to . . . Ms. Gerome." She took a deep breath. "The box was here in plain sight. The thieves grabbed it. It's *gone.*"

Outside, a police cruiser pulled up.

Moncrieff's eyes darted around the store and then back to Tessa. They narrowed to watery blue slits. "Where is it?" he repeated. But his words were thick and seemed to come out with difficulty.

"Stolen, like we told you," said her father.

"They're gone," Tessa said, trying to keep her own voice steady. She gestured to the window and the police car outside. "The police are here to investigate. You can stay and give them details if you want, about the book and the tapestry." She looked the man straight in the eye. The lawyer frowned at Tessa, then stepped toward the storefront window and peered out. He eyed the police officer who was getting out of the cruiser. Moncrieff gave a dismissive snort and seemed about to say something when suddenly he stopped, his eyes fixed on something else outside. Slowly he shook his head no.

All at once the lawyer's face contorted. His neck bulged. His pale blue eyes looked huge and glassy, like marbles, as he glared back at Tessa. "You—you have no idea what she'll do." A stream of saliva dribbled from the corner of his mouth.

"Now, look here—" Jackson said, frowning. His expression turned to alarm. "Hey, Mr. Moncrieff. Are you okay?"

Moncrieff backed away, snatching a handkerchief from his suit coat pocket to mop his mouth. He made a sickening retching sound and held the cloth tight over his face. He pointed a jabbing finger at Tessa, then he clutched his briefcase and staggered out of the store.

Chapter 19

Tessa sat crossed-legged on her bed, holding her cell. With her free hand she pulled at the white, frayed edge around the hole in the knee of her jeans. "Thanks for taking those books home with you," she said.

"No problem," answered Opal. "What's a little grand larceny between friends? At least, I hope it was grand. I wouldn't want to do petty. Sounds, you know . . . cheap."

"It was the only thing I could think of," Tessa replied with a sigh, thinking of her early-morning dash outside to break the window, undo the lock and open the casing. Opal had waited inside to hand things through. They had grabbed a few books from various display cases. Then the two of them had snuck them out to Opal's car in the darkness.

But the tapestry and the *Texo Vita* Tessa had kept. She'd wrapped them together in a bundle and stuffed them under her bed.

"Have the police gone?"

"Just now. The officer interviewed us and looked around, especially on the floor near the broken window and the front door. He said he was surprised we hadn't had trouble before, not having a security system." She didn't think her father suspected anything. "I'll return everything to the store once this mess is all straightened out."

Tessa thought how ridiculous that sounded. Straightened out. Like this was some kind of mix-up at the dry cleaner's. *Yes, ma'am, we seem to have delivered your flying carpet to the wrong customer. You can have fifty percent off your next order.*

And she hated lying to her father. But somehow she felt that the less he knew about Gray Lily, the tapestry and Will, the safer he would be.

Tessa said good-bye to Opal, closed the phone and turned it beneath her fingers thoughtfully, all the while looking at Will de Chaucy from under her lashes.

He stood by her window, watching the movement of cars and pedestrians below, his strong profile backlit by the warm afternoon sun. He'd spent most of the morning poring over her books, expressing disbelief that anyone could have so many. Tessa wished she could bring him downstairs to show him the store, but there was no way. Not while her father was there.

He was wearing a pair of her father's old dress pants, a faded OLD PORT DAYS 5K commemorative T-shirt and Nikes.

It was all she could muster from the back of her father's closet that she felt sure he wouldn't miss. Or probably even recognize. The pants were too big at the waist and hung low across Will's lean hips. The worn cuffs cleared the top of his ankles by two inches. The wrinkled T-shirt was white turned pale pink as a result of an unfortunate washing incident and had a goofy-looking pirate jogging across the front. It was the most ridiculous outfit she had ever seen. He looked completely amazing.

Tessa frowned, considering Will's tall, athletic build, the contours of muscled shoulders and biceps beneath the thin cotton fabric as he leaned against the window frame. It probably wouldn't matter *what* he wore. It was as if he were made of something different from ordinary flesh and blood, something finer.

"You're a very surprising person, Mistress Brody," Will said, turning as if he had been contemplating her and not the traffic outside.

She looked away, hoping he hadn't noticed her doing whatever it was she'd been doing. "Huh?"

"It was a clever ruse, and a daring one," Will remarked. "But did Gray Lily's emissary believe you?"

"His name was Moncrieff," Tessa said slowly. She thought about the way the man's pale blue eyes had stared at her. "No, I don't think he believed me." She gave a shrug. "Would you?" she added, turning back to Will.

"Believe you?" Will considered this. "I would want to believe you," he said softly. He folded his arms and looked outside. "But no. I wouldn't."

There it was again. Why did she get the feeling she was talking about one thing and he was talking about something totally different?

"They'll be back," he said over his shoulder. "Gray Lily will come."

"But what can she do?" Tessa argued. "If you're here with me, and my dad? In broad daylight? In the middle of Portland?"

"I confess I have seen but a small demonstration," Will said dryly, "but I would imagine she can do quite a lot. Anywhere."

"Well, what do you suggest we do?"

He turned around. "Ah. I had hoped you would ask. What I would like is . . . a walk. Down there." He nodded toward the street. "The sea is nearby, I can smell it."

Tessa looked at him. "A walk," she repeated. She'd wanted suggestions as to "What are we going to do about this weird time-traveling-witch-stealing-your-life thing?" Not a social agenda. He was full of surprises. If she had suddenly been thrown into another time and had some kind of evil witch on her tail, she wasn't sure a leisurely stroll would be on the top of her to-do list. She shrugged. Well, maybe it would.

"Okay. But first we've got to get you some other clothes," Tessa said firmly. "It will help make you less conspicuous. You know. Blend in."

"Really?" said Will. He looked down at himself in mild surprise. He shrugged. "Very well. You have a tailor who will attend me?"

Tessa raised an eyebrow. *Welcome to William de Chaucy,* she thought. *Center of the Universe.* She fluttered her lashes and stepped forward to curtsy. "No, Your Highness. I'm afraid we shall have to behoove ourselves down to Ye Olde Goodwill and buy some secondhand attire, like the other peasants."

There was a pause. Tessa peeked up to see Will looking down at her. He turned away and said quietly, "It's ungracious of you to mock me, Tessa, as I am a stranger, and unaccustomed to your ways. I'm far from my home, my time. Nothing is as I knew it."

Tessa straightened awkwardly and reddened. *Ungracious.* The word stung.

"I'm sorry," she blurted out. *Ungracious.* It was exactly the right word for her. Lacking grace, social or otherwise. "You're right." She looked away. Anywhere but at him. "I wasn't thinking about how strange all this must be for you. I'll try to remember. And I won't call you Your Highness anymore," she added.

"Actually, that I don't mind."

Tessa glanced to see Will's expression. His lips curved up on one side and his eyes were alight with something devilish. He was laughing.

"You—you—" Tessa lunged forward, half furious, half relieved and half something else so fluorescently impossible she didn't want to think about it. She reached out to give him a playful shove but found herself unbalanced when he twisted away.

Will caught her by the shoulders, holding her close.

"I don't believe I have thanked you yet, for helping me," he said in a low voice.

For a moment Tessa felt as if she were teetering on the edge of something more than just gravity. She didn't feel herself let go, but she must have; she felt herself supported by strong arms. So why did she still feel as if she were falling?

Will smiled at her and Tessa let herself do what she had been trying not to do: she let her eyes meet his. Head-on. She felt held there for a moment. Caught in a warm, golden trap.

Then something changed as Will stared at her. His look became more intent and his smile faded. She became aware that he was holding something back, something barely restrained behind the careful manners.

"Why did you do it?" he demanded.

"Wh-what?" Tessa righted herself. But he still held her.

"You heard the question, Mistress Brody. *Why?*"

Tessa squirmed. "Let me go. I can't breathe."

Will released her and she straightened. "There is no *why*," she said. "I just pulled a thread. I didn't know what would happen."

Will de Chaucy stared at her for a moment, and then, in a return to the cool, formal manner she was becoming used to, said, "I thank you, mistress."

Was it her imagination or was there a tinge of acid in his tone? "You're welcome," Tessa returned uncertainly. She straightened her shirt over her jeans. "So let's take a walk," she said in an uncomfortably bright voice. Practically a chirp. She slipped past Will, grabbed her purse and made herself take a deep breath. *Get a grip, Tessa,* she told herself.

She didn't even look at him when she piped up again, "Let's go. We'll use the back staircase so we don't have to go through the store." Friendly, but cool.

"Lead on," he said softly as he followed her.

Moncrieff's face was a dusky blue. He stumbled through the open passenger door, collapsing onto the backseat of the limousine that idled outside the bookstore. Foamy spittle dripped down his front and darkened his shirt as he clawed to loosen his tie and collar.

After a moment the other occupant sitting in the shadows of the passenger compartment spoke. "You failed me," she said. Gray Lily faced Moncrieff, regarding his spasms of distress with detachment. She tapped her shriveled fingers against the security glass twice, signaling the driver to proceed. She glanced at Moncrieff as the limo pulled away from the curb. "You didn't get my tapestry," she rasped. "I told you what would happen if you didn't get it."

Moncrieff's blue eyes bulged from his head. He clutched his throat. "Glghhh."

Gray Lily pursed her wrinkled lips and narrowed her small black eyes. "I'm sorry." She leaned forward and cocked her head. "Could you speak up? Oh, I guess not."

Moncrieff's limbs twitched and his eyes rolled wildly. With a jerk his two hands shot forward, as though he were reaching for Gray Lily, to strike or throttle her. But he slapped his palms together and held them, trembling, in silent supplication.

"Very well," Gray Lily said with a sniff. She plucked at

the piece of black thread she held in her lap with her knobby fingers.

Moncrieff collapsed backward, heaving in gasps of air. He twisted to look at her. "Ms. Gerome?" he wheezed.

"Oh. Of course," she commented, looking down at herself. "You haven't seen *this*." She waved a hand to indicate her shrunken, elderly form. "I had a setback."

Gray Lily reached toward Moncrieff. He shrank back, but she only patted his knee. "I'm sorry I had to do that," she said. Her expression might have been that of a teacher who had just reprimanded a child. "Really, I am. But sometimes, Moncrieff, I just don't think that I'm getting through to you. You see, the book and the tapestry mean the world to me." She frowned faintly and her lined face seemed to fold in upon itself. "Consider it a matter of life and death," she said. "Yours." She tilted her head. "We understand each other now. Don't we?"

The man lay huddled in the far corner of the seat. Tears streamed down his face. He gave a jerking nod.

Gray Lily sighed. She took a square of white silk from her purse and tossed it at him. "Here. Clean yourself up," she told him. "Then tell me everything."

Chapter 20

Will set down the bag of clothes they'd bought from the thrift shop and stepped into the road. Now dressed in faded jeans, sneakers and a black T-shirt, Will could have passed for any modern-day teenage guy. Except for one thing. He stood in the center of Wharf Street, staring at the length of paved tar with a line in the middle as if it were a piece of abstract art. He crouched and touched his palm to the blacktopped surface.

"It's warm," he murmured. His expression, as he examined it, was one of startled delight. "Who made this, Tessa?"

Tessa was on the sidewalk, trying to look nonchalant as passersby eyed the strange young man in the road. "Um, I'm not sure," she answered. "The city, I guess. The government?" She hoped he didn't lie down and listen for buffalo.

"It is beautiful," Will said. "So smooth. No ruts. No mud. Verily, coach wheels must fly on such a surface." He straightened up and smiled over at her. "This world is remarkable. I feel as though I am in a dream that goes on and on. Nothing is real." He hesitated. "Except—"

"Car!" Tessa yelled, and dashed forward to yank him back to the curb. A Subaru wagon drove by. Slowly.

"I guess it wasn't that close," Tessa said. She released her clutch on his elbow. "Nothing is real except . . . what?" she prompted. But Will de Chaucy was off again, walking away, like a kid at an amusement park.

He peered into shop windows, looked up into the sky to see a plane passing overhead, headed down the recessed steps of a tattoo parlor and squinted into a grate in the sidewalk. Tessa followed along, watching. Apparently he had to touch everything, she noted with a smile. And everything seemed wonderful to him. Not only was a paved road "beautiful," but garbage cans were "ingenious." Bicycles were "astounding." Streetlights? Forget about it. And they weren't even lit yet.

Confusing questions came up that Tessa would never have expected, leading to weird conversations. For instance, how the Time and Temperature Building didn't actually *control* those things.

They came to the waterfront. The dark water murmured beneath the creaking pier, and hungry gulls wheeled and *scree*-ed overhead. The air smelled of fish and diesel fumes, while chugging ship motors made a constant drone in the background. Will cast an appreciative glance at some older fishing boats rocking against the dock. "I'm delighted to see that wood still floats upon water," he said solemnly.

Tessa's answering smile faded at the fast-food wrappers and Styrofoam debris in the water below them. "There's a lot of pollution in it, though." She leaned on the railing and let her eyes trace the horizon, over the familiar ragged outline of Diamond Island and the faraway blink of the East End Harbor light. "People have really messed up the world," she said. "It must be a lot cleaner where you come from. Unspoiled."

Will, to her surprise, burst into laughter. "Hartescross? Cleaner? I confess that I do not recall it so."

What was his home like? Tessa wondered. His family? She longed to ask, but maybe it would be too painful for him to talk about. He'd been pulled out of a tapestry on her wall only yesterday. She would be freaking out if she were in his place.

What was she thinking? She was freaking out in *her* place.

"You've been handling all this"—Tessa waved a hand to encompass the modern world—"pretty well." When Will looked confused, she clarified. "You seem to be adapting to this time. You're not afraid of anything."

Will shrugged and said dryly, "I have been turned into a unicorn, Tessa. I believe my constitution has been hardened to surprises. Most of them, anyway," he added as an afterthought. "And you're wrong. I am afraid."

He glanced around and up, at the warehouses, office buildings and the steeple of a church that formed the skyline behind them. "But I see much that is fine and admirable."

He turned to her. "Maybe you don't realize how lovely it is"—his voice slowed as he looked down at her—"here."

His eyes held hers. At that moment Tessa had the sudden, nearly overwhelming urge to drag Will de Chaucy close to her. To touch his skin. To know that he was real. So strong was the feeling that she found herself reaching out— *What was the matter with her?*

She glanced away, breaking the spell of his gaze. She lowered her hands and jammed them into the pockets of her jeans. "Yeah, it's nice, I guess." She could feel heat lapping at her neck, her cheeks. So much for cool.

"My father says women who blush are very headstrong." He squinted away from her, out toward distant waters. "They're ruled by their blood."

"Really." Tessa considered this. Will had spoken as if his father were still alive. And somehow she didn't think *headstrong* was the word he'd been about to say. Probably something a little more medieval. Involving lusty wenches, maybe. She gave him a skeptical look. "So your father knows a lot about women?"

"He knows nothing," Will said with a crooked smile. "But he keeps seeking tuition. Diligently."

Tessa smiled, her self-consciousness fading. "My father isn't married anymore. My mom died a few years ago."

"I am sorry."

"It's okay." Tessa laced her fingers together and studied the fine, crisscrossing lines of her palms as she spoke. "She died in a car accident. They never let me see her . . . afterward. It was like she just left and never came back."

"I did not know my mother," Will said. "She died giving birth to me. I am told that I resemble her." He shook his head almost imperceptibly. "My father never speaks of her. Was your mother like you?"

"Like me?" Tessa glanced up. "No," she answered with a rueful shake of her head. "She wasn't like me. She was a famous artist. Well, *pretty* famous, anyway. A painter. But mostly she was just my mom." Tessa remained silent for a moment. She kicked at the splintered beams of the dock and went on. "Sometimes my mom would laugh so hard she would cry and hold her stomach. I used to love that." Tessa smiled softly. "And I feel like she's still here," she whispered. "Somehow." She blinked, shocked at herself. Not only that she'd said something so perfectly lame and sappy, but that it was true. Completely true. And now her eyes were starting to fill up. She focused her gaze straight ahead. "But I have my dad. Things are fine."

"I am glad of it," Will said quietly.

Tessa glanced over at his profile. His eyes were still trained on the sea. Tessa was thankful he didn't seem to notice when she reached up quickly and brushed away the tears.

They stayed silent for a few moments. But Tessa wasn't uncomfortable with the pause. Maybe they each had a memory to think about. And five hundred years or four years, Tessa thought. Or even a day. What was the difference, really?

"Who are your friends?" Tessa asked.

"My brother, Hugh," said Will with a smile. "He's a great, bullying lout of a fellow. You would like him—everyone likes him." He frowned. "Or they *did*." He shook his head and turned to her. "And you? Mistress Opal is your bosom companion?"

"Um. Yeah, I guess," Tessa laughed. "She's my friend. And has a bosom. Wow, she would *love* that you called her that."

"Did I say something funny?"

"Pretty much constantly. Sorry. No. It's just the language thing. We have different expressions."

"Yes, Mistress Opal used many I did not understand." Will tilted his head to regard Tessa. "She seems to know you very well."

"Better than anyone," Tessa agreed.

"What is a control freak?" he asked.

Tessa stared, crossed her arms. "She did *not* say that."

"It is offensive?" Will frowned, looking taken aback. "An insult?"

"Yes. I mean *no*," Tessa said. "And I'm not. I'm just careful, is all. Responsible. And not in a freak way."

"I understand," said Will. He nodded gravely, though the hint of a smile curved his mouth. "I'm sure that is what she meant."

Finally he bent his head back, breathing in the ocean air, then turned to her. The cut over his cheek was still painful-looking, but at least the redness seemed a little less intense.

"Stop worrying," he said, as if he had read her mind. Then he grinned at her, displaying his crooked front tooth.

Tessa caught her breath and smiled back. Will's smile set something loose inside her.

"What is it?" he asked.

"Nothing," she said, averting her eyes.

Was there something between them? More than being thrown together by some crazy witch's spell? Maybe that was just wishful thinking. She looked into his sunlit brown eyes once more. Her thinking certainly *was* full of wishes lately.

A cool, fresh wind blew up, lifting Tessa's hair and lashing it into dark swirls. She grabbed a piece of it and unconsciously twisted it around one finger.

A change came over Will's face.

"It *is* you," he said. The smile left and he stared at her the way he had when he first saw her. With anger and hurt and something else that she couldn't understand. He turned away with a brusque motion and stalked off.

"Hey!" Tessa yelped, but he didn't stop or even slow down.

She stared after him. "So much for easy to be with," she muttered. One minute he was Prince Charming, looking at her in a way that made her breathless. The next he acted as though she had the plague or something.

She ran to catch up. "What's the matter?" she demanded, out of breath.

"Not a thing," Will answered, his long legs covering the pavement in swinging strides and his gaze leveled straight ahead.

"Obviously," said Tessa, matching him stride for stride.

At the corner Will stopped and put a hand out to a brick wall. He took a deep breath and closed his eyes.

"Are you okay?" Tessa asked.

"No. Yes. I do not know. You look like someone. The girl from the village who—" He broke off abruptly and shook his head. "But it can't be. My madness is simply becoming complete."

Tessa wondered who the girl had been. Just a girl, or something more? But Will's expression didn't invite questions. He straightened and looked around. "What is that *smell*?" he demanded.

Tessa sniffed. The aroma of oven-fired dough, garlic and tomato sauce wafted past them as if it were on invisible little Italian legs. She pointed across the street. "It's Vic's Pizza," she said. "C'mon. We didn't have breakfast."

They split a large, gooey cheese pizza—Tessa having decided that traveling to the future, discovering the existence of pizza *and* deciding on toppings was really too much to expect from anyone.

After the pizza was gone, Will slumped back in the restaurant booth with a dazed, slightly goofy expression on his face. "Pizza is . . ." He laughed aloud. "A wondrous food."

"Worth the trip?" Tessa asked, smiling. Then, horrified at what she'd just said, she sputtered, "I mean—I didn't mean— Wow. That was really insensitive. I'm sorry."

"Don't be distressed." Will's face turned thoughtful. "I'm sure there is a reason for this journey. Perhaps it is preordained. Do you think fate has brought us together?" He watched her with an intensity that made it seem the answer was important.

"No," Tessa said without hesitation. It was the one thing she was completely sure of. "It was just a loose thread. An accident." Will didn't seem satisfied with this answer and opened his mouth to speak, but Tessa shimmied farther into the booth and tried to look really absorbed as she flipped through the music selections on the little jukebox at the end of the table. "We need to figure things out," she said.

"Figure? What things, mistress?"

"What to do," she said, making vague gestures in the air. "How to fix this. You."

He frowned. "I was not aware of being broken."

"You know what I mean."

"No, in point of fact. I do not comprehend you in the least. Explain yourself."

Tessa just stared at him for a moment. His imperious tone seemed so formal, and completely at odds with his modern clothes, his shaggy, unkempt hair. He looked like a hot surfer and sounded like King Arthur.

"Well," she sighed. "We need to come up with a plan. For instance, where are you going to go? Where will you stay? What do we do with the tapestry, and the book?"

"Very well," said Will, nodding agreement. "But first I have something to ask you."

Tessa's eyes fastened on his briefly; then she looked away. *Nope. Not again. Do not go there.* His odd reaction at the waterfront was still vivid. She wasn't about to get lured in by the charm only to be squashed like a plague-ridden bug. If bugs got the plague. Maybe that was only rats.

"Hmm?" she replied. She pushed F9 for two Smash

Mouth songs. Exactly what she needed right now for distraction. Something upbeat and friendly but cool.

"Is Tessa short for something?" he asked. When she hesitated, he narrowed his eyes. "Your name. Surely that's not all of it. I'm afraid if you don't tell me, I shall have to guess."

Silence.

"Very well. Is it Theresa?"

"No."

"Elizabeth?"

"Stop."

"Contessa," he said with a knowing nod.

Tessa laughed. "God. Please. You'll never guess." Did she really have to do this? She huffed. "I suppose I'll have to tell you sometime. But it's a secret. A deep, dark secret."

"Really? I'm honored." Will leaned forward. "Should we whisper, perhaps?"

Tessa folded her arms across her chest. "My full name is Tesseract Margaret Brody."

"Tesseract," Will repeated. At least he didn't laugh. But he really did look confused, thought Tessa, with his eyebrows pulled together like that and the full, firm band of his lower lip slightly . . . *Cut it out.*

She rolled a plastic straw—"a fantastic invention"—between her fingers. "When my mom was growing up," Tessa explained, "she was crazy about this book called *A Wrinkle in Time*, and she named me after—"

"A player in the story?" Will tugged the straw from her fingers.

"Sort of." Tessa sighed. "Margaret is the girl's name in

the story. Meg for short. But my first name is . . ." How to explain it? "More like a mathematical idea from the book. A theoretical construct." At Will's puzzled expression, she went on, "My mom was artistic. Not just about her painting, about everything, about life. Unfortunately, that included baby names. A tesseract is"—she recited from long practice—"the fourth-dimensional analog of a cube. A shape formed from two cubes with all their corners connected. Like this."

She took a pencil from her bag, sketched a design on a napkin and showed him.

"Fascinating," said Will. But his eyes were on her, not the paper. "Tesseract. Do you know, in the Greek your name means 'four rays of light'?"

Tessa stared at Will. She was caught, tangled up in his eyes again.

In the Greek? Who *was* he? She realized her mouth was hanging open. She shut it with a snap. "So now you know my secret," she said lightly. "I'm an imaginary mathematical oddity."

"You seem real enough to me." Will reached forward as if to brush a lock of hair from her cheek but checked the motion and dropped his hand.

Tessa let out her breath. He hadn't touched her, but she felt a whisper of warmth on her skin as if he had. Will de Chaucy, she thought. What had ever given her the idea that she knew him? She didn't understand anything about him. He was the almost-perfect stranger.

Chapter 21

Will and Tessa walked in silence from the pizza parlor. As they neared the bookstore, Tessa ducked into the alley that skirted the building.

"This way," she told Will. "You can't stay in my room. My dad would be . . . upset if he knew." Amazing. She had never realized how fluent she was in Understatement.

"Of course," Will replied.

Tessa took a ring of keys from her bag and flipped to one she hadn't used in a long time. "Follow me."

"Where are we going?"

Tessa pointed up. "Top floor. Technically my dad owns the whole building. But we don't usually use this back entrance." They walked in and climbed the set of creaky stairs covered with cracked linoleum. On the top floor Tessa stopped at a closed door. She hesitated for a moment, weighing the small key in her palm, then put the key in the lock, opened it and stepped in. Memories tugged at her like grasping fingers as she walked into her mother's art studio and flicked on the light.

The large, bare-floored open space sprawled around them, lined with canvases propped against the walls. A low table held jars crammed with brushes, their variety of tufted and fanned bristles making weird floral-like arrangements. Crumpled tubes and jars of paints were piled in shoe boxes beneath.

"You can stay here for now," Tessa said, turning to Will. "Until we figure out what to do." Her voice echoed against the vaulted ceiling overhead and came back to her, sounding small and uncertain.

The echoing was no different. But when she was little, she'd always thought the echoes in the studio made it sound big and important. Now it just sounded empty. The smells were still there too: the sharp whiffs of oil and varnish and turpentine and, more faintly, the hint of sawdust from the wooden frames her mother had made. They were stacked in the corner with their taut skins of canvas stretched tight. Waiting. All waiting.

"My father never comes up here," Tessa said. "It will be okay," she added under her breath. She tried to keep her eyes forward as she strode to the middle of the room, but they were drawn, as if by an invisible summons, to the dusty, half-finished paintings that lined the walls. She took in the colors laid down in confident, swirling strokes. An elegant line swept a weeping willow branch over shadowed water. A roughly sketched portrait caught a young girl on a swing in midflight. With a start, Tessa recognized herself as the little girl and tried to remember that moment in the air, with her mother watching her. She found she couldn't. Tessa took a deep breath, or tried to. The air didn't seem to go all the way in.

"You can sleep there." She pointed to a sagging couch in the corner, draped with a crocheted granny-square afghan. "I'll bring over some more blankets and a pillow. There's a bathroom with a shower back there," she added with a nod toward the back of the studio. She ignored Will's perplexed expression, turned away and unlocked the window. She needed air. The wooden frame screeched as Tessa pulled it up and a fresh, sharp breeze blew in. But somehow the cool air wasn't enough to ease the tightness that had taken hold in her chest. A sudden eddy of wind lifted a sketch on the drafting table nearby. It rolled over on itself and tumbled to the floor.

She shouldn't have been there. Not there, among all her mother's things. It felt as if her mother might walk in at any moment. But that was impossible; she was gone. The pain in Tessa's heart swelled up and throbbed in her chest, in her throat, as if it would burst out of her.

"Tessa. What is wrong?"

She didn't answer but brushed past Will, ran to the door and pounded down the stairs. She didn't look back.

❧

Gray Lily let out a shriveled sigh at the sight of herself in the mirror. "Rejuvenating cream my ass," she muttered, and hurled a jar of expensive facial cream into the trash. She tapped her bony fingers on the bureau. A selection of hairpieces, lotions and cosmetics was strewn before her. "None of this helps. Fine clothes look ridiculous on old bones. I'm decrepit. Practically decaying in Givenchy."

She turned to Moncrieff, who sat at a desk some feet away. His stubby fingers wielded a computer mouse as he selected the Transfer Funds option from Lila Gerome's online banking portfolio.

"I need the unicorn back, Moncrieff. Now."

"Yes," said Moncrieff absently, typing in a dollar amount that would cover the cost of running a small city for a year.

"Yes, *what*?" snapped Gray Lily, twisting to face him.

Moncrieff stiffened. "Yes, *my lady*," he said, immediately swiveling the chair toward her and dropping his head to his chest. His heavy blue eyes fixed on a spot on the carpet near her feet. His employer preferred this old-fashioned form of address.

"You mustn't forget your manners." Gray Lily's voice creaked. "I would think your most recent lesson would be fresh in your mind."

Moncrieff made no reply but swallowed reflexively, and nodded. His posture of obedience seemed to mollify Gray Lily, and she went on.

"This girl," she said, turning to look into the mirror once more. "Was there anything unusual about her?"

"No," Moncrieff replied. "Just a girl." But he frowned, and his blue eyes took on a distant look, as though there was something about Brody's daughter that had puzzled him.

"But you think she was lying about the tapestry," Gray Lily pressed.

"She was lying," Moncrieff answered. "I'm sure of it."

Gray Lily's small black eyes slid in the mirror to watch him. "Then she must be the one. She must have released the unicorn somehow. My unicorn."

Moncrieff's fingers hesitated over the keyboard for a split second, but then he continued, completing the transaction and clicking the window on the computer screen closed. The screen saver popped up—a postcard-type scene of an English castle on a green hillside.

"Yes, my lady. I'm sure she's responsible." Moncrieff stood. "What do you want me to do?"

"Nothing. For now," said Gray Lily. She picked up a velvet pouch and opened it, withdrawing a thick green thread from inside. She held it in her palm and stroked it as if it were a pet. "She wants to keep it, does she?" Gray Lily's eyes glittered. "I'll simply send her a visitor." She chuckled. "She won't be able to get rid of my tapestry fast enough. I almost feel sorry for the little snippet."

Chapter 22

She'd never even shown him how to work the shower. Or the toilet. Well, too bad. Mr. Hard Constitution would have to figure out the miracle of indoor plumbing on his own. Tessa swung the door of her room shut behind her and leaned against the solid support with an exhausted sigh. She wondered what Will de Chaucy had made of her disappearing act. She'd run out of there as if Hannibal Lecter were chasing her with a bottle of A.1. sauce.

Letting him stay in her mother's old studio was probably a mistake. Tessa realized that now. Still, it was the best she could do for the moment. She flopped onto her bed and rolled to her back, cushioned and half cocooned in the soft thickness of her comforter as she stared up at the ceiling. So much for control freak. *More like out-of-control freak.* The studio had brought back so many memories. Good memories. But it was strange how good memories could make you feel like . . . well, puking.

Tessa frowned and let her eyes wander over the tiny imperfections of the plaster overhead. Would her mother have resented Will's staying up in the studio? No. Wendy Brody might have been artsy and full of flaky whimsy, but when it came to people, she was practical. It was Tessa's father who kept the studio locked up and unused. He never talked about it. Maybe he had the idea that leaving it untouched would make it into a kind of shrine. But neglect, Tessa thought, recalling the dusty room, had made it look more like a crypt.

With a sigh Tessa hauled herself up and went to her desk. She opened a bottom drawer and rummaged inside until she found what she was looking for. She lifted up a small book bound in red leather and turned it over in her hands. It was her first, last and only journal. Tessa sat back down on the edge of the bed.

She opened the book. Its spine creaked with stiffness, and the clean white pages fanned beneath her fingers. It was beautiful, lined in the front and back with paper whose intricate pattern looked like peacocks' tails. Her mother had given it to her for Christmas two years before she died. It was so pretty, Tessa had been afraid to write in it.

Until one day (a cold, gray day, Tessa remembered) she had grabbed a thick black permanent marker and scrawled inside:

My name is Tessa Brody. This is my journal. I never kept a journal before. I don't think happy people write things down so much.

Tessa took a deep breath and kept reading. The smudgy writing was uneven, and ink had bled through the pages in spots. It was hard to read.

My mother's funeral was today at Culway Funeral Home. I can still smell all the roses—they were disgusting. I never want to see another rose. I have a lot to say but can't say any of it to the people I want to say it to. First of all, I really miss her already, but none of this seems real. Please don't let it be real.

Do you know what the worst part is? Life goes on. Aunt Peggy said that to me. "Life goes on, Tessa." I wanted to hit her. Hit her hard and make her nose bleed and break her glasses. Life goes on. That is so ugly and wrong.

Aunt Peggy was her mother's older sister and looked a little bit like her, tall with straight, flyaway blond hair and wide blue eyes. But where her mother's face had been full and dimpled, Aunt Peggy's was thin, with pulled-down wrinkles at the corners of her mouth and deep worry lines on her forehead. On the day of the funeral Aunt Peggy had said lots of helpful things. Everyone was relieved when she left.

Life should stop. Just for a little while, at least. I hate when I turn on the TV and the news is telling people what the weather is going to be and what the traffic is like on 95. People are going places and meeting in restaurants and planning vacations and shopping.

It's like Mom was never even here.

I think when somebody as special as her dies, everything should stop for a little while. But nothing does.

I want everything to stop.

Tessa still remembered that feeling she had right after they had told her. Her whole life suddenly became a blur. People came and went, conversations drifted past her, over her. The questions, the concerns. The talk. How badly she had wanted everything to stop so she could go back, fix things. But life never stops long enough for you to figure things out, never mind fix them. She knew that now.

Tessa closed the book. That was all she had written. All she had ever written or said about her mother's death to anyone. Until today. With Will.

A faint rustling noise came from under the bed.

Tessa glanced down. "Pie?" She leaned over, hung upside down. She lifted the dust ruffle. In the darkness she caught a glimpse of big, glowing yellow eyes. Tessa sniffed. A dank, wet smell wafted up. Like a dirty fish tank.

Tessa frowned. "Here, Pie. Bad kitty. Come out."

There was a hiss. A green head shot out, straight at her face.

Tessa screamed and wrenched away, feeling something swipe the top of her head. She rolled herself backward and scrambled to right herself on all fours, just in time to see a monstrous snake slither from beneath the bed. It undulated across the floor, its middle section looking as thick as her leg. Its scales, as big as thumbnails, were yellow, mottled with green. They rippled and rose like flexible armor as it moved.

Tessa let out a frightened whimper and sprang up to stand on her bed. The snake coiled around the base of a nearby floor lamp and then, slowly, rose up the pole. The head turned toward her and hung in midair, nearly at a level with her own. A thin red blade of a tongue flicked. Two black-slitted eyes watched her.

A shudder started at the top of Tessa's head and rattled down to her toes. Tessa tried to think. She couldn't get out. Getting to the door would put her within striking distance of the snake. She felt another scream begin in the back of her throat but choked it back. Maybe if she stayed really still, making no sudden moves, it would crawl away.

Slowly, staring at the snake's head, she reached down and pulled the comforter from the bottom of her bed. She inched it up. At least it was something. A barrier between her and the scaly nightmare. She dipped her gaze to the floor for a second. Swallowed. The rest of the snake was still coming from beneath the bed. How long *was* it, anyway? *Just stay still. Don't startle it.*

"Yeah," Tessa reasoned under her breath. "You're probably more scared of me than I am of—"

The snake lunged. Fangs exposed, the pale, ridged flesh of its open mouth gaped and flew toward her. Tessa flung one end of the comforter up. The snake's head bulleted into it, its fangs sinking into the fabric. Tessa fell backward, tumbling off the bed. The lamp crashed to the floor.

Tessa hung on to the thick material, trying to contain the snake's thrashing head. The comforter slipped and her fingers grabbed cool, writhing skin. "Ugh!" she screamed, and heaved the tangle of snake and flowery fabric away from her. Without thinking, she jumped down hard on the comforter and stomped on the wriggling mass. She grabbed the first thing that came to hand: her tennis racket. She turned it on edge and with a choked cry raised it and chopped down hard where she thought the head must be. She felt the metal racket frame connect with a grisly crunch. The foul, dank smell filled the air again, only stronger. The twisted shape on the floor was still.

Tessa leapt to the door, opened it and launched herself into the hallway and down the stairs.

Chapter 23

She bolted down the stairs but stopped short, nearly crashing into her father.

Tessa blurted out the words between gasps. "Dad. Snake. Up there."

"Tessa, hold on. Calm down." He looked into her face. "Is that what the noise was? I thought the ceiling was going to fall on my head."

Wordlessly, Tessa jabbed a finger upstairs. "Big snake," she repeated finally. She closed her eyes and shivered as she pictured it. Her stomach pitched. She would have to burn that comforter.

Tessa opened her eyes to see her father watching her with a perplexed look. "What do you mean? Like a garden snake?" he asked. "How the heck would a snake get up there? Let me take a look," he said, heading up.

"No!" Tessa grabbed him and hung on. "I hit it with my tennis racket. But I don't think— It may not be dead."

"We'll see," he said, gently disengaging her fingers.

Tessa crept behind her father as he climbed the stairs. He opened the door to her bedroom. Inside, the rumpled bed-cover lay on the floor, motionless. He stepped forward and prodded the mess with the toe of his shoe. "Under here?"

"Yes, be careful," said Tessa. She cast her eyes over every inch of the floor, watching for any movement. But the room seemed empty, still.

Her father picked up one edge of the flowered coverlet. With a quick jerk he snatched it back. The floor was empty.

Tessa shook her head in disbelief. "It's gone," she mur-mured. No way could it have slid under the door. It was too big. "I'll check under the bed," her father said, hunching over.

"No!" Tessa grabbed him. The tapestry, she thought, with a sudden sureness. The snake had come out of the tap-estry. And now it was gone. She could sense it.

"I—I think I must have fallen asleep and had a bad dream," Tessa stammered.

"You fell asleep?" Her father glanced at her curiously. "At five in the afternoon? You must be sick." He put his hand to her forehead. "You don't feel hot."

"I'm okay, Dad," Tessa said, pulling away. "I'm just kind of tired. Sorry about scaring you. The snake, I mean. It couldn't have been real. Sorry."

Her father straightened and surveyed the room: the top-pled lamp, the books strewn on the floor. "Must have been some dream," he commented.

Tessa looked down at the comforter. There was a gash torn through the middle of it. "Yeah," she replied to her father, bending to pick it up before he could notice the damage. Even *she* couldn't dream that violently.

"Are you scared, Tessa? You know, about the break-in?" her father asked. "You don't need to be. I'm putting in a security system, new locks, everything. You're safe, honey."

"I know. Thanks, Dad." Tessa righted the lamp. Safe was the last thing she was, and she knew it. But she did her best to give a normal, relaxed smile. Literally lying through her teeth.

Her father left with a shake of his head, and Tessa ducked down to peek under the bed. Cautiously, she dragged the tapestry out, touching only the edges. She unfolded it. There was the snake, appearing exactly the same as before. Except for one thing: it was now lying on the grass in the foreground. It had moved.

Tessa had supper with her father, then told him she was going to make an early night of it. In her room she emptied a gym bag and with quick, gingerly motions stuffed the tap-estry and the *Texo Vita* inside. When she was certain her father had gone to bed, she walked to the back stairway, up to the studio, and knocked on the thin door. "Will!" she whispered. "Let me in."

Silence followed, and Tessa had the sudden, sickening feeling that something terrible had happened. He was gone.

But the door opened and Will stood there. The room was dark, but moonlight washed in from the tall windows and made him a dark silhouette, gleaming around the edges.

"At last," he muttered. "Mistress Brody." He reached out and hauled her into the room.

"Are you all right?" she demanded. She peered around. "Did anything weird happen here?"

"Weird?" he repeated coldly. "In the context of my life the term has little meaning, mistress." He watched her as she dropped the gym bag to the floor. "You're shaking," he said in a softer tone. He stepped closer and took her arm in a firm clasp. "What has happened?"

For a moment Tessa's brain refused to focus on anything except how close he was. How tall and strong he felt next to her. What would it be like, she thought, to take just one step closer? To melt against him, just for a second? The feeling was so strong, she sensed herself sway. It was like standing next to a cliff.

"There was a snake," she said finally, in a low voice. "Like a *Jurassic Park* snake."

"A snake? From a park? I don't understand you."

Tessa closed her eyes. "A really huge snake came from the tapestry. It was in my room."

"Did you conjure it out?" Will demanded. "Did you pull another thread?"

Tessa glared. "No. I didn't do anything. I was reading," she said. "I heard a noise under the bed and then, boom.

Or," she corrected herself, "more like *hiss*. And there it was."

Will gave a grimace and then a curt nod. "Was it of a rather large size?" he asked. "Yellow and green?" In the dim light she could see him watching her intently.

"Yeah. How did you know that?"

"I have seen this creature." Will spoke in a grim, bitter tone. "A frightful thing, but not lethal. Are you all right?"

"Yes. I—I jumped on it. And whacked it with a tennis racket. Yay for sporting equipment," Tessa answered weakly. She glanced around the studio. He hadn't turned the lights on; only moonlight illuminated the room. But it felt safe here. She turned back to Will, who was looking at her as if she'd just grown another head. And not a very attractive one.

"You jumped on it," he repeated. He pushed his long fingers through his hair. "Are you mad?"

"I'll say. My room is trashed."

Will narrowed his eyes to regard her and then shook his head, exasperated. "Did the thought of running away never strike you?"

"Oh, it struck," Tessa replied. "But see, there was this *snake* in the way." She did her best to drip the sarcasm.

"Oh," he said grudgingly.

"Anyway, the snake went back into the tapestry," Tessa said. She stepped away from Will and nudged the gym bag on the floor with her foot. "I brought the tapestry here. And the book. I wasn't sure what else to do." She folded her arms, staring at the lumpy bag, almost expecting to see it move. "Do you think we should destroy it?" she asked. "We could burn it, maybe."

"No!" Will's reply burst from him. "We can't do that."

In answer to her puzzled expression he said, "There are all manner of creatures in the wood from which you released me. They live inside that tapestry. Suppose they are people, transformed as I was? Into beast or bird or flower. I cannot destroy the tapestry, Mistress Tessa. Not even to save myself."

"Oh," said Tessa. She frowned and rubbed the back of her neck. It was unbelievable, and yet she believed it. "I understand," she said. "But then what about the snake? Was that a person?"

Will shook his head. "I do not know. But you said it returned to the tapestry."

"Yes. But in a different place." Tessa shivered, wondering what other surprises the tapestry held. "So what do we do now? We have the book," she said slowly. "The *Texo Vita*. We'll go through it again. Maybe there's something we missed. Something that will tell us how to get them out, or return them to wherever it is they're supposed to be, or . . ."

Will tilted his head, and an amused smile played at the corner of his mouth. "Do you never stop?"

"Stop what?"

"Trying to fix things," he murmured.

"Well, it seems like a good idea," Tessa argued. "What do you suggest? I'm not going to just sit around waiting for Creepy Crawly to come back out for a midnight snack."

"I don't think it will return. I believe it was meant to frighten you."

"Well, it nailed the audition," Tessa huffed. "I'm frightened. But also really pissed off."

Will stared at her.

"Angry," Tessa explained.

"Ah," he said. "Pissed off," he repeated, seeming to consider it. "A colorful expression. I like it." Shadows played over his features as he asked, "Why did you leave me so abruptly?"

The question took her by surprise. Tessa dropped her gaze from Will de Chaucy's stern, tense look. "I—I'm sorry about that. I haven't been up here in a while. It was my mother's space." Tessa's hands searched for something to do. She bounced her fingertips together. "Being here brought back memories. I had to get out."

"I didn't know if you would return."

The hint of regret in Will's tone made something turn over in Tessa's chest. But she ignored it.

"Well, that's normal," she said. "This is a strange place and I'm someone familiar." *That's good,* she told herself. *Go with that.* "Did you know a baby chick will get attached to the first thing it sees when it cracks out of its shell? It thinks that whatever it sees is its mother. A dog, a lizard, whatever. It's called imprinting." Now she was chattering about psychology. Perfect. Next she'd drool on him like one of Pavlov's dogs.

Will frowned, something unreadable in his eyes. "Must you have a reason for everything?"

Tessa shrugged. "It helps."

After a moment Will said, "Leave the tapestry and the book here. You need sleep. Tomorrow you shall repair the world."

"You're making fun of me."

"Not at all. We will apply logic to the problems at hand, find a solution and plan a course of action. If that fails, you shall jump on our attackers, possibly brandishing a statuette or some bit of sporting equipment. Your arsenal seems formidable."

Tessa smiled. "Ha-ha." But she couldn't suppress the wonderful feeling of having him near, sixteenth-century sarcasm or no. "Can I bring you back something?"

"There was a book in your chamber that intrigued me. The language seemed not as foreign as some of the other writings. If you would bring me *A Midsummer Night's Dream,* I should be grateful."

"Shakespeare? I guess that makes sense," Tessa said. Had Shakespeare even been born yet when Will was . . . alive? Close enough, probably. Will would be perfectly at home with all the *thees* and *thous.* Though she couldn't help but wonder if he would like *To Kill a Mockingbird* or *Around the World in Eighty Days,* and there was Sherlock Holmes. And Winnie-the-Pooh! "I'll bring a bunch," she said, warming up to the idea of exposing him to all the great books he had never even heard of.

"Tomorrow. Go and rest now," he said with a smile. "You will be safe."

"Yeah? How do you know?" she asked. She meant it to be teasing, but his smile drifted away.

"Because I will make sure of it," he answered.

So much for sharing, being a team. Cryptic Boy was back with a vengeance.

"Tessa," he said in a low voice as she walked to the door. She turned. Will's features were set into a thoughtful frown as he stared at a place directly in front of him. "Do not run from me again. I do not like it."

Chapter 24

Tessa took a long, scaldingly hot shower, letting the water and the heat pummel her, as if it could drive all the tension and worry away. And maybe even magically make her understand what was going on. It didn't work.

Thinking about him was so confusing. Will de Chaucy had stepped out of a tapestry and taken over her life. Nothing was ever going to be the same. Well, to be honest, he hadn't exactly *stepped* out. He had been yanked. By her. And somehow, it seemed *right* that he was here. Even if he was annoyingly secretive at times. And bossy. And a little stuck-up.

But she had to admit, he had good qualities. When he'd spoken about the other lives inside the tapestry, lives that he wouldn't sacrifice to save his own, she'd seen something else. He was selfless. He was brave, maybe stupidly so.

Braver than she was, that was for sure. She didn't think she could have gotten to sleep with the tapestry in her bedroom. Who knew what could come out of the thing next? Maybe it wasn't the smartest move to have left it with Will either, but her choices seemed pretty limited.

Tessa dried off and slipped into her soft pink bathrobe. As she toweled her hair, she turned to the bathroom door, where she'd hung her clothes. She frowned. Strange. The frayed hole in the knee of her jeans was gone. Tessa stepped closer. No patch, no seam. Almost as if the fabric had been . . .

She froze when she saw the words in the denim. They stood out in tufts of white cotton thread:

Go to a dark glass.

Oh God. Not again. "Cut it out," said Tessa in a shaking voice. She whirled around and cried out, "Gray Lily! Lila Gerome? Whoever you are! Can you hear me? Stop it. Leave me alone!" But nothing happened. And the tiny message woven into her jeans stayed put. With a swat she knocked the clothes from the hook.

She stepped back, sat down on the edge of the bathtub and hugged her robe closer, feeling vulnerable and exposed.

"Go to a dark glass," Tessa said softly. What did *that* mean? A piece of glass? Sunglasses? She looked over at the steamy reflection of herself in the full-length mirror on the door and shivered, despite the warm, humid air.

She remembered her sleepover in fifth grade when Heather Landrigan convinced everybody to play Bloody Mary. Each girl was supposed to go into the bathroom by herself, turn out the lights and stare into the mirror. You were supposed to see the face of your future husband, or Bloody Mary, whoever she was. Tessa had been too scared to do it. She had gone in and sat on the closed toilet seat for a little while, and then gone out again.

But the memory did remind her of something else. *Go to a dark glass.*

"The glass," she said slowly, "is a mirror."

Tentatively she got up, stepped over to the wall and flipped off the light switch.

The sudden plunge into darkness was complete. There was a small, high window next to the shower, but that didn't matter; the sky outside was dark. The bathroom was as black as a cave. Slowly Tessa's eyes began to adjust until she was able to make out the pale gleam of the white sink and stainless fixtures.

Tessa walked to where she knew the mirror hung on the door. She couldn't see it but stood in the darkness, watching the place where she knew it was. She waited.

Gradually she was able to see the outline of the mirror. There was nothing there.

"This is insane," she murmured, and reached toward the light switch.

Just then, Tessa saw a faint flash in one corner of the

mirror. She turned to look behind her at the high window to make sure there was nothing reflecting in from outside. A headlight from a passing car, maybe. When she looked back at the mirror, she jumped.

The mirror glowed with a luminous, neon blue light. Three hooded figures stood before her. They were huddled together, and though Tessa couldn't see their faces, she had the distinct impression that they were staring at her.

"Definitely a mortal," said one of them from the shadowy depths beneath its black hood. Long white fingers stuck out from the ends of its sleeves and made strange little twitching movements.

"Just a girl," said the second, whose dark-skinned hands were calmly folded together.

"Who are you?" Tessa whispered to the faceless shapes. "Did Gray Lily send you? Is one of you Gray Lily?"

"You see?" hissed the first to the other two. "Nothing but senseless questions. We are the three sisters of Fate."

There were several moments of eerie silence during which the three figures regarded her, tilting their hooded heads slightly. Tessa tensed. She had the creepiest sensation they were . . . *measuring* her.

"Return the threads," said one of them in a horrible deep voice. It sounded like something heavy rolling in the bottom of an oil drum. Tessa thought it was the ghostly shroud on the end who spoke, who stood taller than the other two.

"What?" she said faintly.

"Did you not receive our first message?" the resonant voice demanded. "Return the threads."

"Message?" Tessa repeated. "That was you?"

The voice boomed again, "Return the threads!" and the mirror rattled against the bathroom door with the reverberations.

"I—I don't have any thread," Tessa managed to stammer. "Not anymore, I mean."

"Treachery!" screeched the first cloaked figure. She raised a long, trembling finger and pointed it at Tessa. "Who has taught you the weaving of Wyrd?"

Tessa cringed as the skinny digit appeared to come out of the mirror to jab at her. "I don't know anything about weaving," Tessa squeaked. She clutched her robe tighter. "Or weird," she added, repeating the word the creature had used. "I mean, *this* is weird. Of course. But I don't weave. I can barely make a braid. Ask anybody. I pulled on one of the threads from the tapestry and Will came out and—"

"Silence!"

Okay, stop babbling to the angry ladies. Though it was hard to imagine the spectral forms as female, they'd called themselves sisters.

"Alive?" said the deep-voiced one. She raised an enormous pair of scissors in her large, corpse-white hand.

An unpleasant tickle went down Tessa's spine as she stared at the blades. "Huh?" She just couldn't seem to keep up with the conversation.

"The boy. The thread," the dark form in the mirror said tersely. "You said he came out of a tapestry. He came out *alive?*"

"Yes."

"Liar!" The huge cloaked figure somehow made the word sound like a curse. "That's impossible."

"Well, you might want to check on that," said Tessa. Her throat felt dry as chalk, but a little nip of anger strengthened her voice. She wasn't a liar. "I was there. It happened."

Gravel Voice, who, Tessa thought, seemed to be the leader, turned to the others. "I told you. The loss of the threads has created a hole in the Wyrd. She's fashioned a portal, or perhaps another dimension, with this *tapestry,* as she calls it. Who is to say he couldn't pass through?" The others nodded.

"Who are you?" Tessa asked again. She pushed back her damp hair. The air in the bathroom had cooled and the strands felt like cold, wet fingers against her neck.

"We are the Norn, as you know very well, mortal," said Gravel Voice, "since you have been meddling in our realm." She pointed to the smallest of the three, the one with the twitchy fingers. "This is Spyn," she said. "And this is Weavyr." She indicated the hooded figure with the dark hands that stood quietly in the middle. "And I am called Scytha." With this she raised the long-bladed scissors. A sharp white light shot from the blades and lanced out of the mirror like a laser beam. Tessa jerked her eyes away and raised an arm to shield herself. For a moment the bathroom was lit up like a stage with the white-hot glow. "You know the power we hold," thundered Scytha. "Give back the life threads you have stolen or we will wield that power. Your world will be torn apart."

Slowly the painful sensations of light and heat faded. Tessa took a deep breath and lowered her arm.

"Look," Tessa said, her voice shaking, "Norn ladies. I didn't steal anything. I swear."

"Return what was stolen, mortal," said Scytha. "You have meddled in works that you cannot comprehend. Seven threads. Seven lives. The loss of them has caused a rift in the Wyrd. For five hundred years we have searched for what was stolen. Now you have revealed yourself to us. You will not escape."

"I don't know how this happened, but—" Tessa broke off. She swallowed and straightened. "I didn't steal anything," she repeated. "And Will's not a thread. He's a person. He's not going back."

There was silence as the dark, cloaked beings in the mirror seemed to take this in.

"This is your decision?" Scytha asked. "To defy us?"

"Y-yes," Tessa stammered, lifting her chin and stepping back from the mirror.

"It is a foolish one."

The Norn wavered, and disappeared.

Chapter 25

You know your life is completely screwed up when you have to look up the mythological figures who talk to you in the bathroom mirror.

"These women," Tessa told Opal as they sat on the front stoop of the bookstore the next morning. "They called themselves the Norn. They're the Fates who spin and weave and cut the threads of life."

"No way."

"Yeah. Way." Tessa bent her legs, resting her arms and her head on her knees. "I Googled them.

"When Gray Lily stole threads of life, it kind of messed up the scheme of things. The Norn have been looking for the stolen threads ever since. They think *I'm* her. I mean, the one who stole the threads."

After her confrontation with the Norn, Tessa had hardly slept, remembering the three ghostly figures in the mirror. She had stayed awake, expecting an eerie blue glow to creep into her bedroom mirror somehow, even though she'd kept the lights on. She'd also plugged in her old butterfly night-light as well as a Lava lamp, just in case.

"The Fates. The real Fates," Opal repeated. She poked Tessa in the arm to get her attention. "So they could basically . . ." She paused and made a quick slashing motion across her neck with one finger.

"Um. I guess so." Tessa frowned, remembering the scissors and the searing light. "Thanks for the visual."

"Well, don't worry," Opal said. "I mean, I'm sure they wouldn't do anything hasty. I mean, maybe they'd have to okay it with somebody first before they . . ." She glanced skyward. "Maybe fill out a form or something?"

"It's kind of strange," Tessa said thoughtfully. "All these so-called myths and fables. Everyone seems to have the same ones. They cross cultures and continents. Everyone has their own versions of unicorns, witches, even the Fates. Now we know why. Because they're *real*."

Opal nodded. "Makes sense, I guess. Maybe in the olden days people even told those creepy fairy tales to kids for a reason. Maybe there really *were* trolls under all the bridges. Yikes."

They were both silent. Tessa took a deep breath. "I am so scared," she said finally. "What am I going to do?"

Opal's small face pinched up as she concentrated. She tapped one high-heeled boot on the pavement in a staccato rhythm. "What about getting someone to do an exorcism or calling one of those ghost hunter teams from television?" she offered.

Tessa shook her head. "I think this is bigger than anything they could handle. These things aren't ghosts. Somehow they exist right now—just not in a place we can see."

Opal nodded. "Maybe you just have to play along. Give the Norn ladies what they want."

"I *can't*," Tessa said. "That's the problem. They want the thread. And by that they mean Will. I wouldn't give him to those creepy women even if I knew how."

Opal smiled and said something under her breath.

"What did you say?" Tessa asked, narrowing her eyes.

"I said you're smitten."

"Oh, come on," Tessa said with a roll of her eyes, then glanced back and said hesitantly, "Really obvious, huh?"

"Yeah," said Opal, eyeing her. "He smit you good."

Tessa sighed and shook her head. "Well, it doesn't even matter, because this is all some kind of crazy, impossible *thing* that I don't even understand."

"Uh-huh." Opal grinned like a maniac and bobbled her head. "Smitten with the esquire."

"Okay." Tessa held up a hand. "Change of subject. Please? Like if the Norn are so in charge, how did Gray Lily manage to steal Will's thread in the first place?" She stopped, recalling the words of the Norn. "Actually," she said slowly, "they said *threads,* plural." Tessa frowned. "I didn't really think about that before. They're kind of intimidating. It was hard to focus. What are you doing?"

Opal was busy fiddling with something. She turned and slipped the pig bracelet onto Tessa's wrist. "Here," she said, pulling the drawstrings closed. "I don't know how all this is going to end up, but you will definitely need the power of the pig."

Tessa smiled and fingered the simple adornment. It wasn't much to look at. The worn black fibers were frayed here and there, and a couple of the smaller beads were missing. But the chubby jade pig still had that dopey smile on his face. Or his snout, rather. Whatever it was, it felt comforting to have him back.

Opal rocked sideways to nudge Tessa's shoulder with her own. "I'll bet you think of something." She nodded knowingly. "You're tougher than you look, girlfriend."

Tessa grinned. "Thanks."

"Yeah, well, it's not much of a compliment," said Opal with a hint of a smile. "You look pretty wimpy."

"Ha-ha. Come on." Tessa stood with a sigh and picked up a small canvas tote. It was bulging with food and books she'd packed for Will. Her cooking skills were pretty much nonexistent, but that morning she'd sliced bagels and smeared them with cream cheese, steeped three bags of Earl Grey tea in a thermos and tucked it all inside, along with a couple of apples.

Tessa slipped the bag absently over her shoulder, remembering Opal's comment about Will. Maybe she did . . . like him.

Who was she kidding? She could barely think of anything but him. It was as if Will de Chaucy's face, the sound of his voice, even the smell of him had been sizzled into her brain with a hot cattle brand.

It was early, and the Closed sign hung in the bookstore window. Her father was still upstairs. What he didn't know, Tessa decided, wouldn't hurt him. "Okay," she said to Opal. "Let's go get Prince Charming."

They were about to enter the alley to go to the back entrance when Tessa glanced to the side, squinting against the brightness of the morning sunlight. She glimpsed a large black sedan parked near the corner. New York plates. She wasn't sure what drew her eye to the car, but as her gaze lingered, the dark outline of the driver inside shifted, crouching lower in the seat. Tessa veered, immediately changing direction. She put her head down as she hissed. "That's him. Don't look."

"Who?" Opal asked. "Will?" She craned her neck to search the street.

"No! Quit looking! It's the lawyer. Moncrieff. I'm pretty sure it's him in a car behind us. He's watching us." She could almost feel the gaze of those two droopy blue eyes boring into her back.

"Jeez." Opal quickened her pace next to Tessa. "She sent the lawyer after you? Since when do evil witches sue?"

"He's kind of a henchman," puffed Tessa, striding down the narrow sidewalk. "In pinstripes."

"What do we do?" Opal asked. "Try to lose him?"

"Just keep walking."

As they reached the corner, Tessa shot a look back down the narrow street. The black car pulled away from the curb. It was following them.

"Come on!" Tessa sprang into a run as soon as they

turned the corner. Opal gave a yelp and followed. Despite the weight of the tote bag, Tessa dug in, relishing the feel of her strong legs and the sight of the pavement flying away behind her. But after a few moments she jerked to a stop. Opal was lagging behind. The black car had turned the corner and Tessa saw Moncrieff at the wheel, his face looking grim as he drew closer. But he was a few cars back and the line of traffic was crawling, stuck behind a city bus that had lurched to a halt to let someone off.

"Hello?" Opal gasped, coming up beside her. "Heels, here."

Tessa muttered something nasty about fashion statements while she swiveled to look around. "This way." She and Opal dashed in front of the bus to cross the road, and a little farther down they turned onto the next side street. Tessa slowed her steps and threw a glance back.

At the end of the street the black sedan slowed . . . and passed by.

Tessa grinned at Opal. "One-way."

Opal looked back in surprise. "Huh. That never stops them in the movies."

"Yeah," Tessa agreed. "But somehow I don't think this guy wants much attention. Listen, just keep going, okay? I'm going back before he has a chance to loop around."

"You sure?"

"I need to make sure Will's okay and tell him what's happened."

"Okay," Opal grumbled. "But be careful."

"I will." Tessa turned and began to run back the way they'd come.

"And you know all this faithful sidekick stuff?" Opal yelled after her. "It's really not my style."

Tessa slowed and spun around. "I know," she answered, walking backward a few steps. "How about kick-ass best friend?"

Opal's grin flashed. "Now you're talkin'."

Chapter 26

"Return the threads?" Will repeated after Tessa had told him about her encounter with the Norn. "I don't understand. Why would they appear to you? And in a looking glass, no less."

Tessa shrugged. "I don't know. They said that there are threads missing, more than just yours. *Seven threads. Seven lives.* Somehow they knew, or sensed, when I pulled the thread and released you from the tapestry. I guess they think I'm some kind of weaving mastermind. I tried to tell them it was Gray Lily, but they were . . ." She hesitated. "Kind of snippy."

"There *are* others, then," Will said, pacing. He wore a pair of faded jeans and a simple white button-down shirt, the sleeves rolled up over his tanned forearms. His hair fell in slightly messy waves to his collar, and there was a faint stubble over his jaw. "And these stolen threads must be in the tapestry still."

"I guess so," Tessa said. "And the Norn want them back. Like, yesterday."

Will was watching her. "You say that you saw Moncrieff, this legal agent of Gray Lily's, outside your home?" His jaw tightened. "He followed you?"

"Yes. But I lost him. He doesn't know you're here."

"What will you do now?"

Tessa was baffled by his question. "Do?" she repeated. "What *can* I do?"

"Perhaps you should go, while Moncrieff is diverted."

Tessa shook her head and placed the bag on the small kitchenette table. "I don't think he'll be thrown off for long. I think we had both better sit tight for a little while."

"Sit tight?"

"Stay here."

Will nodded. He eyed the canvas bag. "Is there, by chance, any food in that satchel?"

Tessa smiled. "There might be."

Will closed his eyes reverently. "Bless you, mistress."

Tessa smiled and felt her cheeks get warm. As Will wolfed down his breakfast, she wandered around the studio. Morning light washed through the high windows and made warm rectangles of sun on the paint-splattered floor. It didn't seem as overwhelming now, and Tessa went from spot to spot, looking not at the artwork but at the small everyday things, the little places where her mother had been. She drew a finger around a watermark left on a small table, picked up a small palette knife and wiggled the flexible metal between her fingers.

"Your mother's work is truly beautiful," Will said, watching her.

"Yes, I think so too," Tessa answered. She pointed to the framed landscape of Monhegan Island on the opposite wall. "She had shows all over the country."

Her mother's work had been described as "vividly romantic" and "classical in style but with a new age aesthetic." Whatever that meant. Sometimes Tessa wondered if, wherever her mother was, her world had become as beautiful as the ones she'd created in her paintings. Tessa hoped so.

"But there is one that does not fit," Will said.

Tessa's curiosity was piqued. "What do you mean?" she asked. She followed Will as he walked over to a small painting set on the floor in the corner.

"This," he said, and picked it up. Tessa looked at the painting and caught her breath. She had forgotten all about it. It was a small canvas swirled with pure, thick colors. Below, the scene was wild, whipped into spattering waves in colors of electric green and shimmering gold, while above, the sky swirled in a sunset of magenta and orange.

"I have never seen a sea look like this from our shores of Cornwall, and yet it seems familiar to me. As an ocean from my dreams," said Will.

Tessa looked at him in surprise. Funny, that was exactly what she'd thought too. A dream ocean. She had never thought anyone would see it the way she did. He peered at the corner where *Tessa* was painted in vermilion. He traced her name with his fingertip.

"You're an artist," he said, looking up.

Just like that. Not as a compliment or with sarcasm either—a statement of fact. "No," Tessa answered, flustered. "I'm not. My mother was the artist, not me." And this was *her mother's* studio, Tessa thought. Just as her father had reminded her the day he'd discovered Tessa up here, painting in her own clumsy way. He had shooed her out and locked the door. Turned the key as if he could vacuum-seal the spirit of Wendy Brody.

Will nodded in appreciation, then turned back to Tessa's painting. "But you have a talent of your own."

Tessa gave a rueful smile. "You wouldn't say so if you knew how I painted that." Will crooked his eyebrows in a silent question. Tessa raised her hands and wriggled them shyly. "With my fingers. Weird, huh? There's something I love about the feel of the paint . . . the colors." She shook her head. "But when I hold a brush or a pen, I get clumsy. Something gets lost between me and the paper." She tilted her head and looked at Will. "I'm not sure if I'm making any sense to you."

"Yes," he murmured, looking at her steadily. "You do make sense. What else have you painted?"

Tessa looked away. "Nothing. Since then." She had no real talent. And whenever she tried to paint or draw, she was afraid she was just trying to bring her mother back in some small way.

Will made a slow circle of the room with his gaze. "It's a shame such a delightful room is no longer used."

"Like I said before," Tessa answered stiffly. "It was my mother's studio. She was the artist."

There was a silence, and this time it wasn't comfortable.

Will set her painting down carefully, as if it was something precious. "Actually, mistress. I wasn't thinking of painting." He looked around. "This room would also be very suitable for . . ." He came closer and startled her by taking one of her hands in his own. "Dancing."

"What are you doing?" At his touch she all but jerked her hand away. Not because she didn't want to touch him. But because suddenly it was *all* she wanted.

"Simply this: we are trapped here, for the moment, while Moncrieff cools his heels outside. To pass the time, I am offering you all of the benefits of my training with the dance master Monsieur Foquelaire. Come." He pulled her to the center of the large room. He bowed. "We begin."

Will held Tessa by only the tips of her fingers, raised high in front of their chests. The touch was nothing, the merest contact, but somehow she felt as though she were flying when Will began to maneuver her across the open space, pacing beside her.

"Forward," he said, laughing as he watched her feet. "Forward again. Now back. Reprise. Turn. Reverence." He bowed deeply. "You curtsy now."

"Oh, right." Tessa bent her knees, feeling silly.

"This is a *basse danse*," Will said. "It's very proper and suitable for court occasions. During which you must not spit, and blow your nose only sparingly."

"I'll try to remember." Tessa smiled as they proceeded side by side. Once she had the pattern down, she was able to look up across the arm's length between them, where she found Will's eyes trained on her. The silly feeling faded. Tessa's steps became less mechanical as her feet, almost as if by themselves, matched Will's fluid movements. Soon they were gliding, wordlessly in sync. She imagined she wore a beautiful gown that brushed the floor as she danced. Thick folds of blue velvet swirled against her skin when she turned. They were surrounded by candlelight. They were—

"You dance well, mistress," Will said.

His words broke the spell of her imagination, but her heart still did a little flip at the compliment. Tessa searched for something to say. "It seems very . . . slow," she managed.

"It has to be." Will looked forward, head upright. "Everyone's shoes are pinching their toes and they're stepping on each other's trains."

Tessa laughed but Will kept a straight face. "In truth, it can be a most painful ordeal," he commented. "My brother, Hugh, would rather fight the heathen hordes than risk his toes to the dance." He stopped and released her hands. "Now, *this*, my lady, is the *galliard*." He sprang up and landed neatly beside her. "The king himself is a devotee of this particular dance." He kicked out again and jumped. "It is said to be very daring, very athletic."

"Athletic. Yes, I can see," said Tessa, watching him with a smile. "When do you get to the daring part?"

"Just here, mistress. *Lavolta*." Will suddenly put both hands to Tessa's waist and lifted her up. She gasped with surprise and clutched his shoulders. He arched back and she felt her weight resting against the firm planes of his chest as he turned slowly in a circle, looking up at her.

Tessa's heart was kickboxing in her chest. Her eyes stayed focused on Will's as he let her down slowly. But he was tall and it was a long way down.

"You see?" he said, breathing deeply. "Scandalous." He swallowed.

They stood facing each other. Will didn't remove his hands from her waist but leaned closer, his lips only inches from her own. She could feel the warmth of his breath, could smell his skin. She felt herself drawn closer to him. *So this is what it's like to know what you want,* thought Tessa as she raised her lips.

But Will's eyes narrowed as he looked down at her. "Enough," he said. "Now tell me the truth."

Chapter 27

Tessa blinked. Tried to regain her footing. Wait. No, she was standing up.

"The truth?" she whispered.

"Yes, mistress." Will was so close, his warm breath was a caress on her mouth. "Tell me the truth. I can stand this deception no longer."

"Tell you what?" Tessa said, mystified. She was still very conscious of his height, his nearness, but something had changed. His strong, aristocratic features might have been carved from marble. His eyes were cold. Wary.

"You will make me declare it, I suppose." Will released his hold on her waist and walked away. He turned abruptly. "You were there. It was you."

"What do you mean? What are you talking about?"

"You were the maid in the wood when I—" He broke off, staring at her. "When Gray Lily captured me. How can you tell me it wasn't you? Your eyes, your face." He came closer. "Even your hair." With a brooding look he took a soft coil of it and rubbed it between his fingers.

At once Tessa thought of his outburst at the waterfront. He had told her then that she resembled someone he knew. But she felt as if he wasn't seeing her; he was looking *through* her, to the past. She trembled as he swept his hand away. "It all began with you," he went on. "I saw you wander into the northern woods and followed you."

She opened her mouth to reply, to state the obvious. It wasn't her. It *couldn't* have been her. But his words sidetracked her.

"You followed me?" she repeated softly. "Why?"

Will hesitated. "I don't know. I couldn't help myself. It sounds idiotic to you, doesn't it? But even now, knowing what I do about you, I cannot seem to stop. I want to . . ." He took a step closer still. She'd been wrong—his eyes weren't cold, they were like warm honey. Tessa found her concentration slipping. She could forget everything looking into his eyes. But something he'd said—

She put a hand to his chest. And straight-armed him back.

"What do you mean?" she demanded. "What is it you *know* about me?"

Will frowned. "Why do you pretend? You recognized me the first moment you saw me. Admit it."

"Yes," she said, without thinking. She *had* recognized

him. Or at least, she thought she had. But only from the re-
semblance of his eyes to the unicorn's. And from her dreams
or visions, whatever they were.

"You recognized me because *you were there,*" Will said angrily. "Admit what we both know, Tessa. You were there in
the wood to trap me."

Every muscle in Will's lean frame seemed taut with a
barely controlled energy. His voice shook and he sounded
breathless as he spoke: "I was drawn to you, mistress. I laid
myself at your feet. And even bloody and filthy as I was, you
cradled my head. Caressed me." His lips twisted into a sneer.
"And then you watched as the witch shackled me with iron.
And cast me into Hell. Or rather, *wove* me there."

"No," Tessa whispered, backing away. An ugly image
leapt to her mind: a picture in a book of a heartless, stupid
girl. *A virgin in his haunts.* She shook her head in a stricken
denial.

Will was unmoved. "You watched as Gray Lily took the
unicorn's life, *my life.*"

In his eyes she saw the expression that had been puz-
zling her, and finally recognized it. It was accusation. He
blamed her.

Tessa rocked back another step, still shaking her head.
"It's not true." But even as she said it, the violent, vivid images and sensations of her dreams swirled around her. The
dank, rich smell of the woods. The sound of hoofbeats
pounding the earth. The taste of fear.

Only dreams, she told herself. *They were only dreams.*

"I do not know the reasons behind your actions," Will

went on, relentless, advancing on her step by step. "Why you released me from the tapestry. Or why you communicate with Gray Lily and the Norn. Do they have some hold over you? Is that what makes you do their bidding?"

"I'm not doing anyone's *bidding*," Tessa snapped, her own temper finally rising. She was grateful for it. It held back the sharp, hot tears pricking at her eyes as she stopped short and held her ground to face him. "I told you already. It was an accident. A stupid piece of thread. I didn't mean for any of this to happen. I would never do anything to hurt anyone. Especially not—" She stopped, but Will was paying no attention to her words.

He whirled away and paced the length of the studio in long strides. "For five hundred years I have lived as a dumb beast," he said, clenching his fists. "But inside I was yet a man." He stopped, turning to level a glare at Tessa from beneath his disheveled hair. "And do you know what I dwelt on all that time? What device I set my mind to in order that I might keep my sanity?" He came close and nearly whispered the words, next to her ear: "What I should do if ever I had my hands on you."

A drumbeat of fear raced through Tessa's veins at the ragged strain in his voice. He didn't sound like himself. What would being trapped for all that time do to a person? She couldn't even imagine it. "So?" She pulled back to stare at him, trying for composure, even though she was shaken to her core. "What are you going to do?"

Will's eyes swept over her. "I will be damned if I know," he muttered. "I should be afraid of you. But somehow I fear letting you go even more. You are the only tie I have to the world I know."

The world he wants to return to, thought Tessa. *That's the only reason he has stayed. No other. I'm a link, a lifeline; that's all.* "Why won't you believe me?" she asked, closing her eyes in frustration. "I wasn't there. I only know about now. I only care about now."

"*Now* is never going to be a place for me," said Will fiercely. "You must know that as well as I."

"No," Tessa answered. She felt stupid, slow. "I didn't know that." But his words reinforced Tessa's feeling that a distance was growing between them. All the time they'd spent together talking and dancing and nearly— She stopped herself from imagining the kiss that had been only a breath away a moment before. He didn't feel the things she did.

"All this time you haven't trusted me at all," she said in a wondering tone. She frowned. "What did you think I was going to do just now? Swoon in your arms? Confess my dastardly plan?"

Will rolled his eyes and swore beneath his breath. "No. I doubt that you've ever swooned in your life, mistress. But it would be a blessed relief to hear the truth from those lovely lips."

The anger took hold of her and flared. Tessa straightened. "The truth? Okay. Then listen to this," she ordered. Her voice was stronger now, and as cold and smooth as black ice. "I was never in Cornwall. Never sat on my tuffet, waiting in the woods to trap a unicorn. I never met you before I pulled that stupid thread, and *I wish I hadn't*." She advanced, jabbing a finger toward him, and Will was forced back a step. "If you don't feel you can trust me, then you'd better keep your distance," she shouted. "A century or two would be fine." She stopped. Her throat felt so tight it hurt.

Will appeared taken aback by her outburst, and a hint of uncertainty appeared in his eyes. But he tightened his jaw. "I suppose I should."

"Great." Tessa wheeled around. She dragged her gym bag from the floor. She shoved it at Will so hard he stumbled backward. "Then why don't you take the stupid tapestry and get the hell out of my life."

The bag turned over and the tapestry rolled out, thumping to the floor.

"Fine," Will returned with a shout. "I shall."

"And you can deal with Gray Lily and the Doomsday Sisters on your own," she added. Her life would be back to normal again. No more magic towels or glowing mirrors or evil witches. It had nothing to do with her anymore. Correction: it had *never* had anything to do with her. "And I don't care," she said aloud.

"That is apparent," Will agreed. But his voice had lowered. The hard line of his shoulders softened slightly. He looked at her. "Tessa, I—"

"Don't." She cut him off. She crossed to the window and peered out.

There was no sign of the black sedan below. "I don't think he's out there." She didn't understand how her voice could sound so level, so cool. "You can get away now."

"I am sorry," Will said. "I am grateful, Mistress Brody, for all that you have done. Good-bye." He stooped to gather up the tapestry, which had unfurled on the floor. Something caught Tessa's eye.

"Wait." She stepped closer and, with a puzzled look, took the tapestry and held it up before her. But it was too close; she couldn't see it properly that way. She spotted a couple of empty hooks on the wall. She hung the tapestry up on these and stepped back.

"It appears the same," said Will, glancing at it only briefly.

Tessa scanned the tapestry. There was the dark center of the picture where the unicorn had been, the more distant background of woods and trees and flowers. In the morning light the tapestry looked shabby and frayed at the edges, but the muted colors still glowed. Even now she could hardly believe what had happened: William de Chaucy had really come out of a piece of woven fabric. He was real.

Tessa frowned and took a step closer. "No," she said slowly. "I think it's different."

Gray Lily pinched the bridge of her nose and said, "This girl, this Brody person, is beginning to annoy me. Obviously my serpent did not have the desired effect." She turned to Moncrieff, who stood some feet away, his head bowed. Gray Lily raised her hands in clenched fists and shrieked. *"And she still has my tapestry!"*

Moncrieff nodded once. "Yes, my lady." He paused. "The unicorn. Even now, could you not control him as you—"

He broke off, the rest of it not needing to be said. *As you do me.*

Gray Lily jerked her head in the negative. "I can't. The

unicorn is the only thread I left whole within the tapestry. It's the only way I could"—she glanced at Moncrieff—"contain the creature.

"It doesn't matter," she said briskly. "I have other useful threads." She sat down and tugged open the drawstrings of her velvet pouch with quick, vicious movements. "I will have this girl on her knees before this day is done. I will have her blood and her tears." She pulled two coarse, spiky threads from her bag and dangled them in the air. Speaking in a low voice, she murmured a series of incantations.

The threads drifted up and away from her hands and out through the open window.

"There," said Gray Lily. "I have sent the lymerer. The hunt begins in earnest."

Chapter 28

The tapestry *was* different. There were two figures in the upper right-hand corner of the tapestry that Tessa hadn't noticed before. They were so small they were just two dark smudges. She took a deep breath. Stared.

"Will."

"What?" He looked over at her and came closer.

"Look at this," Tessa breathed. Her eyes were fixed on the dark woven surface. "It's changing." She stared at it, trying to see if words were forming. No. Not words.

The figures in the corner were bigger. She could see them clearly now, even though they were only about an inch high. They had taken on faint colors too. One was a man dressed in black; next to him was a shorter form. A dog, held on a leash.

"They're getting bigger," Tessa said faintly. She shivered. The threads of the tapestry were reworking themselves, transforming the wriggling surface of the fabric. The tapestry flapped against the wall, releasing small puffs of dust. Its surface rippled and shook as the figures got bigger. Closer. The grim-faced man had something black over one eye. A patch. The dog was huge and black, with glowing orange eyes and bared teeth.

Tessa heard the sharp hiss of Will's indrawn breath and turned. He stood, white-faced, staring at the tapestry. The jagged cut made a dark track on his pale skin. "Tessa!" Without tearing his eyes from the tapestry Will gripped her arm and pulled her back. "Get away from it. He's a lymerer."

"What's a lymerer?" whispered Tessa.

"A kind of huntsman. They use dogs to track and to—" He broke off and she glanced up. There was a wild look in his eyes. The same look he'd had when he'd come from the tapestry, Tessa thought. A frozen, hunted look.

"Will, what's happening?" she cried. When he didn't answer, she looked back. The figure of the man was in the center of the tapestry now, and bigger still. His face was thick and brutish. He held the leash wound around his fisted right hand. A heavy sword hung from his side, as well as a horn. The threads shifted. *He was moving.*

The dog pulled forward, pawing the air. The picture got bigger with every passing second, filling the tapestry as Tessa watched in horror.

"He's coming here." Will pushed her toward the door. "Get away, Tessa. Run!"

Then it happened. So quickly there was no time to run, no time to think. The room shook, and Tessa heard the rumbling and the tearing sound, the same as before. She stumbled to the door, got one hand on the knob and flung the door open as she twisted to look behind her. "Will!" she screamed.

The teeth came through first.

Chapter 29

Snapping fangs snagged and tore the threads as a monstrous dog pushed his head out of the tapestry.

"Run!" Will yelled, shoving Tessa through the open door.

They flew down the stairs. Will grabbed the rail and leapt over the last few steps, landing with a heavy thud behind her as they reached the bottom floor.

Claws scrabbled above them; then Tessa heard feet pounding down the stairs, chasing them. Thank God her father wasn't here, she thought as she and Will dashed through the back door to the store.

Tessa slammed it, threw the dead bolt and leaned against it as a heavy weight struck the other side. There was a curse and then scratching high on the other side of the door. She smelled hot, pungent odors: dog and drool and human sweat.

"It won't hold them," gasped Will. He grabbed her arm and pulled her, running across the wide, creaky floor of the bookstore. "Get outside—"

"I'll call the police."

"We'll both be dead before they arrive," he snapped, pulling her to the store's front door. The door behind them shuddered with a blow. Will dashed back, pulled a heavy dictionary from a display shelf and smashed the front of a glass case. *Webster's Collegiate,* Tessa noted dully. She didn't understand what Will was doing until, using the book, he began to swipe the shards of glass onto the floor. Without hesitating, Tessa bent to help spread the sharp pieces, brushing them in a wide path.

"Tessa! Not with your hands!" Will cursed and grabbed her by her shoulders. He propelled her through the front door just as she heard wood splintering. The door behind them was being savagely broken down. Will pushed her forward onto the steps. "Run to Opal's house," he shouted over the wild barking coming from inside the store. "It's me he's after. Do you understand?"

Tessa jerked a nod, turned away and began to run. Her heart thudded, as if slowed by fear-thickened blood. Behind her a melee of noises exploded from the store: a door bursting from its hinges, followed by the skitter of glass, then yelping canine cries.

She slowed and turned to look behind her. Will was running down the sidewalk. *They'll catch him,* she thought.

They'll catch him. The thought rammed her fear aside and replaced it with a fierce determination. *No.* She stopped and pivoted, then tore back after Will, running past the storefront again, where she caught a glimpse of the lymerer. His hulking, black-garbed form was bent over the dog, and he straightened just as she fled past. Tessa choked down a gasp as she saw him stand. The lymerer was gigantic; he must have been seven feet tall. He looked like some gruesome giant from a fairy tale.

Tessa raced after Will. To her relief, it wasn't like a dream. She was running fast, covering ground, closing the gap between them. He threw a glance behind him and, slowing, shouted at her. "What the hell are you doing?"

"Coming with you. This way," Tessa gasped, pounding up beside him. They raced side by side, Will nudging at her shoulder as she veered into an alleyway. They tore up the narrow, mud-slicked passage, dodging trash containers and restaurant delivery pallets.

"Up here." She rolled one of the tall recycling bins to the wall, hoisted herself on top of it and grabbed the edge of a fire-escape landing. She hooked a leg up and pulled herself onto the rattling metal frame.

"Faster," Will said. He sounded absurdly calm to her as he kicked the bin away and swung himself up. They scrabbled up the swaying iron steps to the second-floor landing as the lymerer's dog came whipping around the corner and along the alleyway. Unleashed, it bulleted toward them.

Tessa stared. *That couldn't be a dog.* Its thickly muscled haunches must have come up to her waist. A head the size of a cinder block. Sleek black fur, ears flat, muzzle rolled back from red slavering gums. Teeth like sharpened white tombstones snapped the air, and its bark sounded like savage machine-gun fire. Her gaze flicked to the opening of the alleyway. There was no sign of the giant lymerer—yet.

"Down," she tried weakly. "Heel. Sit."

"It's no use," said Will, breathing hard. "A lymerer's dog obeys only its master, and it knows only two commands: 'Hunt' and 'Kill.' "

"Great." Tessa found herself frozen. She was trapped by the monster Hell dog below and the wobbly framework of the decrepit fire escape above.

"Climb!" yelled Will. He put a firm hand on her back end and shoved.

Arms trembling, Tessa climbed the last section: a rusty ladder, bolted to the brick wall. She tried not to look at the sheer drop to the alley below. Tessa slung herself up and over the jutting ledge, onto the flat rooftop.

She rolled from the edge onto her back, panting as Will landed next to her in a crouch. He remained tensed, motionless, as they both listened. Running footsteps sounded below. The dog's barking stopped. Below them, the fire escape creaked.

With a muttered curse Will sprang up and jerked Tessa to her feet. As they ran across the pebbled surface, Tessa took in the limited options for escape. A rooftop garden had been laid out next to a small shed. Beyond this, the building's access door stood in an elevated, wedge-shaped structure. Will reached it and yanked. Locked.

They turned and ran into the garden shed. Will snapped the lightweight door shut. "There's no bloody bolt," he muttered.

"Garden tools don't need to lock themselves in," hissed Tessa. She peered through the ventilation slats of the flimsy barrier. At the edge of the roof the lymerer swung a booted leg up and climbed over. He stood. *Big and ugly* was all Tessa's mind could register for a moment. He came closer, and through the narrow spaces she saw him pause and swivel his gaze over the rooftop. One of his eyes was covered by a patch, and his face was marked with splotchy blemishes. His sloping forehead hung down over a thick, misshapen nose. The lymerer's one good eye fixed on the toolshed. He bared his blackened, broken teeth. It was something like a smile.

In the small, shadowed space, standing hip to hip with Will, Tessa saw the lymerer approach and her heart lurched. They were trapped in here. She turned slightly, trying to make no noise. "He's coming." She barely mouthed the words.

"Find a weapon," Will whispered into her hair. Tessa reached out and grabbed the first handle she touched as Will searched the cramped, stuffy space. In the dim light Tessa saw his fingers racing lightly over the piles of plastic tubs, watering cans and flowerpots. He lifted a bag and turned to her. He pointed to the skull-and-crossbones warning label.

"What's this?"

"Weed killer. Poison for plants," Tessa whispered.

Will nodded his understanding and opened the plastic sack to peer at the white powdered contents. Outside, the crunch of boots on gravel came closer.

"That won't do anything," she said in a desperate undertone. "Not unless you can make him eat it."

"I was thinking of something more immediate," he answered, reaching into the bag.

The door snapped open. Will shouted and flung a handful of the white powder into the lymerer's face. In an explosion of dust the man reeled back with a grunt, clutching his one good eye.

Will and Tessa scrambled out. The lymerer's face was plastered with white powder, and he squinted through one red, blinking eye. He swung a bulky arm, catching Tessa around her waist with such force that the air was knocked from her lungs. He dragged her closer and held her pinned to face him as she struggled helplessly. With a grunt he reached up and pulled off his eye patch. Beneath it, a scar-skinned globe veered in its misshapen socket. The milky, grotesque eye rolled down and fastened on Tessa. The lymerer grinned.

Tessa screamed, "He can still see!" and kicked out her legs, trying to wriggle away. With her free hand she swung the unwieldy weapon she had grabbed in the shed and dragged it across the lymerer's face. The metal prongs of the rake scraped his check, leaving trails of red before he ripped the tool out of her hands and flung it aside.

"Tessa!" Will charged into the lymerer's side. The blow didn't knock the enormous man down, but it broke his balance, and his grip on Tessa. She was tossed sprawling to the ground. Will snatched up the rake and broke it over one knee, leaving a sharply pointed wooden pike in one hand.

The lymerer lumbered to face him as Will grabbed Tessa's hand. "Get back down!" he gasped.

They raced to the edge of the building, and Tessa scrambled onto the fire escape. Will had just done the same when a thick hand reached over the edge and clasped his arm. The leering, dusty face of the lymerer came into view. Below, Tessa looked up and screamed.

She saw Will throw his weight backward to pull free, but the man held on, stretching out from the rooftop to keep his grip. With a desperate cry, Will let go of the ladder. He dangled over the alley far below. Only the grasp of the lymerer kept him from falling. Will thrust upward with the wooden spike. The shaft sank deep into the man's throat.

With a gurgling moan the huge man in black teetered. Will grabbed the ladder again just as his attacker lost his balance. The lymerer plummeted facedown past Tessa, arms windmilling, the wooden spike protruding from his bleeding neck.

There was a sickening, wet thud below them.

Tessa clung to the ladder and looked down. The still form of the lymerer lay in a growing pool of blood as his dog sniffed and whined at his outstretched hand.

Tessa didn't move, afraid the huge man would simply get up again, like something from a horror movie. But as she and Will watched, a faint black cloud began to gather around the body. The cloud grew thicker, hiding the body of the lymerer as well as that of the dog. After a moment the cloud lengthened and became two swirling black threads that trailed up and out of the alley, leaving an evanescent line of vapor in their wake. Soon only the broken wooden pole lay on the ground below them.

The lymerer, the blood and the dog were gone.

Chapter 30

Tessa and Will made their way back down the ladder. It felt as though the rickety thing was going to fall away from the building, but maybe that was only because Tessa was shaking so badly.

"He was real," she said when they got down. She hugged her arms to herself and closed her eyes, picturing the lymerer's gruesome face, the look of naked surprise as he flew past her, on the way to his death. She didn't think she would ever be able to forget it. "But *did* he die?" Tessa opened her eyes. "And what was that strange wispy smoke that came from his body?" She looked down at the bare, empty ground and back up at Will. "Where is he now?"

"I don't know." Will scanned the empty alley. "He may

have gone back from whence he came. Through the tapestry. But you are right. He and the dog were real enough. Both of them must have been people whose lives Gray Lily stole. What you saw leave were their threads."

Tessa began to shiver. Will took a step toward her. "You are safe. It is over, Tessa."

"I know, I know. I'm just . . . I'm afraid of dogs," She confessed. "Even the little yappy ones. Kind of a wimp, I guess."

He frowned. "I told you to go the other way."

Tessa shrugged. "Since when do I take orders from you? Besides, I know these streets a lot better than you do." *And I couldn't just watch you go.* Suppose that had been the last time she ever saw him? The thought made her feel ill.

"Stubborn," Will announced grimly. "And reckless. You are the most unmaidenly girl."

"That's right," answered Tessa with a weak smile. "Get used to it. I can't believe that dog found us so quickly," she added, shaking her head in wonder. "I thought we were safe."

"They track by scent," said Will. "They can smell blood a league away and—" He broke off and his lips tightened. "Show me your hands."

Her hands? Her hands were stinging, Tessa realized. She turned them up as Will took them in his own and bent over them, pulling her closer.

Tessa's palms were scored with small cuts. Blood mingled with rusty dirt and made ugly streaks where she had gripped the rungs of the ladder.

"I guess it was the glass," she said, staring. "I never felt it." But now she did begin to feel the raw throb of pain, and her hands trembled inside his. She realized something else. She was an idiot.

"The dog," she whispered. "It tracked the scent of my blood." She had led it and the lymerer here. "I led them right to you. *That's* why you told me not to use my hands," she said faintly. She tried to pull away.

But Will didn't release her. "That is not why," he said in a low, impatient voice.

He pulled her to him, lowered his head and kissed her.

With the touch of Will's lips to hers, Tessa's world shrank. There was nothing beyond the small, dark space between them, nothing beyond the sensations that enveloped her like a wave. Like an ocean. She was sinking and yet weightless as his breath mingled with hers, his mouth molded softly to her own. She twined her arms up and around his neck and felt herself drawn even more tightly to him.

Their lips parted slightly. "Tessa," Will whispered. His fingers wove into her hair at the nape of her neck, making her skin tingle. She opened her eyes to see Will smiling down at her. Everything had changed and yet everything was right. Tessa smiled back.

Then a brittle voice came from the end of the alley. "So we meet again, young *master*."

Chapter 31

Tessa turned in Will's arms. A stooped figure walked toward them, darkly outlined against the background of the alley entrance. It came closer. Tessa saw an old woman with wiry gray hair carrying a black plastic trash bag. For a crazy moment Tessa thought a bag lady was hailing them.

But Will's eyes widened in shock, and he gripped her arms so tightly she winced. "What's wrong?"

"It's her," Will hissed as the old woman approached. "It's Gray Lily. Get behind me, Tessa, and as soon as you can, *run*." He stepped in front of her.

"But—" Tessa objected.

"Do as I say!" Will snapped.

Tessa looked at the frail-looking old woman before them

and could hardly believe she was a threat. She couldn't have been more than five feet tall, and looked wrinkled and grandmotherly. Her clothes, a blue woolen skirt and white blouse, hung on her frame as if they didn't belong to her.

"I see you dispatched my lymerer," said Gray Lily, gazing at the two of them with small, hungry-looking eyes. She brought a wrinkled hand up to brush back her coarse gray hair in a surprisingly youthful gesture. "It's no matter." She held up a piece of black thread and put it in her pocket. "I shall heal him and call upon his services again when I need him. His diversion did allow me at least to reclaim what is mine." She smiled, or rather, a thin black hollow opened between her lips. Tessa shivered, and stepping forward to Will's side, she reached for his hand. His fingers wrapped around hers, and though her hand still stung from the cuts, the contact felt comforting; she squeezed his hand.

The old woman glanced at Tessa and then raised her eyebrows. "Well. Fancy that," she said.

Tessa stared back at the woman's hard little face. "What?"

But the woman hardly seemed to hear her. "Perhaps that explains why you've been able to meddle with my tapestry," Gray Lily said in a musing voice. "Old connections. Ties that bind. And once again, you've led me to my unicorn."

Will took a step sideways, trying to shield Tessa. "Be gone, witch. Your work is undone."

"Nonsense," Gray Lily laughed. "What weaver worth her salt would give up on a masterpiece for a few dropped stitches? Look what I found, my dears."

Gray Lily opened the plastic trash bag. Inside, Will and

Tessa could see the colors of the tapestry. From the dark interior of the bag it seemed to glow, the colored threads moving as if they were alive. She closed it again.

"Now it is time for you to return to your rightful place, young master." Gray Lily took a step forward and raised her hand. It was almost a friendly gesture, as if she were waving good-bye, but she held it there and then pointed at Will.

Instantly Will's body jerked forward, toward the old woman. Tessa let out a shocked cry. It was as if an invisible rope tied around him had tugged. Tessa tightened her grip on Will's hand. "Stop!" she cried out.

Gray Lily stretched out her hand. Her thin fingers curled slightly, as if to hold on to the ornate silver ring with a yellow stone that dominated her gnarled hand. She shuffled closer and pressed her fist to Will's chest.

Will twisted, struggling against whatever force pulled at him. He looked at Tessa.

"Tessa, I—" he began, but then his words choked off and his body arched back. "Run," he managed to gasp.

Tessa shook her head and tried to pull Will toward her, away from Gray Lily. But she couldn't.

She cried out as she saw a pale vapor seep from Will's chest and writhe away, toward Gray Lily. At the same time Tessa felt a coldness begin to take hold in her own chest. It was as if a splinter of ice had lodged in her heart and was growing, spreading a dull, aching blackness through her. Will's hand slipped from hers.

As soon as the contact was broken, the pain in her chest disappeared. But Will was in agony. She could see it. His face twisted in pain. He let out one sharp cry and slumped to his knees.

"No!" screamed Tessa.

Gray Lily shot a leering grin at her, and a series of foul-sounding guttural growls poured out of her black mouth.

Tessa tried to reach for Will but couldn't move. She was frozen, her mouth open in an endless shout, her hands reaching for Will. She could only watch as the vapor pulled away faster and faster. It rolled out as a lengthening thread and whirled into Gray Lily's hands. Tessa recognized it as the same silvery white thread she had pulled from the tapestry. If only she could pull it back, maybe she could save him. Tessa focused her thoughts on this, and for a moment she thought the thread wavered. No. It sped away. As it did, Will's body began to grow transparent. Tessa could see the bricks of the wall beyond. Could see through him. Then he was gone.

Something, whatever it was that had been holding her, released, and Tessa collapsed to the ground, weeping.

"What have you done to him?" She raised her head and wiped the back of her hand over her wet eyes. "Bring him back."

Gray Lily smiled. "Oh, I will," she said. She wound the long slivery thread over one gnarled hand. "Wait until you see the glory of my unicorn. Much better than a boy."

"Tessa?" A voice echoed in the alley as Jackson Brody came running up. Gray Lily shot a look behind her at this interruption and cursed. She stuffed the glowing silver thread into the trash bag.

Tessa's father bounded over and grabbed her in a bear hug. Relief washed over his worried features. "Tessa! My God. Are you okay? What the hell happened in the store?"

Tessa couldn't speak. She kept shaking her head as she pressed herself into his embrace.

Her father held her, his eyes scanning her torn clothes and bloodied hands. "You're filthy. And bleeding!" He looked up and seemed to notice for the first time the elderly woman standing a short distance away.

"What's going on here?" he repeated in a harsher voice, keeping a protective arm around Tessa.

"Mr. Brody?" said Gray Lily in a warbling, uncertain voice. "I'm Lila Gerome." She raised the trash bag slightly, grimacing as if the weight of it were too much for her. "It's very odd," she said, still speaking in a bewildered tone, "but I'm afraid I saw your daughter staging some kind of a break-in at your store. She ran away, holding this. I followed her here."

"What is it?" Jackson asked, confusion and concern making his usually friendly features crease into hard, nervous lines.

"It's my tapestry." She paused. "The one that you assured us was *stolen,* Mr. Brody."

"Dad, she's lying," Tessa said.

Gray Lily shrugged and opened the bag to show one corner of the tapestry.

Her father looked at her. "Tessa," he said uncertainly, "I don't understand. You took it?"

"Yes, but—" Tessa stopped. She could see the doubt in her father's eyes. How could she explain? She looked at Gray

Lily. "Show him the rest of the tapestry," Tessa cried. "It's changed."

"You're talking nonsense, young lady," said Gray Lily. She looked steadily at Tessa and then turned her gaze to Jackson Brody. "I would hate for there to be any more unpleasantness. For you."

Underneath the false sweetness Tessa could hear the threat. Gray Lily was telling her that she could do the same thing to them that she had done to Will de Chaucy. Tessa had no reason to doubt it. She could still feel the residual ache in her chest. And that was only from the indirect contact she'd had with the witch's power. She couldn't imagine the pain Will had endured. Instinctively, she huddled nearer to her father. She couldn't let that happen.

"She did something awful to Will," she told her father. "He's gone."

"Who's Will?" her father asked, looking confused.

Tessa looked at the ground. "He's—he's a boy I know." She raised her eyes to glare at Gray Lily.

Gray Lily only gave a worried-looking nod of agreement. "Yes. I *did* see a young man running with her. I don't know where he went." Her look to Tessa was pitying. "Obviously he wasn't concerned about your daughter's well-being."

Jackson Brody shook his head and pulled Tessa closer. "Thank God you're okay." He looked at Gray Lily. "Ms. Gerome," he began haltingly. His shoulders drooped as he let out a sigh. "I'm not sure what to say. My daughter has been going through a difficult time." He shook his head, looked at Tessa and repeated slowly, "I just don't know."

"Dad!" Tessa cried. A terrible sense of helplessness

flooded her. There was nothing she could do to prove that Gray Lily was lying. There was nothing she could do to get Will back.

"I'm just pleased to have the tapestry back," Gray Lily said. Her tone was reasonable. "It has been in my family for generations." She gave Jackson Brody a small, careful smile, her lips pressed firmly together. There was no hint of the ugly blackness inside. "Honestly, you have no idea the *sentimental* value it holds for me."

The black bag rustled as if something inside was moving. Quickly Gray Lily gave the bag a shake and pulled the plastic drawstrings tight.

Tessa stared at Gray Lily, shaking with anger and despair. "You lying bitch!" she whispered.

Gray Lily stiffened, narrowed her eyes until they were black slits and focused a stare of such intense hatred on Tessa that Tessa trembled.

"Tessa!" Her father's voice was sharp. "That's enough."

"I'll be going now," Gray Lily said softly. "You see, I have work to do that cannot be put off any longer." Her mouth twisted in a small, secret smile aimed right at Tessa as she turned away. "Just so there will be no hard feelings, I've left a check for the agreed amount at the store, Mr. Brody." She frowned faintly. "It appears that you'll need it. Your daughter has made quite a mess in there."

"Yes," mumbled Tessa's father. "All right." He spoke absently, still holding on to Tessa with a protective grip.

Gray Lily looked at Tessa. "And I will want my book back as well."

She must not have seen it, Tessa realized. *She snatched the tapestry from the studio wall but the* Texo Vita *must still be in the bag up in the studio.*

"I don't know where it is," said Tessa.

"She'll find it," said her father.

Gray Lily nodded. "Perhaps your daughter would be good enough to bring it to my hotel, let's say by Friday evening? I'm staying at the Portland Regency. Then all will be settled." The words sounded so calm, so reasonable, coming from such a frail-looking elderly woman. But Tessa heard the venom hidden within them.

Tessa's father looked at her questioningly and spoke. "Maybe I should bring it—"

"No." Tessa broke in. She stared at Gray Lily. In the woman's sinister black eyes she saw a wicked kind of amusement, and a challenge. "This is all my fault," Tessa said slowly. "I'll bring it. I want to."

"Thank you, my dear. Please don't be too hard on the girl, Mr. Brody," Gray Lily added in a prim tone. "When we're young, we sometimes . . . *tangle* with the wrong sort of people. We get ourselves in trouble." Her eyes slid over to Tessa as she smiled once again.

Tessa's face was streaked with tears and dirt, and she wiped a shaky hand through the mess as she watched Gray Lily walk away.

Chapter 32

"We'll have to close the store while we clean this mess up," said Tessa's father, surveying the damaged bookstore. "It looks like a wild animal came through here."

Pretty much, thought Tessa.

Her father glanced at her as if he thought she might sprout fur and fangs any moment, but Tessa said nothing. In a way, she felt like leaving everything the way it was. Shattered glass on the floor, claw marks dug into the wood, doors ripped from hinges. Everything looked exactly as it should, exactly the way she felt inside. Torn apart.

Tessa couldn't stop seeing Will de Chaucy's face, hearing his voice, feeling his kiss. She could still taste his lips. Her heart had been turned inside out by that one kiss, left open and exposed. And now he was gone? She couldn't think about anything beyond that fact.

She had to fix things. She had to explain this whole mess to her father. But how? She'd seen Will come out of the tapestry with her own eyes and wasn't even sure *she* believed it. Most parents, after hearing a story like that, would have her in lockdown, peeing into a cup.

She approached her father. He was standing in front of the smashed display case. Just standing there, looking as if he didn't know where to begin. "This was the last thing I needed right now," he said.

"I'm sorry." Tessa felt as though she'd said that about a hundred times and it still wasn't enough. "Dad. I want to explain," she began. "I met Will de Chaucy a few days ago. He's from England." *Just keep it simple. No need to specify the century he came from.* "Will was in trouble, Dad. I was just trying to help him."

Her father shot her a quick look, his eyebrows drawn together. "What kind of trouble are we talking about?"

Tessa stared back at him, helpless for words. *Oh, just your usual kind,* she thought. *Witches, time-traveling unicorns. You know.*

"It's not about money or drugs or anything like that," she said at last. "Gray Li—I mean, Ms. Gerome. She was after the tapestry. I had to pretend it was stolen."

"And lie to me?" Her father raised his voice, yelling now. Something he never did. "Why couldn't you just come to me, Tessa? Talk to me?"

Tessa searched for an answer. She straightened the

pile of complimentary bookmarks on the counter with nervous fingers. "You wouldn't have understood," she said at last. "It's complicated. And I thought you might get hurt."

"Hurt? Who's going to hurt me?" Her father pulled at the collar of his shirt. His face was red, as if his outburst had embarrassed him.

Gray Lily, Tessa thought. *And in ways you can't even imagine.* But aloud she said, "Ms. Gerome."

Her father scrunched his hair with his fingers, looking puzzled. "You thought Ms. Gerome was going to hurt me," he repeated.

"Yes. I mean, no. I mean, Lila Gerome is not"—Tessa hesitated—"who she pretends to be."

"I didn't know you'd even met the woman before."

"I hadn't," Tessa admitted. "But Will told me about her. She's evil. She'd do anything to get the tapestry back."

"She paid us ten thousand dollars, Tessa. I don't think she's been exactly underhanded about things. Or evil."

Tessa shook her head. "It's not about the money, Dad. Now that she has the tapestry, Will's life is . . . in danger."

"C'mon, that's a bit dramatic, isn't it?" Her father's anger seemed to have deflated now. He walked over and gave her a gentle rub on the shoulder. "It can't be that bad. Tell me about it. Maybe I can help."

Tessa loved her father so much. She could see how badly he wanted to figure this out. To solve the problem for her, as if she were a little girl again. But this was her problem.

She had gotten herself into this mess somehow. *She* would be the one to fix it.

"I'm not being dramatic, Dad." Tessa tried to keep her voice low and steady, but she couldn't help it. The fear crept in.

Her father just nodded. He suddenly seemed very tired, and years older. "Tessa," he began slowly, "I can understand that you might have a hard time with me having, you know, a relationship. But doing reckless things, getting yourself in with the wrong kind of people—that's not the way to get my attention."

As his words sank in, Tessa gaped at her father, open-mouthed. "You think I did this to get your *attention?*" she demanded.

Jackson Brody nodded. "Yeah. And I understand. It's my fault—"

Tessa let out an angry cry. "Dad! This has nothing to do with you and Alicia. This is about *me* and Will."

"You don't need someone like that in your life, Tessa. Whatever kind of trouble he's in, I don't want him dragging you into it."

"You don't know anything about him!"

Her father rubbed his eyes. "Look. Tessa. I know I've been pretty liberal and maybe not the best parent around. Things haven't been easy since your mother . . ." He shook his head. "But there's got to be a limit. I don't want this guy coming around here." Jackson Brody's face was suddenly uncompromising. All the softness was gone.

Tessa stared at the floor, choking back tears. Her father's

words shot down the last of her composure. *Coming around here?* He hardly needed to worry about that. Will de Chaucy was gone.

"You're wrong, Dad," Tessa whispered. "You've been great. Until now."

Chapter 33

That night the weather changed. An icy blanket of cold air drifted over the coast of Maine. It chilled the moisture on the pavement to a glistening coat of frost and wilted the early April flowers, making crocuses shrivel back to the soil. Even more unusual, the radio announcer talked about snow squalls that had whited out the region as far north as Bangor.

But when Tessa got up, she paid no attention to the weird weather. She was too busy trying to act normal herself. Or at least going through the motions.

She slipped an oversized wool sweater over her leggings and tugged her hair into a high ponytail. Down in the store she brewed coffee and put on her father's favorite playlist of jazz. The familiar routine did nothing to raise her spirits. It was as if she were performing steps to a dance she used to know, but there was no music. Every so often, Tessa would imagine that she wasn't even there anymore. That it wasn't Will who had disappeared, but her.

She was even glad to hear the bell jangle as Alicia Highsmith walked into the store.

"Good Lord," Alicia announced. Her sharp eyes swept over the store, as if she was mentally calculating a balance sheet. "Your father told me it was a little accident. It looks like a bulldozer came through this place."

Tessa didn't know how to answer, so she just turned away and went back to work. A short time later she could hear Alicia and her father talking in low voices. Probably trying to figure out how to cope with his crazy daughter, who was "acting out." She wasn't his sweet, dependable Tessa anymore. Maybe she had never been that girl, Tessa thought. Maybe, deep down, she had always been wild and irresponsible.

Tessa would have loved to escape. She tried calling Opal, but strangely, there was no answer. And there was no call from Opal, no text, nothing.

Alicia stayed, working late into the day, calling a local contractor about repairs to the doors. She and Tessa kept their conversation to a few polite words when they had to speak. It was awkward and awful. But it was better to have Alicia there than to be alone with her father and his disappointment. Later in the day someone else stopped by the store to lend a hand. A fit-looking older man with short, stubbly gray hair arrived, wearing running shorts that showed one of his legs to be artificial. "This is my brother Ed," Alicia told Tessa.

"Big brother," Ed corrected her as he tucked Alicia under one arm to hug her. Tessa found out that Alicia was inspired to go into prosthetics because of Ed, who had lost his leg in the Gulf War. So much for her image of Alicia as an over-achieving, money-hungry CEO.

When everyone had gone and it was just Tessa and her father, they turned on the radio as they sat at the counter, eating from cartons of Chinese takeout. Tessa glanced at her father, who was poking a fork into his container of sesame chicken. He'd hardly eaten anything.

Tessa looked more closely. He was pale, and purplish shadows tinged the skin beneath his eyes. When had he started looking so worn, so beaten-down? She must have been too busy, or just too self-absorbed to notice. She watched as he stood and walked over to settle himself heavily in the corner chair.

"Dad?"

"The rotating racks for the paperbacks," he said. He took a deep breath. "We should put them in the back. For now."

He was breathing funny too, Tessa realized. As if he had just run up the stairs.

"Dad, are you okay?" she asked, stepping over to put a hand to his shoulder.

He shrugged. "I haven't been feeling too well." He rubbed a hand over his face. "Not sleeping these past few nights. Been having these weird dreams. Last night I woke up soaked with sweat. Even had to change my shirt. I think I'm coming down with a bug or something."

Tessa felt his forehead. "You feel kind of warm. Maybe you'd better call the doctor."

"Yeah. I will." Her drew back from her touch and nodded. "Don't worry about it, Tessa."

The next day was Friday. They opened the bookstore back up, and Tessa stayed busy. In the morning she ran the register and dealt with a small but steady stream of customers. In between she reorganized the business cards and messages on the corkboard next to the counter and updated the bestsellers display shelf at the front of the store. At lunchtime when Mrs. Petoskey came in for her shift, Tessa walked down the street to the Moonstone Café to get a sandwich. It was weird that she still hadn't heard from Opal. She must have gone away with her folks for a few days during the school break. Still, it was odd that Opal hadn't mentioned anything about it.

Or maybe she did and I was just too preoccupied to pay attention, thought Tessa. Her head and her heart had been so turned upside down by Will de Chaucy—who knew what had been happening around her? But she needed to talk to Opal so badly. She was supposed to bring the *Texo Vita* back to Gray Lily tonight, and the prospect scared her out of her mind. What was Gray Lily planning? Opal was the only person who knew what had happened. Maybe together they could come up with a plan and figure out some way to help Will.

Tessa walked into the bustling, dimly lit coffeehouse. The Moonstone was a popular place to hang out, with free Internet access and good food, and many of the small tables were filled with people hunched over their laptops. Tessa surveyed the choices on the blackboard, trying to decide between a panini and one of the giant ragamuffins the café was famous for. She decided she didn't want to eat after all and had just sat down at a table with only a cup of tea when she heard a familiar voice and looked up.

"Hey, Opal!" Tessa called with a relieved smile.

Opal stopped and turned with a quick, impatient glance. She was balancing a tray containing a leafy green salad and bottled water. "Yeah?"

For a second Tessa thought she had been mistaken and called to the wrong person. "Opal?" she repeated, staring.

This girl's hair wasn't in flyaway wisps. It had been expertly styled into a sleek, tapered fringe with ultrablond highlights that framed her features. She wasn't dressed in a crazy, colorful mix of clothes but in a pair of skintight, low-slung jeans and a clingy Abercrombie & Fitch T-shirt. Opal was also wearing makeup. And a cold stare.

"Wow," said Tessa warmly. "You look amazing. New look, huh? I've been trying to call you." She pointed to where her tray sat. "I just got this table. There's plenty of room."

"You've got to be kidding," said Opal. Her eyes, outlined in a smoky blue, slid up and down Tessa with doubtful appraisal. "Why would I sit with *you*?"

Tessa's smiled faltered. She heard Opal's words, saw her icy expression, but just couldn't connect them to the person in front of her. She glanced around, looking for the joke, and then looked back at Opal. "Um. Because we're friends?"

Opal gave a snort. "Since when?"

A sick feeling lurched in Tessa's stomach, but she tried to smile through it. "Ever since we met, dummy. First day of second grade," she said lightly. "What's up with you?"

"First day of second grade?" repeated Opal. "You mean the day you wet your pants on the playground? Oh yeah, I remember, Brody. You had to sit on a newspaper in the front office till your mom came and picked you up." She let out a peal of laughter that struck Tessa like shards of glass.

"What?" Tessa gasped. "No. That's not what happened." Tessa's face reddened as she glanced around the café.

"Maybe you just blocked it out," sneered the Opal-who-wasn't-Opal. "Too traumatic."

Traumatic? Tessa remembered the day. She'd fallen off the jungle gym, and it had hurt so badly she . . . Yeah, she had peed her pants a little. But Opal had walked with her to the girls' room, given her an extra set of clothes from her cubbyhole. And had never breathed a word to anybody. On a pinky swear. It wasn't traumatic. It was one of her best days ever. Until now.

"Hi, beautiful," said a deep voice.

Hunter Scoville walked up, holding a tray of food. He glanced at Tessa but then directed his gaze to Opal with a charming, slanted grin.

"Where're we sitting?"

"Far, far away," said Opal with a pointed look at Tessa. She spun on a flat-heeled shoe and sauntered toward a table in the corner, Hunter in tow. As Tessa watched, Opal put a hand on Hunter's shoulder, leaned close to him and whispered something in his ear. They both laughed.

Tessa swallowed and approached their table. "Opal, what's wrong with you?" she said in a low voice. "Why are you acting like this?"

Opal raised a perfectly manicured hand. "Brody, you're the one acting freaky. Why don't you just go over to your loser table and leave me alone?"

Hunter leaned toward Opal. "I see what you mean," he murmured, raising his eyebrows. "Attack of the Living Losers."

Tessa left and walked quickly to the bathroom. She splashed cool water on her face. What was going on? It seemed like some kind of a crazy joke. Opal could never be mean to anyone. It just wasn't in her. Something was wrong.

No, Tessa thought. *Everything* was wrong. All at once she remembered the glowing image of three shrouded figures. And their words came back to her, sending a shiver down her back.

Your world will be torn apart.

Tessa walked home as the air grew thick and damp and the sky welled up with dark thunderclouds. The cold air was gone; the wind that flapped at her sweater and skittered loose papers across Harbor Square was warm. It almost felt tropical.

The store was closed up and there was no sign of her father, but the phone was ringing as she went through the door of the apartment upstairs.

"Hello?" Tessa answered.

"Hello? This is Dr. Robard from the medical center. Is this Tessa Brody?"

The floor dropped away beneath her. Sometimes a voice doesn't even need words to tell you something is wrong.

"Yes?" Tessa whispered. She clutched the phone, feeling incredibly aware of it in her hand. The smooth, cool plastic seemed like a foreign object. The stranger's voice came through, distant and detached:

"Your dad is stable right now, but he's very sick. He's going to be admitted to the hospital this afternoon."

"What happened?" Tessa's voice was faint. "Is he okay?"

"I'd like you to come to the hospital. Right away, if you can, please. So we can talk."

Chapter 34

The medical office building was attached to the hospital. Tessa parked the Subaru in Patients' Lot A and entered the lobby with a feeling of weird detachment, as if she were watching things happen from a great distance, or maybe even to someone else. As she rose in the cool, softly lit elevator to the third floor, she looked at the sign mounted inside. 3RD FLOOR—DR. ROBARD—ONCOLOGY ASSOCIATES.

Dr. Robard was younger than she'd expected. He wore glasses, and a striped blue and yellow polo shirt and chinos beneath his white lab coat. His voice was calm and pleasant. He had a picture on his desk in a clear acrylic frame of two small children sitting on the edge of a sandbox. Framed diplomas hung on the wall. An ivy plant in the corner needed water. It all seemed important for some reason. In her odd, disconnected state, Tessa felt she should try to pay attention to all these things. But first she had to listen to what the calm, pleasant voice was saying.

Acute leukemia.

"Leukemia," she repeated. The feeling of calm, of distance, was suddenly gone. The words crashed in on her as if they would crush her. "You mean cancer? My father has cancer?"

"Yes." Dr. Robard nodded. "It's a type of cancer of the white blood cells."

Tessa held herself tightly. If she stayed completely still, maybe everything would stop. And it wouldn't be real. *This can't be real.* But the doctor was looking at her as if he expected her to say something.

"I don't believe it. It's wrong," she said. Her voice sounded jerky. "It's impossible. Things just don't happen like this out of the blue. Cancer takes years to—" She stopped and clasped her cold hands together. She started to cry.

Dr. Robard said gently, "Believe me, Tessa. We've double-checked everything."

Tears ran down Tessa's face as she leaned forward suddenly. She blinked them back and shook her head. "No," she said, wiping her eyes. "You show me."

"What?" Dr. Robard looked at her in surprise.

"I said show me. The leukemia. The biopsy or the X-ray or whatever it is. Show it to me."

Dr. Robard sat back in his chair. He nodded at her with an expression of sympathy. "Yes. Of course."

Dr. Robard picked up a glass slide. Tessa could see a faint pinkish smudge on it. The slide had a sticker on one end with a number and *Brody, J.* printed on it.

The doctor put the slide into place under the microscope with a faint click. He directed Tessa to look through the eyepieces on her side of the microscope as he turned the focus.

"You see these cells?" he asked. Tessa looked at a bright circle of light filled with small pink ring-shaped cells. "These are the healthy blood cells. Now look here." The image blurred as he moved the slide and focused on another area. A small black pointer appeared. "These are the cancer cells." The pointer, under the doctor's manipulation, circled a large, irregular cell that had spattered blue blobs in it.

"How could this happen so suddenly?" she whispered, still staring through the microscope.

"Sometimes things are happening for a while before the symptoms finally become noticeable. Then things progress rapidly." Dr. Robard lifted his head and leaned back. "Your dad is very anemic. That explains the shortness of breath and fatigue. I know it's hard to take in right now. Give it some time. And meanwhile, please know that we're going to do everything possible to treat the cancer."

Tessa was still looking through the microscope at the tiny cells when some filmy pink material in the background began to move. The wavy pink filaments seemed to swim into focus as if coming to the surface of a pool of water. They swirled together and linked to form a ropy trail.

The pink material coiled into crude words:

Give back the threads.

"It's them," Tessa said faintly. She gripped the side of the microscope. She took a deep breath and felt a sick, hot rush of anger. "It's them!" she whispered. "The Norn. They're doing this!"

Dr. Robard gave her a puzzled frown and said, "I understand, Tessa. It's not easy to accept, but—"

"No!" Tessa cried. "You *don't* understand. Look!"

Dr. Robard hesitated and then leaned forward to peer through the opposite eyepieces. He nodded. "Yes. It's a very aggressive form."

He doesn't see it.

Tessa pressed her eyes to the microscope again. The slide appeared as before. Spatters of pink and blue cells. There were no words. "They're gone," Tessa murmured, and sat back in the chair.

How had she let this happen? She hadn't been paying any attention to her father. Hadn't even been thinking about him. Now they were using him. Punishing him to get to her.

Dr. Robard was clearly mystified by Tessa's outburst. "Okay," he said gently. "Why don't we go over and see your dad now."

Tessa stared at the old man lying in the hospital bed.

In just a day, her father's strong face had been whittled down. The full cheeks were sunken, and loose skin sagged over his jawline. His skin had an unhealthy yellowish sheen beneath the fluorescent lights, and his arms were mottled with bruises. How could that happen overnight? They *made it happen*, Tessa thought.

Your world will be torn apart.

A bag of fluid hung over his bed and dripped through a clear tube into his arm. The oxygen tube fastened around his face and stuck in his nostrils let out a low, monotonous hiss as a TV flickered soundlessly on the wall. And over everything hung the antiseptic smell of the hospital, faintly chemical, metallic. To Tessa, it smelled like pain. Or something worse.

"Dad?"

Her father opened his eyes. "Hi, cupcake," he said in a hoarse voice. He cleared his throat and pushed himself more upright in the hospital bed. He smiled, and his dry lips looked as if they might crack.

"Dad." Tessa bent her head and leaned it gently against the crook of her father's arm. "I'm so sorry. About everything."

"It's okay," he said. "None of that matters."

"Are you— Does it hurt?" Tessa asked.

He shook his head. "Naw. I'm just tired. Feel like I've been kicked all over. But I'm glad they know what's causing it. Probably should have come in sooner." He took a deep breath. "Guess I haven't been paying much attention to anything lately. Including you." He patted Tessa's arm.

"That's not true," Tessa said, closing her eyes.

He pulled her a little closer until their heads touched. "Alicia and I . . . ," he began. "I was going to tell you before this happened. We were going to get married."

Tessa kept her head down and nodded. She couldn't look at him and not cry.

"Maybe it seems sudden to you. But sometimes, you just feel it," he said. "When everything is right."

"I know," she whispered. "She makes you happy."

"Yeah. She does. Now, I know Alicia is"—he began slowly—"not the most motherly type." He gave a weak version of his old familiar grin.

Tessa gently shook his middle. "Who needs that crap anyway?" she said, nearly breathless from trying to sound normal when she really wanted to sob.

Her father gave a dry rasp of laughter. "Right. I forgot. Miss Independent." He let out a deep sigh. "But now *this*. Guess we'll put wedding plans on hold for a little while."

Tessa shook her head. "This is all my fault."

Her father let out a faint huff of exasperation and put his other hand on her head. He ruffled her hair. "Don't be silly. This has nothing to do with you, Tessa. I'm gonna be okay." He sounded out of breath and leaned back as if the words had taken what little energy he had left. "These folks. Deal with this stuff. All the time."

No, not this kind of stuff, Tessa thought. But she nodded in agreement.

He gave her a smile. "I'll take a nap, I think, for a little while."

"Okay," she whispered, and smiled back as hot tears started to roll down her cheeks.

"Store's closed," her father said, shutting his eyes. "Alicia'll look in on the contractors for me. Why don't you stay with Opal for a few days? I don't want you to be alone."

"Yeah. Okay." How could she tell him that she and Opal weren't even friends anymore? That her whole world was unraveling around her? Instead, she said, "I love you, Dad."

"I love you too, Tessa." His eyes were still closed. He looked exhausted.

Dr. Robard stood outside the door when Tessa came out. "Rest assured, we're going to do everything we can," he told her. Even though it sounded like something he had memorized in medical school, it would have comforted Tessa under normal circumstances.

"Thanks," said Tessa. She wiped her eyes once more and nodded, looking straight ahead. "So am I."

Chapter 35

Tessa went into the bathroom, slammed the door so hard it shook, and snapped off the light. She wasn't afraid anymore. To hell with that. How could she be afraid? There was nothing more she could lose. Her anger felt like lightning trapped inside her. She wanted to strike.

"All right," she said, her voice vibrating with fury. "Come out of there. Let me see you."

Slowly the iridescent light shimmered around the edge of the mirror and the three hooded figures appeared. Scytha spoke:

"Mortal, you summon us and yet you have not returned the threads, despite the measures we've taken. Surely you can see that your life is in our hands."

"Shut up." Tessa bit the words out between gritted teeth. "I know what you've done. You've made my father . . ." She stopped, fending off a sob. She would not cry. There was no time. "You made my father sick," she went on. "You've turned Opal against me. Everything is twisted around. You've warped my whole life."

Weavyr raised her dark hands. "We warned you that if you did not return the threads, the consequences would be dire." She sounded almost regretful, as if she were disciplining a small child. "The lost threads must be returned to us," she went on. "They must take their rightful place on the Wyrd and return to their own lives. If this is not accomplished—"

"But it isn't fair!" The words exploded from Tessa before she could think about the wisdom of yelling at the three otherworldly beings.

"Not fair?" Weavyr's head gave a slight shake. "Fairness. Justice. Good. Evil. These are human concepts. *We* are not bound by them."

"What are you bound by?" Tessa whispered desperately.

"Our ways are beyond your comprehension, mortal," Scytha cut in. "Do not ask again. Return the threads."

"But I didn't take the threads!" Tessa yelled at the glass, her face inches from the wavering images. So close that her skin shone with the reflected blue glow from the mirror. "I told you before. It wasn't me. It was Gray Lily."

There was a cold silence. "You lie," said Scytha.

"No. I don't," Tessa snapped. "And I think if you're so damned powerful, you should be able to figure this out.

She's the one who made the tapestry. *She* has your threads. And now she's taken Will's thread away again. He may be back in the tapestry already. I don't know. But I need to find him."

"Why?"

The question came so quickly that Tessa didn't have time to think; she just answered. "Because I need him." Her shoulders dropped and the force went out of her voice. "He's hurting. I can feel it. And I . . . care about him."

Spyn, the Norn with the thin, twitchy fingers, turned to her sisters and emitted a derisive sound, like a snort, from beneath her hood. There was a long pause as the three figures huddled together, apparently whispering to each other. Their muttered tones sounded like the hissing of snakes. They turned to face her once more.

"Perhaps you speak the truth and did not steal the threads," said Weavyr. "It does not matter. It seems that your goals and ours should be the same, mortal."

Scytha's deep voice rolled out like the rumble of thunder. "You must find the stolen threads. Seven threads. Seven lives."

"But I've told you that Gray Lily stole them," Tessa said. "Why can't *you* find them?"

Her question hung there until at last Weavyr answered: "The threads have been removed from the Wyrd. They are beyond our control." The words seemed like an admission spoken with difficulty, and one that Weavyr wanted to pass over as quickly as possible. "You must find this tapestry that Gray Lily has made," she went on, "and retrieve them."

"But how?" Tessa demanded. "Even if I can get close to the tapestry, how do I get the threads out?" What had happened with Will, she was still sure, was some kind of freak accident.

There was a pause. The three hooded figures remained motionless as their collective blue aura swirled like neon smoke. "The tree, Yggdrasil," Scytha said finally. "It is the origin, the source of life. The threads are drawn to it. Look to see if the witch carries a piece of wood, or a twig."

Tessa thought about this and recalled the words from Gray Lily's book. *I have discovered the key.* Could the key the witch referred to be a piece of wood? Tessa didn't remember seeing anything like that when Gray Lily pulled Will's life thread. But maybe she carried it somewhere, hidden. Just great. What was Tessa supposed to do? Strip-search the Wicked Witch of the West?

But Tessa nodded her understanding to the Norn. "Okay. Supposing I do find this piece of wood. Then what?"

"You must find the first thread that was stolen," said Scytha. "That is the only way all can be set right."

"How do I do that?" Tessa questioned. "How can I possibly tell which thread was the first?"

There was no reply. This silent, looming act seemed to be a specialty of the Norn, Tessa realized. She felt like screaming, like smashing the mirrored glass and reaching through to grab the hooded cloaks and *see* what lay hidden beneath them. But she knew it wouldn't do any good. And it certainly wouldn't help her father. After a few moments passed she said wearily: "You don't know, do you?"

"Enough talk!" shrieked Spyn in such a high-pitched voice that Tessa jerked back. "Enough questions. Just get the threads, little human!"

Tessa gathered herself. She had to know one thing more. "If I return the threads, you'll put things back the way they were? My life will be back to normal, right? My dad and Opal and—"

Scytha's roar drowned her out. "We do *not* make bargains with mortals! The only promise you have is this: if the threads are not returned before the full moon, your father will die."

A cold hand fisted around Tessa's heart. She stared into the black murk beneath the hoods of the Norn and imagined cruel eyes looking back at her. She sensed no compassion, no feeling at all. "And Will," she said, forcing herself to go on even though her voice sounded more and more feeble. "If Will's thread is returned to you, then he'll get his life back too?"

There was a pause; then Tessa heard the gloomy voice of Scytha. "Yes. His life will be restored. Just as it was before his thread was stolen."

"But does that mean that—" Tessa began, but stopped. The figures wavered in the mirror.

"Find the first," the Norn whispered together. "Return the seven."

"No. Wait!" Tessa cried.

But the Norn had disappeared.

Chapter 36

Alone in her room, Tessa dressed carefully. She dressed for bravery. Her most comfortable jeans, faded and worn until they were soft as flannel, and patched on both knees with swatches of velvet. A black stretch tank top, and over that a delicately crocheted black sweater with white and crimson roses scattered through it. She brushed her hair until it lay shining in a thick curtain down her back and then braided it, twining a piece of soft red velvet ribbon through it.

She looked in the mirror and saw herself as she never had before. Her blue eyes were bright, and stood out in contrast against the dark arches of her eyebrows and her pale skin. Patches of rosy color stained her cheekbones, as if she were lit from inside. She stopped for a moment to put on earrings: two dangles of tiny pink crystals and freshwater pearls that had belonged to her mother.

She wondered if this was how Will felt putting on armor. She looked down at the jade pig bracelet on her wrist. Somehow it didn't feel very lucky now.

Still, it couldn't hurt.

Tessa walked to the hotel carrying the *Texo Vita,* which she had wrapped in brown mailing paper and twine. The sun was setting and the sky was tinged an eerie purple. It wasn't far to the Portland Regency, but maybe she should have called a cab; fog from the harbor was drifting through the narrow streets. The air smelled of salt and seaweed. Tessa tugged her sweater closer against the damp and quickened her steps.

The hotel lobby was warmly lit with crystal chandeliers; soft piano music played in the background. Tessa walked across the broad marble foyer.

At the desk she said, "I'm Tessa Brody. I have something for Gr—Ms. Gerome."

The desk attendant smiled. "Oh, right. She told us she was expecting someone." He reached beneath the counter and handed her an envelope.

"Thank you." Inside the envelope was a card key and a slip of paper. The paper said:

Room 413. Come alone or de Chaucy will die.

A shiver passed through Tessa, but she stuck the note in the pocket of her jeans and went to the elevator.

On the fourth floor she walked down the carpeted hallway and stopped at 413. She listened. She couldn't hear any voices or movement inside. She hesitated for a moment, thinking. This was probably not the smartest thing she had ever done. But what choice did she have? Her father, Will, Opal . . . Everything she cared for was at stake. She slid the card key into the lock, opened the door and went inside.

"Hello?" she called.

The hotel room was empty and silent. Next to her the door to a darkened bathroom was open. A king-sized bed stood against the wall, and a desk, a TV console and an armchair were arranged against the opposite wall. The room was dimly lit from a small tableside lamp, and the striped drapes were drawn tight. Tessa approached the bed, where the tapestry was spread out.

She fixed her eyes on the frayed square of fabric that had made such a mess of her life, searching. She let out a breath, half relief, half disappointment. He wasn't there. The center of the picture was empty; the unicorn was still gone. The background was different, however. It seemed darker and much more ominous. Woven in thick yarns of umber and black and the deepest of hunter greens, the forest now twined like a thick cage around the grassy clearing. There were no flowers; there was no hint of brightness or life anywhere. The only light in the scene came from a streak of lightning that tore across one corner of the fabric and lit a thundercloud into an eerie, glowing mass. On the distant hillside the dark outline of the castle still appeared, but the fairy-tale quality was gone; the castle loomed over the scene like something from a horror movie.

Could it be a different tapestry? Tessa reached out with a tentative hand and recoiled at the contact. The fabric was as warm as living flesh. Tessa thought she could hear something: a faint thrumming sound was coming from the woven cloth. She peered more closely. Then she saw them—threads that were moving, shimmering and gliding through the interlacing network of fibers.

"So. You can see them," said a low, whispery voice behind her.

Tessa whirled around. "Gray Lily."

The elderly woman stepped out of the shadows. She wore a silky blue dress whose draped neckline dipped, showing too much of a bony, caved-in-looking chest. Again, as in the alley, Tessa had the initial impression of frailty as the haggard woman shuffled forward. But up close, Gray Lily's eyes conveyed strength. Small, black, almost reptilian, and yet filled with a fierce power.

"Good evening, child," said Gray Lily, nodding. "The tapestry draws you, doesn't it? And you *can* see the threads moving, I'll wager. Interesting," she mused, her gaze fixed avidly on Tessa. She gave a nod that might have been grudging approval. "Most people can't."

"What have you done with Will?" said Tessa. "Where is he?"

"The boy?" Gray Lily scowled as she looked at the tapestry. "Truth be told, I'm not entirely sure." She rubbed her stomach, a peculiar gesture, as if she were hungry and were debating what to eat. "Because of your father's impromptu arrival in the alley, I had to put de Chaucy's thread away before I could weave my unicorn. I believe his thread passed through the tapestry. He's inside somewhere." She waved a hand at the tapestry. "But don't worry. I'll find him and have my unicorn back once more." She glared at Tessa and stretched out a hand. "Now give me the book. I'll have no loose ends trailing behind me."

Tessa hefted the package in her arms but made no move to hand it over.

"Give it to me," Gray Lily ordered.

"How can you be so selfish?" asked Tessa quietly. She took a step backward. "And so cruel?"

"Cruel?" Gray Lily gave her an incredulous glare and lowered her hand. "Stupid girl," she muttered. "You think I am the villain? *I'm* not the villain. I was wronged. By *them*." She paused. "You know of whom I speak?"

"The Norn," said Tessa in a whisper.

Gray Lily nodded, then hobbled to the draped window. She stood there for a moment as if mulling something over. Finally she turned.

"I was a girl once, like you." She let out a raspy chuckle. "Full of hope and love and dreams. Can you imagine?"

Tessa narrowed her eyes. "No."

"It's true." Gray Lily nodded. "I loved a young man. John Porter was his name. One summer's day he fell from his horse and struck his head. He died three days later. Three days of torment. I sat by his side, watching him jerk and drool. I was powerless to help him," she said. "Nowadays they can treat such things, but back then—I just sat and watched as his brain swelled and burst inside his skull." Gray Lily's forehead furrowed and her small black eyes blinked. As if she were trying to remember how tears were shed.

Tessa stayed silent for a long moment. "I'm sorry," she said gently. "But if he fell . . ." She shook her head. "It was just an accident."

"No!" Gray Lily shouted. Her face twisted in an ugly snarl. She stamped her foot. "Don't you understand? Even now? There *are* no accidents. It's all them. It's all planned by the Fates. Or the Norn, to be more precise." She bobbed her head at Tessa and said in a low, eager tone, "But that was the day I saw it."

"Saw what?"

Gray Lily's crooked hands wove a trail in the air. "I saw a faint thread drift away and out, through a crack in the shutter. I looked down and John was dead. Everyone in my village thought I imagined it, that I was crazed with grief," Gray Lily remarked. "But I knew what I had seen. It was only later that I *understood* it. It was the thread of John's life. It was his very soul leaving his body. I knew there must be a way to take hold of it. It took me many years, but finally I did it. I learned to control the threads of life. To weave *life*."

"*Texo Vita,*" whispered Tessa.

"Yes."

"How did you learn how to do it?" asked Tessa. "In the book you said you found something. A key."

Gray Lily smiled crookedly. "Girl. I'm not about to share my secrets with the likes of you." She leaned forward. "I took only what I needed to be free. Now I have control of my life. My own world. Instead of them. Do you understand?"

Tessa stared at her. "No one can control everything about their life."

"Ah, but *I* can." Gray Lily looked at Tessa intently. "Do you know what it was to be a woman five hundred years ago? Servitude. Filth. Disease. Spawning children whether or not your body could bear it. Whether or not you could feed them. The Norn made life where none should be. And cut down other young lives like blades of winter grass." Her hands were flexing and fisting rhythmically as she spoke. Her huge silver ring with its yellow stone glinted. "Those hags controlled everything. They still do."

"That's not true," Tessa said. "People make choices."

"No. The Fates decide," said Gray Lily. "Tessa Brody," she went on, "do you want your life back?"

"Yes," whispered Tessa, staring into the hard black eyes. "That's why I have to return the threads you stole to the Norn. They've made my father sick. And changed my friend Opal. Everything is . . . wrong."

Gray Lily let out a bark of laughter. "So that's it. You've become an errand girl for the Norn." She sat down in a chair and leaned back, then pushed her high heels from bunion-knotted feet. "Their threats don't frighten me."

"And why should they?" Tessa said angrily. "It's not *your* life they're destroying. And it's not a threat. My father is dying." Her throat closed around the last word, as if her vocal cords would refuse to produce it. He was *dying*.

"Everyone dies, child. Except me, of course." Gray Lily slitted her eyes to watch Tessa and smiled. "It's interesting. No, ironic, really, that it's you again after all these years. I don't like irony."

Tessa frowned. "Me again?" She repeated. Something lurched inside her.

Gray Lily sighed and rolled her eyes. "You've had past lives, dearie. You think a thread is cut and that's the end? No. They weave you again. Twist you. Do whatever they wish with you. Again and again. You used to be a little slip of a thing with dirty skirts and a willful tongue." She slid a glance over Tessa. "Not much has changed."

"The hunt," whispered Tessa. "I remember the hunt." The visions were real, then. She *had* been there in the wood when Will was captured. That was why she felt such a connection to him. The thought made her light-headed. *The virgin in his haunts.*

"Yes," said Gray Lily. "I tried to get your thread that day as well, but you ran like a rabbit. And now here you are. Not only did you somehow release my unicorn, but now the Norn use you to get my threads. That's irony for you," she muttered. "Biting me in the ass."

"They're not *your* threads," said Tessa, flashing her eyes to the old woman. "They are people's lives. And I will get them."

Gray Lily shook her head. "No, child. You'll just die. And the Norn? They are beyond any pity or compassion. They won't give your old life back to you. Nor those of your loved ones." She cocked her head in a considering attitude. "But I can."

Tessa didn't want to dwell on how confidently Gray Lily had just informed her of her impending death. "How?" she demanded.

"You must help me capture de Chaucy again. I would have my unicorn back."

"No!" Tessa said in a disgusted, angry voice. "He's a human being. Do you really think I would help you do that to him?" Tessa glanced at the dark tapestry and bit at her lip, wondering where on earth Will was, if he was okay. If he was alive.

"He is whatever I make him," said Gray Lily with an impatient flip of her hand. "And as the unicorn he is more glorious than any frail, pathetic man could ever be. With my unicorn fixed once more in the tapestry, I will have Will de Chaucy's youth, his strength, forever." She looked at her own wrinkled hands. "I want those things. I can't last like this much longer."

"I won't do it," said Tessa.

"Then your father will die." Gray Lily yawned. Tessa glimpsed the black mouth and shivered. "I know the ways of the Norn. It will be slow and painful for him. And then you'll be all alone."

Tessa twisted away from the old woman's gaze. She felt trapped and confused. The tapestry lay before her and she stared at it, mesmerized by the mysterious depths. She reached out a hand and imagined she could feel the living threads beneath the surface. *Find the first. Return the seven.* The words echoed and spun in her ears. She blinked.

She thought she had spotted a silvery white thread.

"Will," she said in a low cry. She felt dizzy. She swayed.

Her outstretched fingers were still poised near the surface when a dirty hand ripped through the tapestry. And grabbed her.

Chapter 37

Tessa screamed and tried to wrench free, but the strong fingers tightened on her wrist and dragged her down. Her hand disappeared into the dark threads.

Black fibers opened up, swallowing her like gnashing jaws. She heard a distant, startled screech from Gray Lily. Tessa twisted to look behind her, but a dark mesh was closing in, blocking the old woman's face. The next moment Tessa felt a warm, rushing darkness sweep past her and, strangely, *through* her. She had the sensation of falling, twisting and turning, all the while feeling the indomitable grip of fingers clenched on her wrist. Feathery strands brushed her face and she became aware of colors, like shadowy fireworks, flying past in the dark.

Suddenly she barreled into brightness. There was a rustle and a sharp snap as Tessa tumbled through green, leafy branches. She broke through and landed on something with a thud. It wasn't the ground.

"Oof!"

Tessa blinked. She raised her head. Will de Chaucy was lying beneath her, still holding her wrist. He looked astonished. And also slightly oxygen deprived. She rolled off his chest and he took a wheezing breath in.

"Tessa! Is it you?" He gripped her shoulders as if he thought she would disappear.

"Will," she gasped, lying next to him. "Hi." As she took in his lean, tanned face and the healing cut on his cheek, he smiled. She felt such a rush of relief and happiness, she simply let herself relax and burrowed her head closer to his broad chest.

"I can hardly believe—" he said. "I didn't know what she would do." He cupped her face in his hands, lifted it gently and met her lips with his. He broke away from her, but only to brace himself on one elbow. Pulling her closer, he pinioned her beneath him. "Tessa," he whispered.

She pulled him down.

This time, the kiss was something different. She'd thought he was gone, that she'd never see him again. Now she could let go of the pain she'd tried to deny. He was here. He was real. A smothered cry came from deep inside her as Will kissed her. Her lips parted and there was nothing, nothing in the world, except him. She would never let go.

For a few breathless, blissful seconds Tessa forgot everything. But gradually she became aware of other sensations: the chill of the damp ground beneath her, torn leaves scratching her neck, the sounds of wind and distant thunder. And more importantly, what had happened. Her father.

"Will." Tessa sat up. She looked around.

They were beneath a tree next to a small clearing in a forest. Dark clouds rolled past the treetops high overhead.

"We're inside." Tessa whispered. "We're inside the tapestry, aren't we?"

Will pushed himself up to sit next to her. "Yes."

Tessa reached down to touch the grass. The cool, springy blades brushed her palm. She could smell the rich soil and even the dandelion that had been crushed beneath her elbow. A slight breeze lifted the ribbon in her hair to flutter against her cheek. Nearby, a looming shadow parted from the trees as a large horse drifted closer, calmly pulling up mouthfuls of grass and chewing. "But everything is real," she said. It didn't just *look* real. It *was* real. "How is this possible?"

"Real," said Will, considering her question. "In a way, yes. Everything here has been placed here by Gray Lily. It is her creation."

"It's unbelievable," Tessa whispered. Then, recalling what had just happened, she demanded, "But how did you bring me here?"

Will gave her a surprised look. He reached over and extracted a twig from her hair. "I did nothing," he replied.

"You fell out of a tree. On top of me," he added ruefully, adjusting his neck with a twist.

Tessa looked down at his strong hands. She clasped one in her own. "No. I was in a hotel room. Gray Lily was there. Your hand reached through the tapestry."

Will shook his head to contradict her. "No. I looked up and saw you in that linden tree. You called my name."

Tessa put a hand to her forehead. "Yes," she said softly. She had glimpsed a silvery thread, just like the one she had pulled from the tapestry. She *had* called Will's name.

"I just reached up through the branches and took your wrist," Will said.

"Okay. I don't understand what just happened," Tessa said with a return of her smile. "But I'm glad to see you. So glad." She leaned into the crook of his shoulder and breathed in the warm, leathery smell of him.

"Do you believe now that our fates are entwined, Mistress Brody?" Tessa could hear the smile in his voice.

"I—I don't know," Tessa said uncertainly. She looked up and tried to return his smile. *Fate.* The word brought the frightening conversation with Gray Lily spiraling back to her. Not to mention the directions of the Norn. *Find the first. Return the seven.*

"Ah, yes. I forgot. You believe only in accidents," Will said softly. "Like falling." His face was still and watchful. His eyes traveled to her neck and he leaned closer, until his lips brushed the hollow of her throat. "I believe falling is considered a sort of accident."

Tessa turned away slightly. She could feel her heart

pounding. It felt like an impatient fist, pounding on a table for what it wanted. She finally knew what she wanted, with a sureness that ached. She wanted the impossible.

She looked around, trying to break the spell of Will's nearness. She would have loved to just lie down in the safety of his arms and forget everything. But she needed to get her bearings. And figure out what to do.

"Is this place like your home?" she asked. "Like Hartescross?"

"Yes." Will turned his gaze away from her and scanned the forest with an uncertain expression. "I mean to say—I'm not sure. The witch has made it appear so. It looks much like our northern woods, but I don't recognize any of these paths. I'd been wandering for hours. Until I saw you."

"Hours?" Tessa repeated, puzzled.

"Yes. But you are here now, and with me. It is all I need, mistress." Will got up, brushed himself off and held out a hand to her. He hoisted her to her feet. "We should go. There's a storm coming. It's not wise to linger."

"No."

"What?" asked Will, looking at her with surprise.

"It hasn't been hours," Tessa replied. "It's been two *days* since Gray Lily took you from the alley." Time must be completely out of whack, she realized. Then, with the thought of time passing, Tessa felt a spasm of fear. She only had until the full moon. How much time did she have left?

"Will, I have to get home," she said quickly. "My father—" She stopped and swallowed. She clasped her shaking hands together.

"What is it?" Will searched her face, putting an arm around her. "Tell me."

She didn't want to say the words. She still didn't want to admit it could be real. But she had to. "My father is very sick," she said slowly. "He's dying."

"Gray Lily?" Will asked.

"No," Tessa answered. Panic swept over her. She had screwed everything up. Her conversation with Gray Lily had revealed nothing useful. She had no idea how to get the lost threads back. And now she was trapped in the tapestry herself. Trapped and useless—for who knew how long, maybe forever—while her father—

Tessa broke away from Will and spun, searching. Everywhere she looked, dense tangles of greenery blocked her view. All the lost threads must be here, somewhere. But first she had to find the key.

Think.

"Will," she said. She turned to him. "Remember when we read from the *Texo Vita*? In one of her entries, Gray Lily said something about a key. Do you know what she meant? Think back and try to remember, from the first time she stole your thread."

"No," Will replied with a shrug. "There was no key."

"It might look like something different. Like a piece of wood."

Will shook his head, with no flicker of recognition. "No. She did not carry such a thing." His face stilled, became thoughtful. "But I do remember something from the first time. She had something in her hand." He looked up. "A small yellow stone."

"A stone," Tessa repeated dubiously. She shut her eyes and tried to picture Gray Lily as she had seen her in the alley. She didn't remember the old woman holding any stone when she pulled Will's thread. And it didn't fit at all with what the Norn had told her. How could a stone have anything to do with that tree Igdrazul, or whatever it was called? Could the Norn be wrong?

"Is this key the means by which we can escape the tapestry?" Will asked.

Tessa's eyes flew open. "I—I think so," she answered. "I hope so."

How could she tell him the rest? In order for her father to live, the stolen threads, including *his* thread, had to be returned to the Norn. There was no way she could explain it. She didn't understand it herself. And she didn't want to give him any more reasons to doubt her. She would find a way to fix this.

Tessa looked around. "I'm sure Gray Lily will be coming after us. After you. She wants to turn you back into the unicorn."

Will's eyes darkened. "Of course. That's the only way she can get her youth back." He glanced up at the sky and frowned. "We'd best leave this place. Everything seems different. There was never a storm here before. It bodes ill."

"Somehow I'm not surprised," Tessa remarked. "My whole life kind of bodes ill lately."

Will picked up the horse's reins, which were trailing in the long grass. The horse was beautiful, with a strong neck and heavy build. He had a black silken mane and black tufts on his hooves. His huge, liquid eyes were fringed with feather-duster lashes. "He's beautiful." Tessa reached up to touch his neck. Real flesh, hair. "I never saw *him* in the tapestry. Is the horse a thread too? A person?"

"No." Will smiled. "This is my horse, Hannibal." He glanced at their surroundings. "Not everything here is visible in the tapestry. I don't know how the witch transported him here, or truly how she made any of this world." He patted Hannibal's neck. "But I believe he is just a horse. Though he thinks himself a person ofttimes." Will fit his foot into the stirrup and swung up into the saddle with ease. He extended a hand down to Tessa. "Come."

Tessa looked up at Will, who suddenly seemed very high. Impossibly high. "You mean me? Ride?" She tried to swallow the flitter of nerves.

"That was my intent, yes."

Tessa had never been on a horse in her life. Horses weren't this tall, were they? It must be some kind of prehistoric mastodon horse. She shook her head. "The poor thing," she said. "We can't both ride him. It's too much weight."

"Nonsense," Will said, gathering the reins closer. "Hannibal could bear me and ten stone of plate armor to Galway at a gallop. You will pose no difficulty." Again he reached his hand for her.

Tessa gave a little mewl of nerves and put her hand in his.

"Now your foot there," Will said patiently. "Your other foot. No, there. Right. And hup!" He pulled her up behind him.

The view down looked even worse than the view up.

Tessa felt as if she were balanced on a precarious, moving cliffside. "Okay," she said. She clamped her hands awkwardly onto Will's torso and felt the ripple of lean muscles beneath her fingers. He was still wearing the same modern clothes as when she had seen him last: a white button-down cotton shirt and jeans. "Just so you know, I've never been on a horse before."

"Really, Mistress Brody?" Will turned and gave her an amused look. "I never would have guessed."

Tessa jabbed him lightly in the ribs.

He leaned forward and said something in a low tone and suddenly they lurched forward. The ground, so very far below them, began to move. Tessa abandoned her pride to wrap her arms around Will's waist. After she realized she wasn't going to slide off the animal's back end, she relaxed a little. She closed her eyes. It seemed better if she couldn't see how high they were as she slowly got accustomed to the lurch and sway of the horse's movement. She rested her cheek against Will's warm, broad back. All in all it was not that bad, she decided.

"How fast are we going?" she asked.

"We are walking, Tessa."

"Oh. Right."

The tapestry still lay on the hotel-room bed, but it had changed yet again. A horse was pictured in the center of the dark wood, carrying two figures, a young man and a girl with long, dark hair.

"There she is," fumed Gray Lily. "How is it possible that she keeps doing these inconceivable, infuriating things?" She turned to Moncrieff. He was staring at the tapestry with a puzzled expression.

"What's the matter with you?" Gray Lily said sharply. "Get ready. We're going in after her."

Chapter 38

Will and Tessa rode through the forest, following one small winding path after another, ducking their heads beneath low branches while Will guided the horse over mossy logs and gullies. High overhead the rushing wind swept the treetops and made limbs creak. Rumbles of thunder grew closer.

"Look over there." Will pointed to a break in the trees. "I see something."

They made their way toward the gap in the dense forest. It opened onto a wider, smoother path. "At last," said Will, taking a deep breath and releasing it. "I recognize this."

Tessa was relieved to hear it. The sky was becoming darker with each passing moment, and the air was heavy, as if with an electric charge. The storm was coming. She didn't want to see what this forest looked like in the dark, never mind the wet, cold, thundering dark.

"Hold on to me," said Will. Which was completely unnecessary. Tessa hadn't planned otherwise. He goaded the horse to a faster pace and they surged out of the forest onto a broad expanse of land, where the wind had beaten the long grasses into a green sea of rolling waves. Tessa felt the cold seep through her light sweater, and she shivered and molded herself to Will's warmth.

"Hartescross is just ahead," he said. Tessa looked out across the grassy plain. Her eyes traveled up. A huge stone structure rose against the darkening sky.

"The castle. You live in a castle," she said slowly, taking it in.

"Yes. Well, a small one." Will seemed distracted as he held the horse in place and scanned the surrounding countryside.

Just a small castle, thought Tessa. Okay. Looking at the huge structure looming ahead, she couldn't quite believe, even now, that this was real. Just like the grass, the trees, the horse. Except it wasn't. Everything in this place was woven in a flat, two-dimensional square of fabric. Thinking about it made her brain hurt.

Hartescross Castle sat on top of a small hill. Around the perimeter a high stone wall circled the inner building, interrupted at intervals by jags of stone outcroppings as well as turrets. The inside tower was high and round and pierced with narrow windows. At the top a blue pennant snapped in the brisk wind.

Will guided Hannibal to a road. Actually, it looked like little more than a ridged path of hardened mud. As the horse trotted up the slope, lurching over the pits and rises of the road, Tessa realized why Will had been so impressed with pavement.

Rain began to lash down in fat, icy drops as they approached the castle, and a clap of thunder boomed. To Tessa, the eerie, empty appearance of the castle was more menacing than the storm. Maybe it was the sheer size and somber glitter of the massive stone walls, now stained with wetness to a dark gray.

But menacing or not, any shelter was welcome at this point. The rain sliced at their clothes and they were both cold and wet. At least they were together. Somehow that made things bearable.

"You have a moat," Tessa said, observing the steep, rock-lined depression that circled the castle.

"No. It's a more of a ditch, really," said Will. "We used to pump in seawater but it stank too much in the summer. It still serves the purpose. It's a bloody pain to climb down and out again."

They walked across the drawbridge as the rain started to fall in windblown sheets. The horse's hooves clattered on the huge beams and Tessa looked overhead, awed by the soaring span of stone of the main entry as they passed beneath it. A heavy iron grate was suspended halfway up, held by massive ropes.

They entered a courtyard and Will slipped down, then reached to help Tessa. They ran to a low, sheltered building huddled against the foot of the central tower.

"This courtyard is usually filled with people," said Will, his voice raised against the wind and rain. He pointed. "The smithy here. And over there the wheelwright." He led Hannibal to a dry stall.

"Come," he shouted. "Help me close the gate."

Will ran to a large wooden wheel with crank-type handles on either side, and unlocking it, he directed Tessa to hold one handle as he positioned himself at the other. Together they allowed the thick rope to unwind through its pulley system, lowering the massive gate.

He took her hand and they ran across the muddy courtyard to the tower entrance. "This leads to my family's living quarters," Will said as they ducked into the narrow doorway. It was a relief to be out of the pelting rain and wind. Tessa looked up at a spiral staircase that rose within the tower. The center of each stone step was worn down, smoothed with age.

Will released Tessa's hand and bounded ahead as she ran to keep up. At a landing they emerged in a great room, where a huge open hearth stood against the far wall. Long tables ran the length of the room. Ceramic bowls, cups, cutlery and dried bunches of flowers and herbs were laid, as if awaiting a roomful of guests. Brightly colored tapestries hung from the stone walls, and large barrels and boxes and sacks were stacked in the corners. The huge room was as dark as a cave except for the high, narrow windows, which were periodically lit with streaks of lightning.

"Everything is the same," said Will. "She has put my home in the tapestry."

"But none of the people." Tessa looked around the expansive hall. "There *are* other people trapped here in the tapestry, right?"

"Yes, I believe so." Will went to the hearth and poked through the blackened coals. A dull red ember flared. "Someone has been here," he observed. "The fire has not gone cold. The lymerer, perhaps."

The thought of seeing the gruesome one-eyed giant again made Tessa's stomach churn. But he was one of the seven threads too. He was a person. "Seven people," Tessa said. "That's what the Norn said. Gray Lily stole seven threads. Seven lives. And they have to be returned. Or else . . ."

"Or else?" Will prompted.

Tessa rubbed her eyes. "Or else my world will fall apart. It sounds crazy. But it's true."

Will came to stand before her. When he spoke, his face was grave. "I believe it. What the witch has done here is foul and unnatural. No wonder it wreaks havoc with nature. This world may appear familiar, even beautiful, but make no mistake: it is a prison. It is not my home." He looked away, as if trying to find the right words. "It is like the bubble of glass in your bedchamber."

Tessa frowned. "Bubble of glass? Oh. The snow globe."

Will was watching her. "Gray Lily's spell must be broken, and the threads returned. That is why you are here, Mistress Brody, is it not? To fix things."

Tessa searched for some flicker of confidence inside herself. It wasn't there. "I'm lost, Will," she replied. "I have no idea what to do."

"You must get dry and eat," he said. At the hearth Will fed bits of straw and bark to the embers until a small, guttering flame sprang to life. Soon he had the fire burning steadily, heaped with split logs from a huge pile in the corner. Tessa was grateful for the crackling warmth and light. She could see steam rising from their wet clothes in the cool air.

From the fire they lit thick stubs of candles that made small, trembling lights flicker over the gloomy stone walls. Tessa shook her head wonderingly. She could hardly believe it; she was in a medieval castle. She listened to the rain and the keening wind whistling through the windows. High overhead, somewhere in the dark recesses, she could hear the flap and coo of birds.

"There may be dry clothes upstairs," said Will. "Come."

He led her up the spiral stairs again, and this time they came to a set of spacious adjoining rooms laid out like wedges of a circle.

In one of the rooms was a tall wooden wardrobe that, when opened, gave off the dry, pleasant fragrance of a flowery herb. Lavender, Tessa thought. Inside hung dresses on pegs. In the dim light Tessa could see the rich fabric of long gowns, sashes and veils. Velvet headpieces that looked like small caps were adorned with tiny pearls. Jeweled buckles and brooches sat on a small shelf above.

"I can't," she said.

"Please." Will dismissed her questioning glance with a brief smile. "Take whatever you desire." With that he left.

Tessa held her candle higher and peered into the

wardrobe. She found a thin shift of what felt like soft linen. Tessa peeled off her sodden clothes and gratefully slipped it on. She also discovered a less ornate dress buried in the back of the wardrobe. It was made of deep blue velvet, and its fitted bodice was stitched with golden thread in a delicate pattern of vines and flowers. The dress fit her but was snug in the waist and the bust, with a neckline cut low and square across her breasts. It was also a little short, Tessa realized; the heavy, flared skirt fell only to her ankles. It was probably just as well. She felt awkward enough without tripping over her own clothes.

She unbraided her hair and fingered it loosely over her shoulders so the dark, wavy tendrils could dry. She smiled when she saw the pig bracelet on her wrist. It was such a silly little thing, but it made her think of home, of Opal and her father. She wondered suddenly if she would ever see them again.

"Cut it out, Brody," she said, blinking back the tears that threatened to fall. She looked around for some shoes. In the bottom of the wardrobe were small embroidered slippers with tiny heels, but they never would have fit her, so Tessa walked back to the great hall in her bare feet, stepping quickly on the icy-cold stone of the castle hallways.

She thought she heard Will catch his breath, but he said nothing as he watched her walk toward him. He stared at her as if he had never seen her before, and made no move to come closer.

"What's wrong?" said Tessa. She tugged the neckline of the dress a little higher. She probably looked ridiculous.

"Nothing." Will nodded. "You are beautiful." But somehow the compliment sounded cool and detached, as was his formal bow. "You do Hartescross a great honor, mistress." He turned away. "I'm sorry you see it in such a state. Usually this hall is ablaze with warmth and color. And noise," he added ruefully as his voice echoed through the damp darkness around them.

"I've found what I could from the larder," he said. "Come and sit."

"Food?" asked Tessa. "The edible kind?" She shook her head at the concept of how this was all possible. Gray Lily had meant it when she said she'd made a world inside the tapestry.

They ate from heavy pewter platters that reflected dark-veined, silvery images of their faces in the dim light. Will cut rich, creamy slices from a wheel of cheese, and they shared bowls of dried apricots and apples. There was also a tough, dried-out loaf of heavy brown bread. They broke off chunks of this and dipped them into a small bowl of honey. Finally Tessa tried a swallow of what Will called sweet March ale. It was so heady it made her choke. "Maybe I should stick to water," she gasped, and reached for the earthenware pitcher nearby.

As she sipped, she stole a glance at Will. The candlelight played over his face and brought every strongly angled feature into stark relief. His face was troubled and pensive and his eyes dark, shadowed by a fall of unruly hair. Will usually seemed so confident, so full of life. Seeing him so desolate now made Tessa realize how traumatic the day had been.

She had been completely focused on her own troubles, and so awestruck by the strange splendor of this place that she had nearly forgotten. This was Will's home. Or at least a shallow replica of it.

She tried to imagine growing up in such a huge . . . fortress. Surrounded by servants, riding across the countryside, free to do whatever you wanted. "You must have had an exciting life here," said Tessa, trying to lighten his mood.

Will seemed to consider this. "I would not have called it so." He shrugged. "I am the younger son, not in line for my father's title, which goes to Hugh. I had not yet found a place or a calling of my own." He frowned. "I didn't even have an inkling of what it should be, though the choices were plain enough." He ticked them off on three fingers: "marriage, to a girl with a large estate and a larger dowry; soldiering; or the priesthood."

Tessa watched and listened, trying to figure out which of these choices appalled her the most. It was a toss-up.

"What—what were you leaning toward?" she said lightly.

For the first time that evening Will smiled, his teeth flashing at her in the near dark. "I had thought to leave my decision up to fate, mistress."

When Tessa said nothing, his smile faded. He leaned across the table, his expression intent. They stared at each other. Tessa felt her chest tighten; it ached with every breath she took. At that moment she felt they were alone, adrift in a black sea of dreams. There was no castle, no world. Nothing existed beyond this small pool of light and Will.

She must have trembled or made some small sound, because in the next instant Will stood and rounded the table.

"You're cold." He scooped her up in his arms and walked closer to the fire, her heavy skirts trailing. He sat in a chair, holding her so close that she could feel the steady drum of his pulse. He looked at her, and Tessa felt the cold melt away in the heat of the fire and Will's gaze. She watched the firelight reflected in his eyes and then rested her head against his shoulder. Every part of her was warm: her feet, her hands, her heart.

The storm had stopped. A beam of light sliced across the floor.

"The moon," whispered Tessa. She could see the pale globe through the window. "It will be full soon, won't it," she said.

"Tomorrow night," said Will, following her gaze.

"That's when the Norn said my father would . . ." Her voice trailed off as she tried to picture her father, to imagine what was happening, what he was feeling. She should be there.

"Is his illness painful?" Will asked quietly.

"I don't know. I don't think so. But it's just . . . it's awful not knowing what's happening. I don't know what I'm supposed to do."

That wasn't exactly true, she told herself. She had to return the threads that Gray Lily had stolen before the full moon. And she hadn't told Will everything.

Will was watching her. "Perhaps you won't know what to do until the time is upon you," he said. "There must be a reason for all this." There was an expression of grim determination on his face. Or maybe hope.

"You were the one who released me from the tapestry," he finished.

He said it as if it were some feat she had accomplished, had planned. "But—" she began, protesting miserably.

"I know," he interrupted with a weary smile, and dropped his head back to rest on the chair. "It was an accident. But just consider the possibility that it *wasn't*. That there is a *reason* you were able to release me." He angled his head to look at her.

"Okay," Tessa whispered helplessly. "Give me a reason."

Will pulled her close and kissed her.

Chapter 39

Sweet. The taste of honey from Will's mouth. The smell of fire and flowers. The feel of his hands holding her. Touching her. Tessa lost herself in the kiss. Everything she had, everything she was, she offered to Will. Nothing mattered but tonight, she told herself. The fierce need to be close to him, to love him, drove everything else out of her head. Her purpose in life was to kiss Will de Chaucy. It was a calling, she decided.

They slipped to the floor, pulling down fur pelts and cushions to make a soft, if haphazard, bed against the cold stone. The warmth of the fire seemed nothing to Tessa compared to the heat of her own skin. Somehow, the bodice strings of her gown were loose. She threw her head back as Will traced kisses down her throat and eased the velvet from her shoulders.

She loved him. As impossible as it was, she loved Will de Chaucy, and at that moment, she could believe in anything. She *would* believe in anything. Karma, destiny, fate or invisible leprechauns.

She loved him. She had to tell him everything.

Tessa drew back from Will's arms. "Wait. Please. I have to tell you something more," she said, and brushed back her tousled hair. "You were right. It was me. I was the girl who trapped you."

"I don't understand," Will said, his voice ragged. He pulled her closer, taking her hand in his own and putting her palm to his chest.

"It was another life, but it was me," Tessa said slowly. "And lately I've been remembering what happened. And Gray Lily says if I—"

Will's face was flushed, and Tessa could feel the wild beat of his heart in her hand. But he went very still and his gaze slid away from hers. "If you what?" he asked in a low voice.

"If I—" Tessa's mouth had suddenly gone dry. "If I bring you to her, help to capture you as the unicorn, she'll give me my life back." She raised her eyes to his. "And my father's life."

Will let go of her and stood. "Why did you not tell me this before?" he said.

Tessa shook her head. "I don't know. I was confused. I didn't think it mattered, because I would never *do* that, Will." She gathered the gown over her bare shoulders. She was suddenly cold. She turned away from Will, stepping closer to the fire, which had burned down; the coals glowed a dull and angry red.

Will shot out a hand and gripped her arm. "So. What is it you plan to do now?" he asked.

"What do you mean?"

"You have to trap the unicorn to save your father. That's why you came here." He placed himself directly in front of her, raised his hands briefly and let them drop. She wasn't sure if it was a gesture of challenge or defeat.

"No. You don't understand," Tessa said faintly. "I don't know what to do. I just wanted to find you."

They stood facing each other as the silence grew. Will looked at her as if she were a stranger. As if there were worlds between them. Just as there always had been, Tessa thought.

"You wanted to find me," he repeated to himself. "And so of course, you have. I am a complete fool," he went on, shaking his head. "It was as I thought. You are here only to trap me once more."

Will's lips curled in a faint, mocking smile. His eyes swept over her and down to the rumpled furs where they had been lying only moments before. "You are still the virgin in the wood. Virtue dangled as bait."

Tessa stared at him. "What?"

"No more lies, Tessa!" he shouted. He gave a suspicious glance around the darkened room. "Where is she? Where is Gray Lily?"

Tessa shook her head. How could he believe that? When he kissed her, when he spoke to her, his lips grazing her ear, she could swear that he loved her. In fact, they had just been very close to making—

The thought struck her like a freight train. She felt the world twist away.

She put a hand to her throat. "You never trusted me," she whispered, barely breathing the words. "You told me before that I was the one who trapped you. You even used the same words. The *virgin* in the wood."

"Yes," he said, his eyes unreadable.

She stared at him, replaying in her head every word, every glance, every kiss. "You never trusted me," she repeated. "Not even after . . ." *Not even after I fell in love with you,* she said to herself. She thought of all the times when he had distanced himself, kept himself apart. Cool, aloof. He had been protecting himself. From her?

A virgin in his haunts, Tessa thought. Only a virgin could lure the unicorn into the snare. Only a virgin. And then the obvious finally sank in.

"And what if I wasn't?" she asked.

"What?" Will asked.

"What if I *wasn't* a virgin?" She said each word distinctly, slowly. "You'd be safe from me if I wasn't a virgin. Is that what you thought? Is that why you kissed me? Why you would have—" She stopped, daring him with her eyes to deny it, to lie to her.

"Don't be absurd." Will's face looked ashen, but Tessa wasn't going to be fooled again.

"How stupid am I," she said to herself, turning away and covering her face with her hands. "Stupid. Stupid."

She heard Will mutter a curse under his breath, but

she didn't look back until he grabbed her and spun her toward him.

"Stop it," he said. He was breathing hard. "Tessa. It is not that way."

She shoved him away as hard as she could with both hands. "Leave me alone!" she cried, and ran across the dark hall.

"Where are you going?" he demanded.

"Don't you know already?" she said sarcastically. She swiped at the tears streaking her face. "I'm going to set a trap for you."

Tessa ran through the darkened hallways, her bare feet pounding hard stone. She didn't care where she went or what happened. She just ran. The tears felt cold on her cheek as she made her way deeper and deeper through the dark. She climbed a passageway so narrow that the walls seemed barely wide enough for her to pass. She had to slow down finally when it became too dark to see. Her hands scrabbled against rough, unfamiliar forms as she came to the top. She spied a small room to her right, lit from a narrow window with a faint streak of moonlight. A low wooden bed stood in one corner.

Tessa collapsed onto it, exhausted.

Chapter 40

The thin mattress was stuffed with feathers—mostly the pointy, quill part, it seemed. Tessa opened her eyes. Between the crying and the goose feathers poking her all night, she felt raw, inside and out. She rose and went to the window. Outside, the low hills rolled away in a soft, rich palette of greens and browns. The day had dawned crystalline blue, with no hint of the ravaging storm the night before.

"It's beautiful," she said to herself. But beauty didn't particularly impress her this morning, and she turned away, only to see Will standing in the doorway watching her.

Silently he came and stood next to her.

Tessa gazed out across the landscape, afraid to look at

Will. He didn't seem willing to speak about what had happened the night before. Or what hadn't. Tessa knew she had overreacted.

Overreacted? She'd gone crazy, she thought, remembering her outburst. Will de Chaucy wouldn't sleep with her to save himself. That was crazy. But what *wasn't* crazy was the fact that he didn't trust her. The idea hurt so much she could hardly breathe.

"Tessa," Will said. "Look at me."

"It's all right," she said quietly. "It doesn't matter anymore." Tessa pointed to a small figure approaching. "She's here. Gray Lily is coming."

"Then we had best prepare to meet her," Will said shortly. He turned away.

Will gathered weapons from the wall. He selected a long wooden bow and quiver of arrows, both of which he slung over one shoulder; then a short, bone-handled dagger went into a sheath on his belt. He grabbed a huge sword in a heavy leather scabbard and fastened it around his waist. He was perusing a variety of round, hammered-metal shields when Tessa's impatient huff finally caught his attention.

"Well?" she said pointedly. "Aren't you going to give *me* something?"

Will looked taken aback but then surveyed the choices and passed a critical eye over her. "I don't suppose you have ever used a crossbow."

Tessa set her jaw. "Just show me."

"Here," he said as he handed the hefty and archaic-looking weapon to her. The weight of the crossbow surprised Tessa, and she threw Will an uncertain look.

"Don't worry. You only need to aim and fire." He strode to a chest, from which he took a handful of short arrows. He gave her one.

"Pretty heavy for an arrow, isn't it?" Tessa said.

"It's called a bolt," said Will. "And it's iron. Now watch."

He took the crossbow from her. He bent over, put a foot into a leather stirruplike piece and, holding the bow steady, straightened himself and pulled the bow upward until the string caught in the notch and the bow seemed taut to the point of snapping.

"Lock it here," Will said while Tessa watched intently. "The bolt lies here in the groove." He slid in the sharply pointed, ugly-looking missile. "Keep your fingers clear of this." He pointed to a firing mechanism. "This is a short-range weapon—it's best to wait until your target is close, but it fires true and can pierce armor at fifty yards.

"Unlock this only when you're ready to fire." He indicated a small wooden catch. He put the crossbow in Tessa's hands and guided the padded end to her shoulder. "Aim along the body and release this trigger to unloose the bolt."

"Okay," said Tessa, feeling her hands quiver. She frowned, straightened up, tightened her hold and sighted along the path of the bolt. "Like this?"

"Good." Will nodded.

She took the extra bolts from him. She didn't have a belt, so with a shrug she tucked them into the embroidered sash at her waist.

"Okay," she said with a satisfied nod. Then, sensing Will

watching her, she looked up at him. "Do I scare you?" Tessa asked coolly. She wasn't sure why. Maybe to provoke him, to make him feel as unsettled as she did. Though he didn't look afraid, Tessa decided.

"You always have," he murmured.

They climbed the stairs to the battlements of the guard tower. They could see Gray Lily standing on the grassy slope, about a hundred yards distant. She began to walk toward the castle. Tessa squinted against the bright sunlight.

The old woman advanced to the grass near the edge of the moat and peered up at the battlements. She was dressed in a long gray dress and cloak.

"You! Girl! Send down the young master," she called imperiously, "and you can go back to your world unharmed. I only want my unicorn."

Will snarled a curse.

"You thought this would be a quaint, pretty place, eh, girl?" Gray Lily went on. "Welcome to reality. Actually, reality would be much worse. Now send down the young master," she growled. "Or I will come fetch him."

Tessa and Will looked at each other. Something strong and sure passed between them in that moment. Something that didn't require words or promises. Tessa grinned. She was suddenly stupidly happy.

Will gave her an answering smile, then nodded and turned to Gray Lily. "Be on your way, old woman," he shouted. "Perhaps you can peddle your wares farther down the road."

Gray Lily let out a slew of profanity in reply. But she didn't leave. She pointed a finger toward the distant horizon and began to speak. The sound was horrible. Tessa stepped back from the castle wall.

"I think we should get inside," she whispered, reaching for his hand.

"No," said Will, watching Gray Lily's motions. "Best to know what we're dealing with."

Tessa peered into the distance. A tiny dark thing fluttered against the blue sky. "I've seen that before," she said, frowning. "In the tapestry. It's only a bird."

The bird flew closer. It was odd, Tessa thought. Usually you couldn't hear birds flapping like that. *Whoomp. Whoomp.* She stared with horrified fascination as it got bigger. "It's not a bird," she whispered nervously. "Is it?"

"It's the dragon," Will said.

It flew closer, its long body writhing in a serpentine trail across the sky. It looked like a giant snake on which someone had sewn gargantuan, floppy-jointed bat wings. As it swooped closer, the wings unfolded like huge, veined fans and blotted out the sky overhead. The wings could have touched both goalposts of the Prescott High School football field, Tessa thought. A gust of foul wind knocked her and Will backward as the creature hurtled past. It screamed. It was a deafening, almost human-sounding scream except for the sibilant ending—a hiss, like whistling steam.

"Dragon! Why didn't you tell me there was a dragon?" shouted Tessa, against the roar of the wind.

"I didn't think it necessary," Will shouted back, helping her to her feet. "It has never troubled me before."

The dragon flapped closer. Tessa saw a cerulean eye and the shutterlike flick of a membranous lid—the dragon was watching them as it lifted past, flying nearly straight up in the air.

"I think it wants to make up for lost time," Tessa muttered.

The creature soared upward, its long body undulating, its spiked tail whipping the clouds. Its searing breath quivered the air into heat waves and left in its wake a blackened double contrail that looked like train tracks against the blue sky.

"Right." Will swallowed. "I believe we've seen enough. Come on." They scrambled back, running into the central tower just as a wall of fire blistered the space behind them. Tessa turned to see a ball of orange flame fill the doorway and blast toward them like a cannon shot.

She dove to the side just as the fireball roared past. The whole tower shook, and the walls were blackened where the fire had licked stone.

"Up!" Will's hand reached for Tessa's as she clutched the crossbow in the other and raced on, up the spiraling steps.

They came to the top of the castle's tower, emerging onto a walkway that was girded by a chest-high wall with narrow chinks in it. Below them Gray Lily looked tiny, but Tessa sensed the repulsive dark eyes locked on them with hatred.

The dragon wheeled in the sky and approached again. It plummeted toward Tessa and Will, seeming to watch them like a raptor would its prey. At the last second it veered away, firing another blast of flames from a fanged, gaping mouth. Will and Tessa ducked and flattened their backs to the outer wall as fire shot over their heads and blasted the tower wall facing them. Will held the bronze shield over them. Tessa closed her eyes against the heat, but when she opened them she saw Will drop the red-hot shield with a curse. He shook his blistered left hand as the molten center of the metal sagged.

"Jesu," Will breathed.

A burst of twittering erupted overhead as a flock of doves flapped out of one of the tower windows, driven from their perches. A few unlucky ones fluttered across the dragon's path. A moment later, roasted carcasses, looking like black frizzled lumps, dropped to the ground at Will's and Tessa's feet.

The poor things, Tessa thought, but there was no time for more because she saw Will stand up, draw his bow and fire a shot at the dragon, all in one fluid, lethal motion.

The air split with the dragon's scream as the arrow struck the underside of one spread wing. The dragon hurtled toward them, its wounded wing folded.

"Get down!" Tessa hissed.

The dragon slammed against the tower and one of the huge, heat-cracked stones snapped free from the top of the wall and tumbled downward, planting itself deep in the ground below with a reverberating thud.

Meanwhile, Will and Tessa watched as the dragon coiled its long body and tail around the tower, clinging to the walls like a lizard with its clawed feet.

"Maybe it's too hurt to fly," said Tessa.

"Maybe it just wants to eat us," retorted Will.

He pulled Tessa inside the turret and ducked down beneath one of the windows in the circular room. Outside, the dragon's head hovered like a giant parade balloon as it passed the window opposite them. They straightened up and circled to get out of its line of fire as puffs of black breath from slitted nostrils blew ash and charred feathers into the room.

"How do you kill a dragon?" gasped Tessa. "Don't they teach that stuff in medieval school?"

"Truth be told, mistress," panted Will, "this would be my first." He readied another arrow in the bow and aimed it at the far window, holding himself as taut as the bowstring itself while he waited for his target.

Slam! The room shook as the dragon heaved itself against the tower. Tessa and Will were both thrown to the floor. Another slab of stone plummeted past the window. "He's going to knock the tower down," Tessa said in disbelief.

Then an idea occurred to her, and before she could talk herself out of it she hefted up the crossbow and dashed down the stairs, yelling instructions to Will as she ran.

At the bottom of the tower Tessa braced herself in the open doorway. Above her hung the dragon's pale green belly. She aimed the crossbow and released the latch, then held her breath. She fired. *Ffft!* The recoil of the crossbow bit into her shoulder as twelve inches of sharpened iron flew into the beast's scaly armor and was buried to the hilt.

The dragon shuddered and let out another scream. It

twisted down, its huge reptilian head dropping to Tessa's level. It didn't let go of the tower. It wasn't mortally wounded. Only really pissed off.

Tessa froze in the archway of the tower, facing the dragon, and for a moment she thought she could not carry out her plan. It was something she saw in the dragon's leering eyes. Something almost human.

But then the dragon drew in a slithering breath, and Tessa knew she would be incinerated on the exhale.

"Now!" she screamed.

A handful of tiny stones and dust pattered onto the dragon's head. The creature blinked and almost seemed to sneer at her with a triumphant flare of its nostrils. It opened its jaws just as a massive wedge of granite fell and crushed its head.

Chapter 41

The dragon lay sprawled on the ground, its huge green skull hollowed in by its own tombstone. It let out a last hot, hissing sigh and died. Just as with the lymerer, the dragon's body was soon enveloped in a shroud of vapor.

Will flew down the stairs and arrived panting at Tessa's side. He turned to Tessa, his face stricken, the skin around his lips pale white. "The next time you have a plan," Will heaved, catching his breath, "Please. Just *don't.*" He hugged her to him. They both watched as a coil of swampy-colored green thread drifted away and the dragon disappeared.

"Another thread," said Will. "Another life to be gathered back in by Gray Lily."

Tessa, covered with dust and splatters of rapidly disappearing dragon blood, was still dazed as Will pulled her tighter. She sagged against him, grateful for the support. Every muscle in her body seemed to be quivering from either exhaustion or relief. And after seeing the thread of the dragon drift away, she felt impossibly tired. What the Norn wanted her to do was more than impossible. It was hopeless.

"Now listen to me." Will spoke into her hair, and maybe he sensed her despair; his voice was fierce and low. "I don't care what happened before. I don't care what happens tomorrow. You will do whatever you must. I trust you."

The words filled Tessa with a pure, strong joy.

He drew back and looked at her. His eyes were blazing. "And I love you. I have loved you from the first time I saw you."

"That was a long time ago," Tessa murmured, looking into his eyes. "Some things change."

"Some things don't," Will answered. He pulled her into a tight embrace and kissed her.

After their lips parted, Tessa whispered, "I love you too. Today and always."

Will stepped back and smiled. "I think we can hold out here against whatever Gray Lily sends," he said. He took her hand and they climbed to the tower window once more, lugging their weapons.

"I think you may be right, Esquire de Chaucy," said Tessa. It was true; suddenly she felt that together they could handle anything. She smiled to herself. Together they would find a way. She stole a glance at Will, remembering something. *Marriage to a girl with a large estate, soldiering or the priesthood.*

"By the way," she said. "I was thinking about those three career choices you mentioned?"

"Hmm?"

"You can forget about two of them."

"Which two?" he asked, cocking an eyebrow.

"You figure it out."

"Ah."

They came to the window and looked out at the grassy expanse. Tessa's smile faded.

Down below, Gray Lily was no longer alone. Beside her stood a man dressed all in black. Tessa could see a frizz of reddish hair and a pale, freckled scalp.

"Moncrieff," she gasped. She turned to Will. "That's Moncrieff. The lawyer."

Will narrowed his eyes. "Really?" he remarked. He watched the man, who began to walk slowly toward them and raised his head. "He doesn't look very . . ."

Will trailed off and let out a low, strangled cry. Tessa looked up to see his face contorted in a disbelieving stare.

"What is it?"

Will spun away and raced down the steps. "It's Hugh!" he shouted. "That's my *brother!*"

Chapter 42

Moncrieff, or the man who had once been called Hugh de Chaucy, stepped across the drawbridge and let out a weary sigh. He turned and looked across the green hills, the meadow. This place reminded him of home so much that his chest ached. He had once been Hugh de Chaucy, stocky and strong and a match for anyone, man or beast. But no longer. He was barely human anymore.

Will raced down the stairs two at a time and reached the heavy iron gate of the castle, his eyes fixed on his brother's face. "Hugh!" he shouted as the other man approached. He pushed his arms through the grate and clasped his brother around the shoulders, pulling him into an awkward embrace.

Standing behind Will, Tessa saw the man she had known as Moncrieff freeze, his pale blue eyes wide with shock. He stared at Will through the metal bars. For a moment he only moved his mouth in silent, quivering shock. His voice, when he spoke, was nearly gibbering:

"W-Will. Will? No, by Christ, it is a ghost. More of her witchery."

Will tightened his grasp on Hugh's arms and gave him a shake, as if to wake him up from a dream. "It's *me*," Will said.

Hugh flinched in his grip. Will's face registered surprise as he held the flabby, withered arms of his once-ox-strong brother.

"What has happened to you?" Will whispered. "How do you come to be here?"

"You are *not* my brother." Hugh breathed the words, but he didn't back away. He reached up and pulled Will closer to inspect his face wonderingly. "My brother is dead," he said at last, blinking as if the sight of Will stung his red-rimmed eyes. "He was killed by a unicorn."

Will shook his head. "It was only Gray Lily's conjuring and lies that made it seem so. She transformed me. *I* was the unicorn." A sharp moan of pain came from Hugh de Chaucy's mouth, as if he had been struck.

Will lifted a hand to the fading scar on his cheek as the two men stared at each other. They were united in the memory of another encounter, one as distant as a fable yet as close as a fresh wound.

"Will." Hugh's voice broke on the name. "I did not know. I swear it. All this time. I didn't know."

"I know that, brother," said Will. Hugh straightened

almost imperceptibly, and for a moment Tessa could imagine the man he had once been. Even his speech, the inflections of his voice, seemed to now hint at the heritage he shared with Will.

"What did she do to you?" Will whispered, looking at Hugh de Chaucy's sagging, lined face and blotchy skin. The face that, Tessa could see now, must have once been robust and strong.

Hugh's reply was curt. "What she does to all her victims. She took my life. Or at least a piece of it. In the form of a thread by which she can control me. I have served her for centuries, and she has twisted this old body so many times that I hardly recognize it myself."

"You're one of the stolen threads," said Tessa. She went a step closer to the brothers.

Hugh nodded a sober greeting to her. "Yes. But not in the tapestry. She has kept me by her side all these long years." The statement seemed to amuse him somehow, and he let out a dry gasp of laughter. "I have served her and she's kept me alive. But then you found the tapestry. And released the unicorn. Its loss has diminished her." He gave Will a grim look. "She'll do anything to get it back."

"We should get you inside," Will said in a low, urgent tone. He made a movement to release himself from Hugh's embrace. But Hugh held on.

"Hugh," said Will, staring at his brother.

Hugh looked at his hands and an expression of twisted apology crept over his face. "I'm sorry, brother," he said softly. His fingers tightened.

Will stared at his brother in confusion and tried to jerk

away. "Let me go, Hugh. We'll raise the gate and bring you in."

Gray Lily drifted up behind Hugh, as silent as a shadow. "Hold him," she muttered.

"She kept you whole," he whispered to Will. "But me—she took my thread after the hunt was done. Sh-she keeps a piece of me in her pocket." Hugh choked out the words as he clutched his brother in a viselike grip. "I'm sorry. I have no choice."

Tessa ran to Will and pulled as hard she could to separate the brothers, but Hugh's grip seemed superhuman.

Gray Lily snaked her ringed hand through the bars and pressed it to Will's chest, even as he struggled to wrench away.

Tessa screamed and held him, even as she began to feel the icy pain in her chest. Just like before.

Will's face spasmed in panic and fury, and his voice cut into her like a blade. "Tessa!" he roared. Thick cords stood out from his neck as he strained against the pain. His tall, strong form arched back like a whip.

But already the silver thread was being drawn. Tessa held him, enveloped in pain herself, and saw the beautiful thread wind away from his weakening body, drawn by Gray Lily. With what seemed like the last of his strength, Will pushed Tessa away from him, breaking the contact and lifting the cold ache from her. Will sagged in his brother's grip and his head slung backward. His eyes turned and fixed on Tessa. "Destroy the unicorn, Tessa. Kill it."

She stood frozen; she couldn't look away. She kept

staring into Will de Chaucy's eyes as they became transparent and disappeared. But his last look still burned through her.

Hugh's eyes closed and his face grew red and wet, but he maintained his grip on his brother's body until it was gone and his hands clutched empty air. Gray Lily turned away, weaving the silver thread through her fingers and whispering.

Tessa crumpled to the ground. It felt as if everything inside her had been ripped out. Slowly she pushed herself up and saw Gray Lily standing on a small hill of grass some distance away. A silver cloud of smoke seemed to gather around her as her hands worked the thread of Will's life.

As the smoke cleared, Tessa saw the unicorn: a living dream, strong and graceful and proud. It tossed its head as it came nearer, and its mane made a line of tattered silk that rippled on the breeze. Its long spiral of horn rose from its sculpted head. As the unicorn came closer, Tessa could see his eyes. Warm golden brown fringed with dark. Will's clever, beautiful eyes.

The unicorn reared up against the sky, tearing the air with its hooves. As Tessa and Hugh watched, Gray Lily's body grew taller, straighter. Tessa stared as comprehension came to her: Gray Lily had woven Will's thread into the form of the unicorn while he was here, inside the tapestry—so now she had her youth again. Will's youth.

Gray Lily tossed back her head, sending shiny blond hair flying. Her delighted peal of laughter rang out.

"God help me," Hugh de Chaucy said, staring at Gray

Lily and the unicorn. "It was Will. All these years I truly believed he had been killed by the unicorn. That's why I helped her. I thought she had trapped the monster that murdered my brother. *She* has been the monster all along."

"But now?" Tessa whispered. "Hugh, how could you do it?" She lifted her tearstained face to him. "To your own brother?"

"You still don't understand." Hugh said wearily. He leaned against the bridging bars as if they were holding him up, as if every particle of strength had left him. "Her power is absolute over anyone whose thread she holds. No will is strong enough to oppose her. She can twist the body, the mind, the form. She is as a god." He hung his head.

"I don't believe that," said Tessa. She looked through the heavy gate at Hugh's sagging, lined face. "Help me, Hugh. Tell me how to get him back."

"You can't get him back," Hugh said. "We are lost. She is too powerful."

"No," Tessa said. "She *has* something that makes her powerful. What is it, Hugh? What is the key?"

Hugh made a fist and let it fall against the iron bar closest to him. "I don't know."

"You must have noticed something," Tessa insisted. "Is there a piece of wood or a rock that she carries with her, or wears?"

"No. There's nothing like that." He hesitated, frowned. "Only that silver ring she wears. It never leaves her finger." He suddenly backed away from the gate, as if he had been jerked on a leash. "If you do as she says, she will send you back to your world," he said, his words rushing out. "Do it, Tessa Brody, and forget this terrible story. For that is what it will become in time, just a story. And you'll remember us only in your dreams."

"It's too late," Tessa said. "I love him."

There was silence for a moment before Hugh spoke. "So do I," he said. His gaze seemed to shift inward as he turned away. "Perhaps she will allow me to stay here with him. There might be some peace in that."

In the distance there was a whinnying cry. Tessa covered her ears—she couldn't bear it. Gray Lily strode toward the castle gate once more. Tessa stared. The witch's figure was curved and supple beneath a clinging, sheathlike garment of green silk, covered by a lavishly embroidered robe. But her eyes were the same, and Tessa shuddered as they flicked over her. Like those of a snake sizing up its next meal.

"It is done. What a relief." Gray Lily ran her hands over her bosom, and down her waist and hips. "I feel wonderful," she said with a long, stretching roll of her shoulders. She looked at Tessa. "Come out of there, girl."

Tessa backed away from the heavy metal bars that separated her from Gray Lily. Somehow they seemed impossibly flimsy, not nearly protection enough from the creature on the other side.

"Why?"

Gray Lily raised a finely arched brow. "Because I have what I want. My unicorn is returned." She gestured to the castle, the sky. "From the outside, the tapestry will have been restored and will show the unicorn as before. He lives within the tapestry once more, and his eternal youth is mine. Now," she said briskly, "we must leave. I'd like to be in Rome for breakfast." She gave Tessa a sly smile. "And *you* don't belong here."

"No one belongs here!" Tessa cried. She threw her arms up. "It's not real. It's not life. You can't put people in here, trapped like . . . *specimens*. It's evil, don't you understand?"

"I didn't *put* you here, pet," snapped Gray Lily. "Somehow you did that yourself. Remember? The fact is, I want you out of my tapestry. You cause far too much trouble. And as for evil," she said with a sneer, "my tiny machinations are nothing. Not compared to the bloody carnage those three sisters have wreaked. Have you forgotten that your father lies dying? We can save him if you come with me now." Gray Lily gripped the gate and gave it an irritated heave, but the massive structure didn't budge.

Tessa shook her head and stepped away. "I haven't forgotten anything. But I'm not leaving Will here. Or any of them."

"Fine. Your choice," spat Gray Lily. "We'll have to do it another way. This will hurt a bit." She shot a hand through the gate, and a *ping* rang out as her silver ring clanged on the metal. She pointed a slender finger at Tessa and began to mutter in a guttural voice.

Tessa gasped as she felt a tiny spear of pain strike her chest. She scrambled backward. The pain subsided. A look of fury passed over Gray Lily's countenance and she stretched her arm as far as it would reach through the square grating. "Come back here," she muttered, and clawed at Tessa.

Gray Lily wasn't close enough, Tessa realized with a sigh of relief. She must have had to be within a certain distance of a person to pull their thread.

With a grunt of disgust Gray Lily withdrew her hand. "Come along, Moncrieff," she snarled. "She'll come out of there. If she doesn't want me to hurt the unicorn."

Hugh stared at the ground, his shoulders slack. At Gray Lily's words Tessa saw him mouth a word, silently. *Will.* When he looked up, he had a strange, lost expression on his face. But he trudged away, following Gray Lily, walking toward the distant forest, head bowed.

Tessa was alone. She was locked inside a fortress of stone and there was nothing left to protect. She made her way to the wide, dim space of the great hall and slumped at a table strewn with wilted flowers and candle wax. Here, only the night before, firelight had flickered over Will's face as he had kissed her. She closed her eyes and traced the memory of the feeling on her lips with a finger. Why did that seem more real than anything that had happened since?

Hugh said she would forget. He was wrong. The person Tessa had tried to dismiss as a fantasy was the only part of reality she cared to cling to. There would never be a place for her in a world without Will.

She thought of her father; she would never see him again. Or Opal. They were from another life, another world. She hadn't returned the threads; maybe the world she knew wasn't even *there* anymore.

Everything had been taken from her now, Tessa thought. She was gutted. Empty of everything except, apparently, tears. She raised her head and squeezed her wet eyes shut and flexed her cold fingers nervously. Will was gone. She would never have the chance to show him how much she loved him.

I will never go back into the tapestry. I would rather die. Destroy the unicorn, Tessa. Kill it.

Or maybe . . . She frowned and interlaced her fingers. Maybe if she was strong enough, she would.

Chapter 43

She couldn't get the castle gate up. She couldn't turn the ponderous wheel even an inch by herself. Finally she wiped the sweat from her eyes and wiped her stinging palms on her dress.

"Idiot," Tessa said. She ran to get Hannibal from his stall.

"Okay, big boy," she murmured. Nervously she looped a harness over his gleaming black chest and led him out into the courtyard. She fastened a heavy rope to the harness and to one of the handles of the wheel. "C'mon." She tugged him forward until the rope stood taut. Hannibal stopped.

Tessa pulled, trying to urge the massive horse forward with a combination of giddyups, threats and tentative slaps on his rump, which he disdainfully brushed away with his tail. He just stood there. Finally, getting weepy again with frustration, she begged him.

"Please, Hannibal." Tessa rested her head against the horse's muscled shoulder in exhaustion. "Please open the gate. For Will."

As if he had been waiting for her to speak his language, the proud war horse surged forward. Tessa leapt out of his way and the heavy, rattling gate began to rise.

With a yelp of relief Tessa secured the locking mechanism and unhooked Hannibal. She had no clue how to saddle the huge animal, so she stood on a high wooden stool, slung the crossbow over one shoulder, tucked a handful of her skirts up into her knotted sash and climbed onto his bare back.

Hannibal trotted out with Tessa clinging to him like a limpet. Her hands were knotted in his mane, and her sneakered feet dangled below dusty skirts while the crossbow banged against her back. Her old clothes had been in a damp, tangled pile where she'd left them, so she had decided to stick with the dress.

"Go find Will," she whispered to the tufted ear below her. Hannibal seemed to require no further orders and broke into a gallop, across the grassy fields and toward the forest.

Tessa rode through dappled shadows into the cool dark of the forest, green on green. The sweet, cleansing scent of the trees drifted over her. She could hear the twitter of birds and, somewhere distant, the trickle of water.

She sat stiffly upright, jumping at every twig snap beneath Hannibal's step and turning her head from side to side, cautious of every silhouette they passed. Anxiety drummed inside her, making her pulse beat and her muscles stiffen with tension. Tessa swung the loaded crossbow forward across her lap. She was thankful for the ugly weight of it, and for the remaining bolts that jabbed into her thigh if she leaned forward too far.

Then she heard the dog. It was the yelping bark of the lymerer's dog, coming from up ahead. The sound brought back every memory, every visceral sensation of the hunt. A knot of fear crept into her and settled deep inside, a cold weight in her gut. But rather than stop Tessa, it whipped her into frenzied action.

"Go! Go!" she shouted, and leaned forward on Hannibal's neck, kicking at his sides. She clung to his back, tilting and lurching awkwardly, but she hung on. They raced toward the sound and broke through the dense trees into a small clearing, where Hannibal shuddered to an abrupt stop. Gray Lily stood before them.

She stood, hands on her hips, and looked up at Tessa. "Here she is at last," she said. "I knew you would come."

Tessa's glance swept the rest of the clearing as Hannibal stepped toward the center. The huge, brutish lymerer stood there, silent and grim, practically at eye level with Tessa as she passed. His Hellhound pulled at its leash and growled. At Tessa's glance the lymerer brought a grubby hand up to his throat and ran a thick tongue over his lips.

Tessa stiffened and looked away. Hugh de Chaucy was there, near the edge of the grassy circle, sharpening a spear with some kind of flat stone. He did not look up at Tessa but continued to hone the point with rapid, methodical movements.

"Where's Will?" Tessa demanded from her precarious seat on Hannibal.

Gray Lily gave her a tight-lipped, smile. "You mean my unicorn, don't you? I don't know. He's off somewhere." She shrugged. "Grazing, perhaps. Leave him alone. He's happy."

Tessa thought of Will's tortured look when he imagined going back into the tapestry. His love of life, of freedom. "He's *not* happy," Tessa hissed. "He's a prisoner. Let him go."

"This is becoming tiresome. Get down from there, girl." Gray Lily barked out the order. "I have what I want. I am ready to leave."

"Suppose I just shoot you instead," said Tessa. She raised the crossbow and angled it over her forearm, fingering the safety latch. She aimed the pointed barb of the iron bolt at Gray Lily's chest. Her palms felt slick with sweat. Hugh de Chaucy raised his head and gave Tessa a speculative look. Gray Lily eyed the crossbow. She made an exaggerated pose of fright before dropping it and letting out a high-pitched trill of laughter. It sounded like bats swarming from a dark cave.

"That won't have any effect on me," Gray Lily advised, indicating the crossbow, "and you would waste valuable time." She looked up at the twilight sky. "Evening is coming. The moon rises soon."

"I'm not afraid of the dark," Tessa said. She rested the crossbow lightly on her thigh so they wouldn't see the way her hands shook. "Whose was the first thread you stole?"

"What an odd question. Why must you always be so difficult, girl?" Gray Lily's small, dark eyes narrowed on Tessa's face. "I am trying to help you, you know. Do you want your father to die? The Norn are your enemy, not me. They have wronged us both."

"That's not true," Tessa said. "The Norn will restore the lives of the people whose threads you stole. They've promised." She pointed the crossbow at Gray Lily once more. Anger and fear made her voice come out in a jerky, breathless shout. "The first. Whose was it? The snake? The dragon? Tell me!"

Gray Lily only folded her arms. The light was fading, and shadows crept from the line of trees, turning the colors in the clearing to deeper shades of emerald grass, dark wood, black earth. There was no time left. Tessa aimed the crossbow, her finger pressed to the release mechanism.

"You make yourself sound like a victim," cried Tessa. "But you're a monster!" Hannibal's ears flattened and he tossed his head as he stepped in place. Tessa gripped his sides with her legs and went on, "You took Will's life. You've trapped him in this tapestry for hundreds of years."

Gray Lily made a sharp, derisive noise. "You know nothing about it. I *protected* his life."

"What are you talking about?" Tessa said slowly.

"Do you know what came to Cornwall a fortnight after I took the young master?" Gray Lily asked. When Tessa answered her with only a silent, distrustful stare, she went on. "A plague of smallpox. The entire village was wiped out. They all died, with bleeding pustules and fever and racking pain." Gray Lily paused and watched Tessa. "Will de Chaucy was to die. That was the *life* the young master had to look forward to."

Tessa stared. "You're lying," she whispered. But she lowered her weapon.

"Look it up," Gray Lily said tersely. "You'll find no modern village of Hartescross. No descendents of Gervais de Chaucy. Or," she added, perhaps seeing the flicker of uncertainty cross Tessa's face, "you already have. Yes. You know that what I say is true."

Tessa swallowed. Her throat felt parched. She stared at Gray Lily, trying to take in what she'd been told. Smallpox.

"You had no right. He might have lived," Tessa said, but her voice carried all the weight and conviction of smoke from a dying fire. In the Middle Ages people did die from plagues of infection. It would explain why the village was wiped out, gone from history. Why there were no descendants of Will's family. Tessa's grip on the crossbow slackened.

Gray Lily shrugged. "If I hadn't taken him, he would have been laid rotting in a shroud before another month had passed. And you? You would never have seen the unicorn in the tapestry. You would never have met him. Do you regret that?" Gray Lily pressed.

"No," answered Tessa dully. "I don't regret meeting him."

"Then why not let him live on? Here. It is your only choice."

Choice? Tessa saw no choices anymore. Everything was going too fast, and there no time left for her to think. If the stolen threads were not returned, her father's life, her whole world, would be destroyed. And if Will's thread went back to the Norn, what would happen to him? Would he go back to suffer and die with the plague?

What can you do when you have no choices?

At the edge of the trees a twig snapped. The unicorn stepped into the clearing. It was Will. Without a doubt. His eyes were fixed on Tessa, and his breath blew in gusts of vapor against the cool air. The strong columns of his legs were spattered with mud, and bloody scratches marred the milky white shoulders and flanks.

The unicorn seemed to light up the dusky gloom of the clearing as he stepped forward. Tessa could only watch in heartbreak as the beautiful creature came closer, elegant and strong. "Will," she whispered.

"Of course," muttered Gray Lily. "I should have known he would come. You are the virgin in his haunts."

"Except I'm not here to trap him," whispered Tessa. "I'm here to save him." She swept a cold look at Gray Lily. "And it's got nothing to do with being a damned virgin."

Gray Lily gave her a curious look.

"He came here because he loves me."

Dizziness washed over Tessa, and she stiffened her body against it. She closed her eyes. She *had* been here before. She took a breath, recognizing the herbal scent of the wet grass and the sounds of birds. Other visions, other dreams came back now, crystalline and real. Running in terror from the woods. Tearing off a bloody gown that didn't belong to her. In another life, in another time, she was the girl who had trapped Will de Chaucy. An aching sense of loss invaded every part of her.

Kill the unicorn, Tessa.

Find the first. Return the seven.

Was Will's thread the first that Gray Lily had stolen? It made sense. His thread had given her power and youth.

"Do as I say, girl, and come here," Gray Lily demanded, interrupting Tessa's thoughts. "Or the unicorn will suffer. Would you like a demonstration?"

She clutched a thread in her supple fingers and twisted. Hugh de Chaucy stepped out of the shadows. Tessa saw the glint of the spear tip as he raised his weapon. Aimed at the unicorn.

"No," Hugh whispered. He turned a pathetic gaze on Gray Lily. "I beg you." His head shook back and forth as if he were having a seizure and was trying to control his own limbs. Gray Lily made a small flicking motion with her fingers.

"Hugh," Tessa screamed. "No!"

The spear shot through the air.

Chapter 44

The spear struck, quivering into the unicorn's arched neck. The animal screamed and rose on his hind legs as the pole of the spear dangled to the ground and blood sprayed out.

"Will!" Tessa screamed. She leapt down from Hannibal's back and ran. She heard a dull, distant twang as she flung down the crossbow.

The unicorn staggered forward. He buckled to his knees in front of Tessa and sank to the ground. As he dropped his head, his long, spiraled horn impaled the ground.

"Do as I say, girl," said Gray Lily. "I can make him bleed forever. Or I can heal him. Which shall it be?"

Tessa knelt beside him. The spear jerked in the grass as

the unicorn's body shuddered. With every movement more blood seeped from the animal's neck. Tessa took hold of the spear in a trembling hand. One thrust deeper and the unicorn would die. This was the reason she was here.

Will's thread would be freed if he died. If Tessa could prevent Gray Lily from taking it, he would be released. His must have been the first thread stolen; it only made sense. She gripped the cold weapon and closed her eyes. *Kill the unicorn, Tessa.*

"No!" With a hoarse, sobbing cry Tessa pulled out the spear and fell to her knees. She couldn't do it. "I'm sorry," she whispered. The blood flowed freely from the unicorn's neck, crimson against pure white. Tessa pressed her hand on the jagged wound to try to slow it down, but bright blood ran slick and hot over her hand. The unicorn's head slumped to her lap.

Tessa stared. The moment froze in her head and she couldn't move. She thought of a picture in a book—it seemed so long ago now—of a pathetic girl with sad eyes who just sat there while the unicorn bled. Tessa fisted her hands in frustration. She let out a cry of rage and sadness. She would not be that girl, that heartless, stupid girl.

"Will." She whispered his name over and over, crooning reassurances to him and burying her face in the thick tangle of the unicorn's mane.

But she'd failed. To find the key, to find the threads. She had failed at everything. She couldn't take care of herself, or anybody else, for that matter. She wasn't in control of anything and she couldn't fix anything. She was just a puppet on strings.

Gray Lily stepped forward and, reaching out, offered her hand to Tessa. "Come now. He will be all right."

Tessa blinked. She looked down at her hands. She had been stroking the unicorn's soft cheek, all the while smearing blood. Her hands were covered. The unicorn's eyes, Will's eyes, were closed, but the rounded belly moved with shallow breathing motions. He was still alive. Tessa raised her eyes to look up at Gray Lily. Slowly, gently, she slid the unicorn's head from her lap. With mechanical motions she forced herself to stand. Her bloodied hands clenched, she stood for a moment. Then, with a fierce scream, Tessa launched herself at Gray Lily.

But Tessa's body slammed to a violent stop when Gray Lily lifted her slim, beringed hand. She touched Tessa's chest lightly with her fingers. "Come," Gray Lily said. Tessa looked down at the golden yellow stone that glowed in the center of her ring. Gray Lily's fingers pressed harder. Tessa cried out as a needle of icy cold pain shot through her.

"At last," muttered Gray Lily. Her gentle tone was gone, stripped away like a discarded bit of costume jewelry. "I'm going to be rid of you once and for all, girl. You're not going back, not after what you've done."

Tessa made herself look into Gray Lily's eyes. Eyes so filled with hate it seemed that they should burst. Gray Lily opened her dark mouth and begin to spew words. The noise rattled and coiled around Tessa like chains.

"No," Tessa said. She tried to back away, but she couldn't move. Pain arced through her body, a hundred times worse now than it had been before. The pain brought tears as she stared down at the spot where Gray Lily's hand, wearing the silver ring, touched her.

Tessa stared at the ring. She tried to focus on it, even as her vision became blurry. The stone was large. Pretty, Tessa thought with an odd detachment. Her head drooped toward it and she saw details within the polished stone. It was a rich, glowing yellow with a dark brown fleck deep within it. Like a splinter. Snatches of words buzzed in her head.

A piece of a tree.

Stone from wood.

She carried a little yellow rock.

Then a realization broke through Tessa's muddy thoughts like a beam of light through darkness. "Amber," she whispered. The key was a piece of amber. A piece of petrified, ancient sap. Sap that held a tiny fragment of wood from an ancient tree.

Tessa raised her hand toward the luminous stone. "The key," she gasped.

"Yes! I hold the key and the power," shouted Gray Lily. "Can you feel it, girl? Can you feel your life spinning away from you?"

With a faint cry Tessa reached up and grabbed Gray Lily's hand. She tried to pull the ring away, but the cold was filling her, spreading from her core to her fingertips. Tessa could hear her own pulse pounding in her ears. It was slowing, as if her blood were freezing solid. Her heart felt like a tumbling block of ice. Tessa saw a flicker of something smoky drifting around Gray Lily's hand, around the ring. The smoke was pale blue.

Gray Lily was pulling her thread.

"Hugh," Tessa cried out. "Help me! Please."

"Moncrieff," shouted Gray Lily. "Hold her still." She glared at Tessa and her lovely face twisted into a horrible, furrowed caricature of a woman's. "I'm going to cast you off!" screamed Gray Lily. "You'll go into the Void, into a forever of nothing. Go. Drown in blackness."

As she heard Gray Lily's words, a pinprick of black swam before Tessa's eyes and swelled. And then she saw it. She saw the Void. The cold, black vastness of it stretched out before her, and she could feel it. The ravenous loneliness. The crushing weight of . . . nothing.

A sudden movement flashed off to Tessa's side. She felt a shiver pass through Gray Lily's hand, felt the witch's grip loosen for just an instant. But it was enough. Tessa reeled back as Gray Lily's hold on her thread was broken. The pain lifted from Tessa's chest, and she saw the blackness of the Void retract and wink out.

Gray Lily grunted and looked down at herself. A spear protruded from the green silk of her gown. Blood oozed around the wooden shaft. Her head shot up and she stared across the span of it at her henchman. "Moncrieff," she choked out.

"My name," Hugh gasped, still holding the other end of the spear, "is Hugh de Chaucy."

"You know you can't kill me," snarled Gray Lily. She winced.

"No. But I can hold you for a little while. You took my brother from me, you cursed bitch." Hugh twisted the spear and shoved it deeper into Gray Lily's gut. Fire raged in his eyes. "Get the key, Tessa."

Still wracked with pain, Tessa reached for Gray Lily's hand. She grabbed the ring and pulled.

With a shriek Gray Lily wrenched her hand away, sending Tessa sprawling to the ground. Gray Lily twisted, trying to loosen herself from Hugh de Chaucy's spear. Her elegant form looked like a worm writhing on a hook. Finally she narrowed her eyes and gripped the spear, then lifted it, still protruding from her body. She tossed Hugh into the air as easily as she would have thrown a rag doll. He fell in a crumpled, splayed heap yards away. Tessa looked back at Gray Lily with horror as the witch took hold of the spear and wrenched it out of her side with one sharp motion. It was true; Hugh couldn't kill her, Tessa thought weakly. Nothing could kill her.

Through the trees Tessa could see the glowing orb of the moon. The light washed over the grass, giving it a sparkling sheen. Gray Lily whirled on Tessa. "Now you die," she gasped. She held out her hand. And stared. Gray Lily's middle finger was empty. Tessa looked down into her own cupped palm. The amber ring glowed up at her. She hadn't even felt it. She slipped it on her finger. "No. I don't think so," Tessa answered breathlessly. Without thinking, she reached out her hand.

A look of stark terror filled Gray Lily's face. That was when Tessa saw it: a faint purple shadow hovering near the wound in her side. Tessa peered at the shimmering form; it looked like waves of heat rising from a hot highway, or wisps of steam from a cooling but still-warm teakettle.

It was Gray Lily's thread.

Somewhere in the distance Tessa heard Gray Lily's screaming curse, but she hardly noticed. She stepped closer. Slowly a purple vapor was coiling out from Gray Lily and winding toward her. Tessa had no craft, no words, no potions. But she could feel that thread. She concentrated her whole mind on the faint, wispy substance. *Come to me,* she told it. She knew it would. She could already feel the livid color of it, the texture of it in her fingers. She took hold of it and felt warmth glide along her arm.

"Let go of me!" screeched Gray Lily. Her demeanor changed; she wore the expression of a cringing, frightened child.

"Not on your life," Tessa whispered.

"Lymerer!" groaned Gray Lily. "Come to me."

But at the edge of the clearing Tessa could see the huge man staring with horror at what was happening to his mistress. He made no move to help her. Or perhaps Gray Lily was simply unable to work his thread, to force him to do her will.

Tessa pulled Gray Lily's thread with both hands, faster now, and watched as the woman's already-weakened form began to shrivel. Her skin wrinkled. Her body twisted and shortened. A look of torment made Gray Lily's face grow rigid, and her mouth opened wide in a gaping scream. "It's mine!" she screamed. "It's mine!"

Tessa closed her ears to the unearthly noises from Gray Lily's widening black mouth. The gaping maw grew larger until it seemed to engulf Gray Lily's face; the lips rolled back, and it swallowed itself.

319

Gray Lily was gone.

Tessa held the purple thread, and for a moment she felt it. Felt the power of holding a life in her hands. She knew that she could do things with it. She could have control. What could a person do with power like that? Anything.

The thought was intoxicating.

And terrifying.

Tessa dropped Gray Lily's thread. It twisted away from her, snaking through the dark air, then floated up into the night sky and finally disappeared.

Hugh de Chaucy stood up. Before Tessa's eyes he seemed to straighten and grow taller. He held a hand before him and gripped it into a fist. Then he threw his head back and laughed, his milky blue eyes transformed into bright, twinkling crescents.

"You've done it, Tessa Brody. You have released us. Thank you," Hugh said in a rich, booming voice. Before the final words left his mouth, his thread was already winding away. Hugh's body became transparent, and a gleaming crimson thread floated into the night.

The lymerer and his dog drifted away in black coils that were nearly invisible against the dark sky. And from the woods, two other threads rose. The snake and the dragon, Tessa thought. All the threads rose higher, twisting and gliding their way free. And then Tessa understood what had happened. She'd found the first stolen thread after all.

The old weaver, whose life had been broken by tragedy, had wanted freedom from the Norn. She had wanted control of her own life. So the first thread that Gray Lily had ever taken was her own.

It was just as the Norn had predicted. Once the first stolen thread was returned, the others were released. Six threads returned. Only one to go.

Tessa turned to the unicorn, and through her tears, she saw it. The pale, silvery thread of Will's life began to rise up and wind away from the beautiful creature's lifeless form. The silver thread, lit by the moonlight, looked like a ribbon of liquid mercury.

"No!" Tessa ran forward, reached out and caught the swirling thread. Simply caught it.

The force that pulled the thread skyward was incredibly strong. And there was pain. It wasn't the cold pain of having her own life pulled, but warmth that threatened to burn her. Tessa cried out as the heat lapped her fingers like an invisible flame. But she couldn't let go. She knew what she wanted. It was Will. She would never let go.

"Seven threads. Seven lives."

Tessa heard the eerie voices of the Norn break through the darkness.

They were telling her to let go. The Norn were trying to take him. For what? To go back to his own time and die of smallpox?

No.

Tessa looked down at her wrist and saw the thin, frayed threads of her bracelet. The pig. Double lucky. Tessa dragged the silver thread closer. She wound it tightly around her wrist, wincing as the burning heat enclosed her skin, and finally, with shaking fingers, tied Will's thread to the bracelet.

"Double lucky," she cried. "Please hold him." She gasped the words and then repeated them, like a chant. Or a prayer. "Double lucky. Please hold him." She stared at the worn, tattered threads between the beads. The simple bracelet was nothing, and yet what it represented was everything. And suddenly Tessa imagined what it was made of: not just threads. To her, the frayed fibers were people. Her mother. Her father. Opal. And Will. Family, friendship and love. She imagined the threads of everyone she loved and cherished. She called upon every bit of love she had ever been given and asked love to make her strong.

She held on. She would not let go of what she loved. She would give anything to save Will. She would give herself. She would be the seventh thread.

"Take me!" she yelled up to the sky, sobbing. "Take me instead of him. Take my life."

Something snapped; Tessa fell backward with the sudden release. Will fell to the ground beside her, gasping, holding her wrist in the same spot where she had tied his thread.

"Tessa," he said, hugging her close. Tessa felt the earth rumble as she wrapped her arms around Will. He was real and warm and smelled, as he always did, of leather and smoky wood and spice. The ground pitched beneath them. A tearing, ripping noise filled the air as the world around them, Gray Lily's world, seemed to unravel. Trees splintered apart

and leaves whirled up to the sky. The moon dissolved, bub-
bling away across the sky in a streak of light.

Tessa clung to Will. "I'm sorry," she said, whispering into
his ear. She hung on to him, ready for the end.

But that didn't happen.

Chapter 45

Actually, Tessa couldn't understand *what* happened next. It was as if the sky split open and another world washed over the dark one that had just disintegrated. A great, bright wave of it knocked Tessa over, submerging her. She felt herself torn from Will. She screamed, waiting for liquid to fill her lungs, to drown her.

But it wasn't water that engulfed her. Tessa stood up and breathed. She was alive.

"Where am I?" Her voice sounded unnaturally loud, and echoed back to her. She looked around. She stood on a green hillside. Far beneath her the land ended in a dense cloud, blocking any view of how high she was or what lay below.

But it was dazzling. Each blade of grass at her feet seemed distinct and beautiful. And the colors. This world had colors Tessa had never seen and had no words for. The air around her was as intricate as lace. She reached up and the air seemed to quiver, sending a wave of the noncolors rippling away from her. She looked around for Will, but he wasn't there.

She could see a small plateau cut into the hillside in the distance; it held a pool of glassy green water on which two swans floated. Nearby stood a huge tree whose stark branches made a tangle against the sea-blue sky. As she walked closer, Tessa heard another sound in the quiet, and somehow she thought it was coming from that tree. It was a sound like breathing.

Three cloaked figures were walking toward her. Tessa recognized them from, well, her bathroom mirror. The Norn had arrived.

They were still cloaked in dark robes, and the only hints that Tessa had of their faces were vague, shadowed features and an occasional flickering gleam of their eyes.

"You have succeeded, mortal," said one of them. Tessa recognized the deep, hollow voice of Scytha. "The stolen threads have been returned. All except for one."

For a moment Tessa froze. *All except for one.* Will. A panicky sense of confusion overtook her. His thread hadn't drifted away like the others. She'd held on. But where was he? She tried to hide her fear as she replied to the Norn.

"You can't have that one," Tessa said.

"We can't—" Scytha's booming voice repeated, only

to break off in amazement. "Foolish child. What are you saying?"

"You lied to me," Tessa said steadily. "You told me you would give Will his life back. But you lied. He would have died of smallpox."

"It was not a lie," said Scytha. She drifted closer and Tessa saw the piercing shine of the huge shears in one heavy hand. "It was his fate. He must return to it."

Scytha came even closer and Tessa felt a sense of stillness, of time suspended. She wasn't aware of breathing or blinking or even having a pulse when Scytha loomed over her. Maybe she didn't.

"Where is he?" Scytha raised the shears. The sharp blades sang as they opened wide. Tessa tried to avert her eyes against the blinding glare but couldn't. The light seemed to cut right into her. The shears hovered over Tessa's head.

One of the other Norn stooped to touch something at her feet. "Stop," said Spyn. She pointed. "He's here."

Tessa saw that a vast fabric had appeared, swirling around the feet of the Norn. Or perhaps it had been there all along; she wasn't sure. It was made of myriad threads of colors she knew and colors she had no words for. She could see no beginning or end to it.

"She has done something," said Scytha in a puzzled tone. "Her thread is intertwined with his. Tied together. I can't cut one without cutting the other."

Tessa heaved an inward sigh. Will was alive. The feeling of relief was so intense, she felt her knees sag beneath her. Somehow the air supported her.

Spyn wriggled her long fingers at Tessa. "You love him."

"Yes," Tessa said. "I love him."

"It wasn't a question," remarked Spyn with a sniff.

The last cloaked figure, who had been regarding Tessa silently from the dark recesses beneath her hood, finally spoke:

"Do you try to cheat fate, mortal?" Weavyr asked quietly.

"I'm not cheating," Tessa answered. She pointed to the endless fabric. "You just said his thread is there. Returned."

"But not to where it *should* be. He belongs to another time."

Tessa shrugged. "I guess you should have been more specific."

There was silence as the Norn contemplated this, and then, for the first time in the memory of the world, Scytha's shears slowly closed—without cutting anything.

"Very well," said Weavyr. "I suppose we owe the girl something for returning the lost threads." She bent to examine the Wyrd. "Some semblance of order seems to have been restored."

"And my father," said Tessa. "He'll be all right?"

Scytha gave one slow, emphatic nod. "All will be as we promised, mortal. Just as we extend no pity, neither do we hold grudges. You shall be returned to your life. And Gray Lily will be punished in a manner that is . . . appropriate."

Tessa hardly heard what the hooded figure was saying. Having learned that her father was safe, she was weak with relief. She'd come so close to losing him. Just as she had lost her mother, suddenly and without reason. The old hurt welled up inside her. It felt like a hole; it could never be fixed, and it would never go away.

Tessa looked down at the swirling fabric that the Norn had made of human lives. The Wyrd, they called it. "You have all this power," Tessa said. "You control everything. Why do you do the things you do?"

When no answer came, she pressed them. "My mother," Tessa whispered. "Her name was Wendy Brody. She was young. An artist. Why did she have to die?"

Spyn shuddered and put her spindly fingers to her head. "You see," she said. "It's always the same question. Why? Why? It buzzes in my head."

Scytha answered. "Your mother died because it was time for her thread to be cut."

"But why?" Tessa demanded. "Because *you* decided?"

"I told you once before," said Scytha. "Our reasons and our ways are beyond your comprehension."

Tessa shook her head and replied quietly, "You should try us sometime. You might be surprised."

There was silence for a moment as the three cloaked figures seemed to mull this over. Finally Scytha shook her head. "Good-bye for now, mortal. Go and live your life," she said gloomily. "You shall see these blades again one day."

Then there was a tearing noise and Tessa plummeted into rushing darkness.

She landed, with a muffled crash, on a bed. There was an instant of stillness as motes of dust settled around her; then the frame collapsed to the floor. Tessa pushed herself up, wide-eyed. She was back home. Well, not home, but close. The hotel room of the Portland Regency was just as she had seen it last.

Through the open window wafted a cool breeze, tinged with the scent of brine from the sea. The sound of a car horn blared outside. Tessa stood up, dazed, and looked around. Other than the demolished bed, there was no sign that anyone had been here. The tapestry was gone.

Tessa took several deep breaths and put a hand to her head. It was aching and warm, but otherwise, she was okay. The events of the last few days unfurled in her thoughts. The unicorn tapestry, Will, Gray Lily. Had she been sick and imagined the whole thing? Maybe none of it had even happened.

She stumbled over to the full-length mirror on the wall. "Oh yeah," she said. "It happened." A bedraggled, black-haired girl dressed in a torn velvet gown stared back at her. On her finger glowed a brilliant ring of amber set in silver.

When Tessa touched the band of polished metal with a tentative finger, the burnished stone glowed as if a tiny flame flickered inside it. Tessa clasped her fingers tightly around it.

"Thanks," she whispered, knowing that the Norn probably couldn't hear her. And that they probably wouldn't care if they did. She turned to go and spotted something beneath the corner of the bed. She picked up the thick black book and walked out.

Chapter 46

Two weeks later Tessa was in her favorite chair in the corner of Brody's Books. She stretched out, letting her gaze roam around the updated décor. She had to admit, Alicia had made some good suggestions, including the addition of a small café area, which had brought tons of customers in. Tessa took a sip of her frothy latte. The new espresso machine wasn't too bad either.

Opal sat crossed-legged on the floor beside her, fingering a tune on her battered acoustic guitar. Her hair was tied up in a twisted silk bandana, and her lilac-painted toes tapped in time to her music.

"So what are we going to do this summer?" asked Opal. "It's gonna be boring around here, with no imminent death and all. And I never even got to meet my evil twin."

"That suits me fine," said Tessa with a smile as she saw her father pacing the balcony above them, his glasses dangling from his mouth. His face was fuller and healthy-looking. He had a huge book in his hands. Tessa squinted. It looked like an antique-plumbing supply catalog.

Life was back to . . . well, *life*. Her father had been discharged from the hospital after what the doctors were calling an amazing spontaneous remission. He and Alicia were planning a wedding in the fall. And Opal was Tessa's best friend again.

Everything was perfect.

Except *it wasn't*.

Things had been made right. The stolen threads had been returned. Somehow Tessa had thought that everything would be fixed. She'd had this wild, crazy hope that the things in the past that shouldn't have happened would have been changed. And yet her mother was still dead. The accident had happened, and nothing was going to change that. Did that mean that somehow in the big scheme of things her mother was supposed to die? That there was a reason? Tessa didn't know. And apparently the Norn weren't going to bother explaining things to a mere mortal. She had to live with it. Just as before.

Tessa had started to paint in the studio again, with her father's blessing. Mostly big colorful, abstract stuff in her own weird style. But the paintings pleased her, and somehow it didn't feel as if she was trespassing on her mother's memory. It felt as if she was honoring it. She'd even been accepted by the Maine College of Art.

She should be grateful for her life, for her father's life and for Opal's friendship, Tessa thought. And she was. But she couldn't control what her heart did. And it had decided to break.

There had been no word, no sign of Will de Chaucy. She'd made efforts to find him, but it was as though he had disappeared from the face of the earth, or more precisely, had never been there at all. She had to accept the fact that she would never see him again. But it felt as though she was leaving something precious behind, a part of herself. The part that was the best she would ever be. It hurt so much. But it had to be enough, she told herself, that he was alive, somewhere. The Norn had said so.

He was in the world. He just wasn't in hers.

The bell over the door jangled and a tall, well-built young man strode into the store from the bright sunlight of the Old Port Square. He wore a crisp white shirt and tailored dark suit. Tucked beneath his arm was a large package wrapped in brown paper. He walked over to the counter and took off his dark glasses, glancing coolly around the bookstore. As his eyes passed her way, Tessa dropped her mug to the floor with a clatter. Opal's guitar twanged as she got a finger stuck under one of the strings.

"Holy Armani," Opal whispered. "Isn't that—" she began.

Tessa stood up. She began walking toward him slowly. Her pace got quicker as she went closer. The lean, chiseled features, the tawny hair. Brown eyes flecked with gold. It was Will. She ran the last few steps and only stopped short of launching herself into his arms.

The young man frowned down at her, looking slightly alarmed. "Good morning, miss." The accent was more modern English than it had been before, impeccable and clipped.

Tessa's heart took a downward spiral.

He didn't recognize her.

"Uh," Tessa said, backing away. "Uh, hello. S-sorry, I thought you were someone I knew."

"Lucky chap," he murmured.

"Can I help you?"

"I do hope so," said the young man. "My name is William Chase. I'd like to speak to Mr. Brody."

"Um, sure," said Tessa, staring at him. William Chase. No wonder all her searches for William de Chaucy had led nowhere. But this was him. It had to be.

"Uh, I work here," Tessa sputtered. "Er—maybe there's something I can help you with?" she stammered. Maybe she could form a sentence that didn't start with a caveman grunt. Closing her mouth would be good too.

"Perhaps," said William Chase. He drew a sheet of paper from his suit pocket. "I'm inquiring after a book that was recently sold at auction."

"A book," Tessa repeated.

"Yes, a book." He glanced around. "I've been led to believe this is a bookstore." A flicker of a smile turned up one corner of his mouth.

Tessa grinned like an idiot. "We have lots of books."

"This one you would remember, I'm sure," he said. "An archaic text, leather-bound and handwritten, in Latin. It was mistakenly placed with a number of items sold from our estate in Cornwall. I'd like to retrieve it as quickly as possible. It's very important."

"Yes, my father bought that book about a month ago," Tessa said almost absently. She was too busy absorbing every facet of his face, his voice. Her eyes caught on one detail. "You have a scar on your cheek," she said.

William Chase put a hand up to touch it. "Oh, that. I've had it forever. My older brother gave me that." He spoke as he unrolled the package on the countertop. "The book has always been stored with this tapestry," he said. Inside was a tapestry with a coat of arms woven on a blue background.

"It's very handsome," said Tessa, examining it.

There was a unicorn in the tapestry, but it was small and flat-eyed, emblazoned on a golden shield. There was no life in it.

"A unicorn rampant has been our family's crest since the Middle Ages," William Chase told her.

Tessa peered more closely at the medieval insignia. The most lifelike thing in the picture seemed to be a small flower that was shown crushed beneath the hoof of the unicorn. A pale, faded flower.

"A gray lily," Tessa said aloud. In the back of her mind she remembered words spoken on a distant hillside. *She will be punished . . . appropriately.*

Tessa reached out her hand to touch the tapestry but pulled it back again. "I'd better not."

"What's wrong?" William asked. He had a strange, still expression on his face as he turned to her.

Tessa shook her head. "I got into trouble that way once."

Will looked into her eyes. "Tessa," he said.

Without thinking she answered, "Yes?"

"You know, I do have the strangest feeling that we've met before. In fact . . ." He pulled her close and kissed her gently. "I'm quite sure of it, mistress." He let go and stood back.

Tessa swayed slightly, a dazed expression on her face. "Oh," she said deliberately, "I am *so* going to kill you."

"Nonsense," he said. "You couldn't do it before."

With a cry Tessa hugged him to her, feeling the warm strength, the bones of his shoulder blades flexing beneath her fingers as he put his arms around her. Tessa breathed in the warm green scent of him and let out a choked whimper.

"I am sorry, mistress," Will said. "I wasn't sure that you would remember me when you were returned to your world. I wanted to be sure before I did this." He kissed her again, deeply.

"But where have you been?" Tessa demanded when they finally broke apart. She stepped back and took in the clothes, the expensive watch on his wrist.

"It will take time to explain," Will said with a smile, "but thanks to your deeds, I have a rightful place in this world. I have a home. I even have a history. It seems that in 1511 Hugh de Chaucy was the only survivor of a terrible plague of smallpox in Cornwall. But he survived to be the Earl of Umbric's heir. He married and had twelve children."

Tessa clapped her hand to her mouth and laughed. She was so happy for Hugh.

"My family's name, our lands and title all survived. I have a place in the world, Tessa. Although"—he ran a hand through his hair in a familiar gesture—"the path ahead is not certain."

"It doesn't matter. We'll figure it out." A feeling of happiness swept over her. "It's really you," she whispered. Then she yelled, "Dad! Come down, please. There's someone I want you to meet."

Will hugged her, and his lips grazed her cheek as he bent down and whispered, "So you finally accept it. We are destined to be together?"

"Uh-huh."

He smiled and pulled her closer. "I thought you didn't believe in fate."

"I didn't before," Tessa said. She took his hand and, looking down, wove her fingers into his. The connection felt strong. It felt right. "But I've learned a lot," she said slowly. "Every person makes a difference. And the choices we make, the things we do—they matter." She looked up into Will's eyes. "And now I *do* believe in fate. Especially the kind we make ourselves."

EPILOGUE

Beneath the tree Yggdrasil, the Norn spoke to each other after a long silence.

"How has she done this?" said Spyn. "Having the key alone would not have twisted his path so."

"They shared a connection from the past," said Scytha.

"Perhaps—"

"No." Weavyr shook her head. "She has the gift. It is the only explanation."

"Does she know?" Scytha asked in a dismal tone.

No one answered. The Norn stood silent for a time, pondering this question. Then they returned to work.

ACKNOWLEDGMENTS

I am grateful to many people who helped bring this story to life. I thank my family for the love and support that allows me to write and encourages me to think I can. My wonderful critique partners, Angie Frazier, Amy Henry and Dawn Metcalf, all gave me invaluable feedback and helped an early draft take flight. My lovely editor, Michelle Poploff, and her assistant, Rebecca Short, asked all the right questions, even if they were sometimes hard to answer! I especially owe a loving debt to my writing friend Marissa McCarthy Goodell, who read *Warped* from the very beginning and always wanted to know "What happens next?"

ABOUT THE AUTHOR

Before beginning her writing career, Maurissa Guibord worked slinging pizzas, alphabetizing things, and practicing medicine. Now she writes fiction for young adults who love the same kind of story she does: mysterious, romantic, and with a touch of humor. She lives on the coast of Maine with her mysterious cat, her romantic husband, and three kids who make her laugh. *Warped* is her first published novel.